14 HANDS TO FREEDOM

GLEN VETTER

ISBN 978-1-63961-737-1 (paperback)
ISBN 979-8-88540-000-8 (hardcover)
ISBN 978-1-63961-738-8 (digital)

Christian Faith Publishing, Inc.
832 Park Avenue
Meadville, PA 16335
www.christianfaithpublishing.com

Printed in the United States of America

CHAPTER 1

Captain's Arrival

The morning had not yet started, and the clanking of dishes from the kitchen assured me that Mother was already busy in the kitchen. The house was warming, and even the addition of my bedroom was warming, which meant Mother had been up for quite some time. Mark shared my room and usually had the house fire roaring before anyone got out of bed. The smell of fresh bacon was finally enough to get Mark out of bed. I always waited for the soft touch and gentle voice of Mother before I uncovered from a warm homemade quilt. Captain had added my bedroom on the south side of our house a few years ago. The loft was filled with four sisters and was located above Mother and Captain's room. Mark had started to sleep in the barn; that's when Mother insisted on another bedroom. Although Mother was firm and sometimes distant, she preferred the entire family under one roof, especially when Captain was away. My father, whom everyone referred to as Captain, had been gone for seventeen days. Mother ran the farm with a firm voice and a big stick. Although I had never seen her actually use a stick, she had surely threatened the older kids a few times. Not one of us had ever actually defied her enough and would never think of it; the threat of Captain knowing our wrongdoings was enough to get the results Mother wanted. I did not get to hear or feel my mother's voice today, but when Mikey came through the front door, I was willing to get out of bed.

Mikey was our first cousin and was well known for his maple syrup. Once I heard his voice, I knew blueberry pancakes, bacon, eggs, and fresh juice were waiting; I decided I would get out of bed before Mother said anything. Mikey was Mother's nephew and had lost his entire family to the plague. Mikey's sister had come down with the plague, and it wasn't long before everyone was sick and later died. Mikey loved the trees and was in charge of tapping the maple trees for maple syrup. He spent a few days at a time there and had a summer camp on the way north end of the maple trees. He would tell the story, "I came home after a few days in the trees. I had two big barrels of syrup, and another two coming." He made so much syrup that it was a major part of his family's income. As he was pulling his syrup in the yard, he read a sign, "Infected with the plaque. Stay out." His mother came out to say goodbye but would not even come close. She instructed him to take the syrup to town and sell it and not return for at least thirty days. Mikey went on to explain, "I immediately did leave the farm that day. I had good demand for my homemade syrup as soon as I got to town, and I did really well. I needed a lot of supplies if I had to spend an entire month in my summer camp. After selling my syrup, I bought everything

I needed and still had money left over, and I have plenty more syrup." You would think he would be a lot more elated, but Mikey was in the maple tree grove for over a month. After a month, he came home to find his parents farm completely burned to the ground—all the farm animals killed and not even a funeral for anyone. The plague was killing farmer after farmer completely devastating the families.

The Russian army and cavalries were assigned by King Nicholas to execute everyone who was sick and to burn everything down. No one was going to church. No one was visiting. It was sad times. We lost two sisters, and I had been very sick. Mother insisted on saving me and the rest of the family. I believe through prayer, her strong German will to live, a really good doctor, and her willpower, she saved our family. Captain was also a well-known man and captain of fifty men in the Russian cavalry. No one, not even the local sheriff or doctor, would cross Captain. So, when they decided to execute the sick, our farm was not touched.

After a hearty breakfast, which lasted for a long time, we were reminded of our chores and were directed to get started. But instead, we visited Mikey for a long time. He talked about his maple trees and how they produced so much syrup that even the bears couldn't wipe out his supply. He told the story of a giant bear, "This big black bear must be eight hundred pounds, and he is not afraid of me. He never lets me get a good shot at him, and he loves syrup and has tipped over more syrup jugs than I can count." This morning, we must have eaten fifty pancakes. We were all happily stuffed and willing to do our chores. Mother allowed us to visit Mikey a lot longer than expected. We ate as much as we wanted.

Mother and Mark were both waiting for the sun to burn off the dense fog outside. Mark was the oldest and was almost like the captain when it came to designating chores. Most of us knew our part and knew what chores needed to get done, and Mother was clear this morning. Mark and Mikey were to round up all the horses and bring them to the west corral. Diane and Carol were directed to round up every cow and put them in the east corral. The milking cows were impatiently waiting as Strike had the milkers waiting to get in the barn, somewhat an odd request, but we had learned just to do as we were told. With Mikey and Mark rounding up all the horses, I was certain that Captain was on his way. We housed fifty cavalry horses, and all of us kids had our own horse and were allowed to ride as often as we wanted as long as the chores were done. We also had the field horses that we used to pull the wagons and work the fields.

The fieldwork was done, so bringing all the horses up to the corral seemed even more peculiar. I fed and watered the chickens and fowl. We had butchered the majority of the birds so only the hens that laid the eggs and a few pesty roosters were left. Four turkeys and some wild guinea still stayed distant in the trees. There were also a few ducks and geese in the pond, but we did not feed them anymore. I was done rather quickly with the birds and headed to the barn for milking. Mark and Mikey had put the horses in the corral and were already milking. I was to haul the milk to the dungeon; I called it that anyway. It was scary, and I had to go down a steep staircase and put the milk in where it stayed cold. I carried two buckets from the barn to the stairs but only carried one at a time to the dungeon; spilling was not allowed.

Janet stayed in the house and did the dishes and reset all the plates. She was instructed to set all the plates, which were twenty, so now we all knew Captain and his men were expected soon. I figured the worried look on Mother's face was because of the dense fog and that Captain was not home yet. Linda and Carol were to gather the pigs and bring two of them to the butcher shop; another odd request, as we had just butchered four pigs last week. Our cellar was full. Our garden vegetables were all canned and stored. It was a banner year, and all our bins were full. We had an abundance of wheat, so we even had a big pile on the ground, uncovered. We had several stacks of hay, all ready for what was expected to be a cold winter. This was the most I had ever seen, and Mark assured me this is the most we have ever had. Mark was proud, and he knew he would make Captain happy when he would see all the hay was put up for the winter.

We did get a late start on chores, and yet as we were finishing the morning chores, the fog still had not lifted. The sun, now up in the sky, was struggling to fight the fog. Mother continued to announce more chores. Mark was to prepare the smoker after he hung the pigs in the slaughterhouse. The girls were to get started butchering, and Janet was told to stay in the house and start preparing brine. She was told to make ham brine, jerky brine, turkey brine, and chicken brine, so it was obvious that we were butchering a lot more than could fit in the cellar or the dungeon. I was told to catch the remaining turkeys and guineas, but I knew I would not catch them on my own, but Mother was clear, catch them or get the shotgun and kill them. I loved the shotgun, and although it was Captain's, I referred to it as my gun. I did not even try to catch any with by bare hands and a net once I got the okay to use my shotgun. Everyone was busy, and although the fog was still thick, I made quick work of the turkeys, ducks, and guinea. I had put my gun away and was heading to the butcher shop when Strike started barking to alarm us that there was a rider approaching.

Strike was the family farm dog and was loved by everyone and is a great companion and my second best friend. Flash was my horse and my best friend. On any other day, we would see who was coming. The fog was too thick to see, but we all knew who it must be. The steady stride of Captain's horse was undeniable. I made for the gate and had it opened as Captain rode through. He did not miss a step but smiled and gave me a reassuring head nod that he was home. He normally showed up with ten or so soldiers, but I did not question. I was happy to see him, as was the entire family. The chores came to a halt, and we all joined Father at the table.

He had been wounded, and Mother was now more concerned than ever. As Captain drank fresh coffee and before he could even say hello to Mikey, the pancakes were on the grill. Mother bandaged Captain and began to ask questions of course. "Where are the men? Are they coming? Are they okay?" Mother wanted answers and would not get the answers she wanted with the family in the house. Captain did not answer, and although we were happy to see him, we were told to go outside and continue our chores.

Captain did not speak about his war and battles with any kids around. His worried look told us that his last battle was bad and many men were wounded and lost. Captain looked very tired; after he ate, he rested. I have never seen him not help with butchering. When Mother told us to get outside and get the work done, Captain gave each of us a hug, and tears swelled in his eyes. I was the youngest and last to get a hug. I had never seen my father cry; his tear-swelled eyes said it all. For several hours, we did not see Mother or Captain, but we knew he had had a long ride and a tough battle. All of us had a full day of chores ahead of us, and we were not going to stop before we were done.

The morning remained foggy, and in the afternoon, the wind started to pick up, which helped to clear some of the fog. Once again, Strike began barking, and we could hear more riders approaching. Captain had fifty men in his command, and all of them knew where we lived. Our farm was hidden in the hills, but from atop the farthest hill, our house was plain to see on a clear day. This day was less than easy to find our farm. As Strike continued his bark, the soldiers found their way. Again, I met them at the gate. This time, I left the gate open as only six riders were here. With twenty plates set and butchering in full swing, I knew more men were coming. I accompanied the men to the corral where they unsaddled the horses. Mikey did most of it, pulling saddles; removing the bridals and turning the horse in with the others, he did make sure they all got a good drink of water and some fresh hay. The soldiers and the horses looked tired and worn.

I led the men into the house where Janet had plenty of food prepared. Mikey got some more syrup from his barrels and joined us in the house. Once again, I was told to go outside and help with the butchering, and Mikey wasn't far behind. There were private matters to discuss, and Captain was pretty particular who he let hear what his plan was. As I was leaving, a soldier I recognized, and he me, commented and gave me a hug. It seemed odd, but he said, "It's nice to see you again. I'm glad you are up and around." He asked if I remember him from when I was sick. I answered of course, and he asked, "Do you have the same horse, and is he still fast?" I remembered him from when I was sick, and he told me stories of his fast horse. I was unsure what to say or even if I was allowed to speak to him without getting scolded. To my surprise, Captain, Mother, and even the other soldiers listened attentively to my story.

I told the soldiers, "My horse is the fastest in the corral, and he is the fastest horse in the entire county, and how even Mark said I can ride him faster than he had ever seen anyone on a horse." My story was short, and I really didn't know what else to say. The soldier's name was Christopher but usually went by Chris; he was one of Captain's top scouts. He smiled and gave me a hug, which was something I really did not expect, and the others laughed a bit, but I could tell they all had a tough ride home and enjoyed my company.

Captain then stopped me with a smile and confirmed, "You have become an accomplished rider, and I am proud to hear about you winning the county fair horse race." I was very proud to hear him say such a thing. He did not compliment much, and I never remember him talking to me with soldiers around. Captain told me to go to the corral, find my fast horse, saddle him, and ride him up to the house. Of course, I was excited to show the men how fast I could ride.

I exclaimed, "I am faster than the wind!" But before I left, I asked both Mother and Captain if I could saddle Flash now and finish chores later. To my surprise, Chris said he will help finish my chores once I was done riding.

Captain said, "The chores can wait. I have an important task for you and your horse. So get him ready to ride, and then I will give you the details." I was more than excited now, and I ran to the corral. The soldiers loved my enthusiasm and all cheered as I ran out the door. I quickly arrived back at the house. Flash and I were ready. Most days, I rode without a saddle, but today, I was told to saddle him up and get ready to ride. Mark also saddled his horse and wanted to ride with me. Flash was fourteen hands tall, looked a bit thin with long legs and looked too big for a smaller guy like myself on his back. Flash was quite spirited and love to run!

It wasn't often this situation happened, and Mark had dreamed of being in Captain's cavalry. Mark is older and a much better rider but wasn't near as fast. Mother did agree that it was best for Mark to go with me. When Captain and the men came outside to see our mounts, they were impressed. We had saddled our horses and were ready to ride as fast as any soldier. Captain had a rifle in each hand. He gave both Mark and me new rifles. He commented they were both loaded and to be careful. We had both shot a lot and were near marksman already. Mark once claimed anything I could see, he could hit. Of course, it was not quite true, but he has an amazing shot and was ready to join the cavalry as soon as Captain said it was okay.

Mother was not ready to let her oldest son join the cavalry. He was too valuable on the farm. She had lost two daughters and was not going to lose any more children. To now see both her sons on horses holding cavalry rifles was not what she wanted to see. She went inside and did not wait to hear what we were being sent to do. It was still foggy, and there were still soldiers looking for the farm. Our task was to ride out to the trails and hills looking for the soldiers. If we encounter anyone but Captain's soldiers, we were to ride as fast as we could home and sound off with our rifles if we got lost. I looked at Mark, and he knew what I was thinking, "We will not get lost." We have played cavalry and have ridden every inch of those hills. We knew every trail, every hole, and every water hole, and besides that, our horses knew the way home as we pretend to be wounded and our horse had to take us home in the dark.

We were excited to ride off and disappear into the fog. It was not long before we found a small day camp filled with soldiers. We approached quietly, but Mark recognized the cavalry horses right away, so we rode into camp. We explained we were out looking for them and to mount up. "We will take you to Captain's farm." There were wounded men; some could ride and some could not ride any longer. My idea was for me to ride home as fast as possible. I would get a wagon and return with food and water. I wanted to ride as fast as I could. The soldiers quickly squashed that idea. The wounded men agreed that they would stay behind and wait for Marcella. She was Captain's sister and private nurse. She was coming to meet everyone and was bringing her wagon. Marcella knew the way to our farm, so we helped the soldiers that could ride saddle up. Their horses looked badly worn and were thirsty and hungry. We first led the men's horses to a nearby water hole and let the horses get some water. It was starting to get dark, and the men were also worn, and they worried if they were ever going to find our farm. We arrived home with fourteen more soldiers. The wounded went straight into the house, and Mark and I took care of the worn-out horses.

The smoker was rolling, and the smell of fresh smoked ham was a welcomed aroma. The men, once inside, complimented us and commented on what a good job we did getting them here. I figured to ride some more and look for more men. Captain was still short thirty men. Mark too said we hadn't looked way up north. "There is a trail that often gets missed, and more men could be up north." We filled our canteens, grabbed a saddlebag full of jerky, and off we went. Strike was barking, and as we started heading north, we eyed Marcella and her entire family, two wagons, and several horses heading toward the farm. She had found some of the remaining men that were injured and were camped on the south trail. We were not turning back; we headed north. It wasn't long before we found the remaining men. They were on the north slope where even in the daylight you could not see the farm.

We fed the men some jerky, gave them our water, and hurried for home. By the time we got home, it was full-on dark. We had found fifteen more soldiers. They told us that the rest went to their own farms and were gathering their things and families. We did not ask why and instead quickly led the men to the farm. The few words we heard before we went to bed were not good. Captain had lost ten men, and several had been wounded in his last battle. He was fighting a well-equipped Russian army, and they were coming. They were coming for any man, women, or child that was German. As mother shut our bedroom door, the last words we heard were "Our time in Russia is done. We must move!"

CHAPTER 2

THE RIDE

Our home looked like a hospital. There were seven wounded men, three who needed a doctor immediately. Mother had been awake most of the night and now was in the kitchen. Mikey had been up for hours, and his pancakes and syrup was the only food on the menu. Marcella had not slept since her arrival. She has been caring for the wounded all night but needed a break and a doctor. She again asked Captain to send for the Doc. Captain was adamant that he could not spare a man to risk riding forty miles one way and then getting a doctor to ride back home and help the wounded. Captain assured her that he will think of something and soon. The farm looked like a military camp, with every man busy with his own task. Captain had everyone on task, and during the night, several wagons and families arrived. There were now twenty-five wagons in the yard; the men were working on repairing and preparing the wheels. Captain had pulled our old wagon out from behind the barn, and every old wagon wheel, every harness, and every rope and saddle were being worked on. Men were making rope halters; the horses were being shooed, and preparation to travel was definite. It was exciting and scary. There was not one person without a task.

Our morning chores were not a priority, and both smokers were roaring at full capacity. All the farm animals that were not making the trip had been harvested. All the eggs had been collected, and some girls whom I did not know were butchering my chickens. I sat down to have some breakfast; Christopher was at the table. He talked to me like I was a green soldier and was making a plan with me. I was shocked but excited; I was being asked to ride with Chris. Mother was against me riding that far in a dangerous area. King Nicholas has been looking for Captain and his men and was burning villages. Dr. Schweitzer was a forty-mile ride to get to, and we were sure to ride through the Russian resistance. Captain agreed that I could ride with Chris, explaining, "Glen knows the hills and trails well." We were to ride to retrieve the Doc. "Without him, we are sure to have more men die, and Glen knows Doc. He enjoyed his visits when Glen was sick." We also had to convince him to pack his gear and not return. His wife had died recently, and it was rare to find him sober or even to find him at all. We had to do all this and return by nightfall. Captain made it clear to Chris and myself that he would not wait. There was no option but to return with the Doc, and before nightfall. I ate feverishly and put five pancakes and some jerky in my saddlebag. I filled my two canteens with fresh water and had Flash ready to ride. Before I left the house, Mother insisted that I pack what I need for the trip. I told her I was packed and everything I needed was already in the wagon. I no more than rode up, and Chris was ready as well. Captain once again gave us the instructions. His concerned look was different than anything I had seen before. His youngest son was riding off with a cavalry scout—a ride that that had to be done and yet was not one he expected to send a thirteen-year-old farm boy to do.

We headed east and rode hard for an hour; we did not see anyone. We veered off the trails anytime we neared a farm, and finally after an hour, we slowed some, but Chris would not let up much. I had never ridden this hard, this fast, and for this long. I had been in this area quite a few times, but the land did not look familiar. After three hours of hard riding, we were nearing the village where Doc would probably be. We watered the horses at the last creek crossing, and although they were winded, they were not worn down. We had made it forty miles in three hours. It seemed like more than forty miles as we left the trails to eliminate being seen. The small details of the ride that Chris was teaching me were valuable. I listened and learned; everything he said was important. He would say, "Ride as one with your horse, and try to resist his movements as little as possible. He will last longer on long rides." We did not speak a lot, but when we did, I was at full attention.

We rode into town and straight to Dr. Schweitzer's office. It was still morning, and his office was closed. We did not want to ask the sheriff or even be seen by him. He would surely ask questions why we need the Doc. So we left Main Street and rode behind the buildings. We rode quietly to the tavern, which was just being opened and where Doc had spent the night. He was in no condition to ride.

Chris was amazing and did not give Doc the option. He was adamant and stern. "Doc, you are coming with us, and you have no choice but to come along." We hustled Doc to his office, poured a pot of coffee down his throat all while explaining to him that his expertise was needed immediately. He was to pack everything he needed to make it through an extended trip. Doc did not want to ride that far and definitely did not want to pack all his gear. I explained to Doc, "Several men were wounded, and Captain did not give us the option to return without you." Chris was busy packing every bit of medicine and bandage in the office. Chris had also quickly picked up another horse from the stables. Doc was not happy with his choice of horses, as it was not his. Chris picked the biggest, healthiest horse he could find, and it was definitely not Doc's old stag. The saddle looked good, and Chris was already packing Doc's gear onto the horse. Doc had finished the coffee and had been pouring whiskey into the last several cups. In all, it took about two hours to convince Doc to ride with us and get his gear packed.

Once packed, we immediately headed back west. Unfortunately, a few people saw us leaving. Doc's horse was packed heavy along with mine. It is exactly what Chris was trying to avoid. We did not want people to see or know about what we were doing. We were riding out of town as quickly and quietly as we could. Unfortunately, it did not go unnoticed. Once we were passed the town's edge, we picked up the pace. Doc did not like it and questioned everything, "Why are we riding so hard and why are we avoiding every farm and tavern?" He complained the entire way.

We had travelled ten miles when Chris noticed we were being followed. It was probably just a nosey farmer, but we could not risk being found by King Nicholas and his men. We veered to the north into the rough terrain through several steep hills and tricky riding areas. Doc was visibly upset and refused to ride deeper into the dangerous forest. Mountain lions have killed many riders, and the threat was real. We found a water hole to stop at and have something to eat and to rest the horses. Chris did not rest much and rode ahead and found an area to see who was following us. We had lost our followers in the woods, but we were also off track. Traveling through these trees and hills definitely slowed our return. Chris returned with some bad news. It was King Nick's men, and it looked as if they were heading the same direction and destination that we were. Our lunch break was cut short, and the ride continued. It was now as hard of a ride as I have ever heard of, and Doc was not even drinking whiskey anymore. He committed to the ride and now was riding hard to get to our farm before the Russian soldiers. Chris barked out directions and details as if he were Captain. He had a plan to detour the following soldiers. I was to ride and ride as fast as I could. Doc had a solid mount and was told that he should follow me and try to keep up. Doc wanted to rest. We made conversation of when I was sick and how I've grown and how I was so young to be in the cavalry. I did not deny that I was now in Captain's cavalry. It made me feel good, grown up, and scared all at the same time. Doc convinced me to stop and water the horses again.

While in the meadow, watering the horses, we heard gun fire from the south. It had to be Chris, so we both quickly mounted and rode off. No words were said, and Flash was running hard. Doc was behind and falling further back. I slowed some when I recognized where we were. We were not far from the farm, and it was near Mikey's maple grove. The trees were still tapped for syrup, and his north summer camp was just ahead. I circled the camp to make sure it was empty, but Doc was not as worried and rode right into camp. He was thirsty for some whiskey and ready for a nap. I thought, *There couldn't be much danger.* And so I followed Doc into camp. Doc was adamant about resting, starting a fire, and getting a meal in us. I did not want to stop, so I rode ahead to find Chris. There was no sign of him, and I was now alone in the hills. My mind was playing tricks on me, and I remembered Mikey talking about the hungry bears in the area. Bears were not afraid of Mikey, so now I was riding with my rifle in hand. I found the trail that I had been on several times, a trail that went almost straight to the farm. There was still no sign of Chris but no sign of Russian soldiers either. I returned to Mikey's camp in the maple grove where Doc had a fire going and food prepared. His whiskey bottle was mostly gone, and he was seemingly passed out. He opened his eyes as I rode in. A scared look with rifle in hand and trembling, Doc knew it was time to ride on. I did eat some of Doc's porridge or whatever it was. It had mostly boiled syrup and oats. It smelled good but did not taste very good, and so I was quick to announce that we were leaving. I told Doc that it was only ten miles to my farm, and I knew the trail well. As he began to saddle his horse, I knew there was something wrong. The horses had become wild, jumpy, and very nervous. They would not stand still and threw Doc's saddle to the ground. Doc was cussing at the horse as if it was the horse's fault. "Stand still, you long-legged bitch," he muttered under his breath. He was too drunk to saddle a horse, but Doc was certain it was the horse's fault.

He finally got the saddle on the jumpy horse, and that's when he looked up at me; I was on point. A large bear had the horses spooked, and the hot syrup was a smell the bear had smelled before and was coming right for us. I moved my horse forward three steps; I gave Flash a tight squeeze. I had never killed a bear before. I had only heard about them. I was trembling in fear as I aimed at the large bruin. It seemed like the bear was barely moving, but I could not get a definite kill shot off. Doc was not moving and was now only a few feet from the intruder. I finally got off a quality shot and turned the bear away from Doc. Now it was running right at me. I made a second shot when the beast was only a few feet from me. The second shot was the kill shot. I hit him right between the eyes and dropped the big black ball of fur directly between me and Doc. The horses did amazingly well. The dead bear laid in Mikey's camp, right next to his fire and remaining syrup barrels.

Doc was shaking a bit and took a large drink from the whiskey bottle. He offered me the bottle, but I denied. As he took another big swig, he laid it on the ground. As soon as he had, he finished sinching up his horse; he mounted and rode ahead a few steps. My third shot shattered the whiskey bottle.

I was visibly upset; Doc had nearly cost both of us our lives, and now there was a good chance the Russian soldiers had heard the gunfire and were heading this way. Most of the day had passed, and as we rode to the farm with the sun on the horizon, I reflected on my day. My first day as a soldier seemed like a lifetime of events. I had calmed down some and returned my rifle to its scabbard. I made sure to reload my gun, and my trembling had stopped. I was riding tall in the saddle and feeling very accomplished. I knew I had done well, and Captain would be proud. I have a story to tell, and every soldier I knew will be proud of me. Doc and I rode into the farm before dark, and the smell of the smokers were once again a welcome sign for sure. There were twenty-five wagons lined up in a near perfect line and were loaded as full as they could be. My story had been rolling in my mind since we left the maple grove, but now it was confusing. The farm did not look the same. Strike had spotted me and now was running next to me almost as if he knew his best friend had accomplished one hell of a ride and was a success. I rode in tall and proud. I was only at the farm for a few minutes, and soldiers gathered around to hear my adventure. As I was only getting started telling my story, Christopher was spotted riding hard and heading this way. I smiled as my worry for Chris and his safety felt resolved. We had made it before nightfall, and we were safe with Doc.

CHAPTER 3

OAK GROVE

Captain and Mother, along with the girls, had the entire wagon loaded mostly of food and cooking utensils. The second wagon was completely full of supplies—spare wagon wheel, rope, and a box full of rifles and ammo. Mother was to drive the wagon, and her sister Viola was to follow in the supply wagon. Every one of us had our own mount. We were accomplished riders, and Captain had insisted that every person learn to ride and ride well. I was still bursting with pride as my ride was still fresh as the sun fell on our farm. Captain was speaking loud for everyone to hear, "We must leave tonight at midnight." He explained, "We have a hell of a trip ahead of us, and where our next stop will be is several hundred miles ride." We were to travel as fast as twenty-five-loaded wagons could go with all the gear and not lose anything. Mark and John, another scout in Captain's cavalry, had not returned. They were sent ahead to find a safe trail to travel at night. Mark knew every trail and had ridden most of them in the dark. It was only a matter of time before they returned. Although I was tired and was wondering why we are leaving in the dark, I did not question Captain. I was able to get some rest and a good meal. Flash was resting too. I made sure he got fresh water and something to eat.

Dr. Schweitzer was busy in the house. He had to remove some war bullets, and although Marcella had the wounded well prepared, it was a bloody painful reality. After several hours, he exited the house, bloody and worn out. He was talking to Captain and was worried about the lieutenant who had a bullet lodged in his hip and could not get it out. Doc complimented Marcella and Mother for the fine job they had done. He explained without their preparation, none of the wounded could be moved. He also said that the lieutenant should not be moved for several days. This was not an option, as the entire division and families were leaving at midnight. Captain would not change his mind. He told Doc to prepare all the men to ride.

Mark and John returned, and the journey was upon us. Everything was loaded. The smokers were now extinguished and all the stock was ready for travel. The girls were tired as they did all the loading of the food, but everything was in the wagons. Our cellar was empty, the dungeon was empty, and our house, although still filled with wounded, had been cleared out. To my surprise, Captain ordered Mark and the six scouts to start the ride west. They were to stay miles ahead of the main wagon train but report back as often as needed. Mark was very happy to get started. The others did not have his enthusiasm and continually had to slow him down.

All the soldiers had their own ride and were all cavalry mounts. The men with family stayed with the family wagons. Marcella had the lieutenant with her in her wagon. There was a total of forty soldiers, all riding except the injured lieutenant. He was in a covered wagon, and his horse was tied to the wagon and was following along. There were thirty women and twenty-two teenagers. There were only two girls under the age of ten, and they were in their family wagon with their mother. Ninety-four mouths to feed along with seventy horses, four cows, and four pigs. Strike followed, and by 1:00 a.m., the entire caravan was on the trail. The first several hours were through the hills; it was an easy trail to follow and not a lot of danger. Captain expected this and knew come daylight the entire caravan would have to travel at a much faster pace. The entire caravan had made it through the hills without incident, and as the sun came up and the trail narrowed, Captain insisted, "Everyone pick up the pace. We must ride faster." The scouts were on lookout, and Mark and John were still riding point and doing a very good job directing the caravan. Chris and a few others were to follow and double back to make sure we were not being followed. I wanted to ride with Chris, but I did not complain a lot when I was told to ride guard with my rifle. I knew the threat was minimal, but I was quite tired. Flash walked, and he too was tired; he had been riding for almost two days straight.

All day the caravan continued as Captain pushed and pushed, and the only stops were at water crossings where he allowed the horses to water and rest. The women made a quick lunch, and that was it; back on the trail we went. Captain wanted to ride straight through to the oak grove of trees. That meant riding all night and all day again. Mother convinced Captain to stop against his better judgment; the caravan came to a stop just after sundown, and the wagons were circled, and the horses and stock grazed in the middle. No one was allowed to unpack anything as It was to rest and get some sleep only. At first sight of sunrise, we were to continue west. The scouts had returned with good news—we are not being followed. Mark and John returned with good news as well. The next forty miles were easy and without any water crossings. Captain was uneasy. He was resting and wondering that if the next forty miles could be done at night, why were we resting.

The morning came fast, and the sun was on the rise. Captain had all his men on their mounts. He had Mother and the girls ready to travel and were on their way immediately. Unfortunately, Mikey was one of the slowest and was following Mother but just could not travel as fast. He had his wagon full of syrup barrels and had his pack mule packed as full as one can pack a mule. His team of horses also pulled the water wagon. Altogether, it was a big load, which was slow. The caravan was rolling west before the sun came over the horizon. Although some did not like Captain's insistence on traveling fast, no one ever questioned him. The entire caravan crossed the forty-mile sand fields and entered into the hills by dark. There was no way Captain was stopping come sundown.

Mark reported back that there were some rocky and rough terrain ahead, and it would definitely slow us down. We had traveled one hundred miles in thirty hours. The caravan was slower than expected, and Captain started pushing hard. "No one is to stop," he said with authority.

The slow travelers fell behind, and the first wagon wheel was now broken. Captain insisted on the entire caravan continue. He gave the Millers a spare wagon wheel and had four soldiers change it and get them back on the trail asap. The majority of the caravan had made it through the rocky pass. Once through the pass, most of the trip was a slow downhill slope. Lots of rocks, but downhill.

Chris and the other scouts also returned. They did not have as good a news as Captain wanted. They went on to tell Captain that the Russian army had found his farm, and they were burning it as we spoke. It also meant they would easily find our trail and were not far behind. The news traveled quickly through the caravan, and the pace had to increase. It was downhill and rocky; Captain now pushed harder and harder. "If any wheels are to break at this time, others will have to make room, as we do not have time to change wheels." He shouted, "It is imperative we make it to the oaks before the Russian army catches up!" The entire caravan traveled all night; they traveled fast and quiet. The downhill trail helped the pace, and the horses were pulling a little easier.

It was rough on everybody. While tired, worn, and hungry, the entire caravan forged on. The scouts continued to report back. The Russians were not gaining on us and had stopped to camp before riding into the rocky hills that we had just traveled through in the dark. Fog had once again set in, and Captain seemed to be relieved as we could travel nearly undetected. "At least no one will see us," I heard Captain say to Mother. Mark and John had been directing the entire caravan and doing a great job. They were finding a trail in the fog, but that would prove to be *not* as easy. We were now past the area Mark knew. No one knew actually, but Captain did know that there was a large grove of oak trees ahead that would provide shelter, cover, and safety. Although Captain had been there before, it was several years ago and not in the fog. Captain encouraged Mark and the scouts to continue on. The sunlight could not break through the fog, and the caravan traveled all day, pushed hard into the evening. John reported back to Captain that the grove was only twenty miles ahead. Unfortunately, Chris reported that the Russians were through the rocky pass and were following and gaining.

We still were hours ahead, but Captain was not content, and he insisted that we all must now run or trot. We had to push harder now than ever. If we could get to the trees before we were detected, we could mount a defensive and eliminate the followers altogether. Mikey was left to trail behind, but several soldiers stayed with him. The rest began to run or trot through the rocky terrain. It was very rough on the wagons, and the dangers of such a ride had now become evident.

We had our first tragedy, and it was a horrible one. One of the youngest of the girls had fallen out of the wagon, and she was killed almost immediately. Doc tried to help her, but she had died instantly from a sharp blow to the head. The soldiers dug a quick hole, a small box for a casket was erected, and Sally was buried. A few short words and a few prayers were said, and the caravan continued. The lieutenant in the wagon with a bullet in his hip was fading, and Doc did not think he would make it much further. Captain worked the entire caravan that was now spread out over a mile. He pushed and pushed. "We all must make the grove and prepare for a battle." He could not be more forceful as he coached the wagons to keep riding.

Mark finally reported that the grove was just ahead and we were near. The first wagons started into the trees right where several of the soldiers had already found a perfect ambush spot. We needed to get the entire caravan into the grove of oaks before we were detected by the chasing Russian army. One wagon after another wheeled in, and the horses and most of the families looked worn out. It was a long, hard three days of travel, but Captain had done it. He has everyone, even Mikey and his wagons and mules, in the trees. The soldiers were busy hiding the families and wagons. Captain's cavalry were experienced soldiers and had been in many battles, and yet there still was a nervousness among them all. The battle was planned, and no one expected to see any of the enemy before sunup. Once the ambush was set, the men joined the families. A good meal and plenty of rest was welcomed by everyone.

Every soldier was up before dawn. Every rifle was prepared, checked, and double-checked. Although every soldier was battle tested, never had they fought for the life of their immediate family's that was only a couple hundred yards away. As the Russian army came marching into the grove, the surprise attack had worked. Once Captain announced the attack and the bullets started flying, the battle was quick. I did not take place in any the shooting, but I kept every soldier loaded and plush with ammo. Every Russian soldier was killed, and the battle was over in only two hours. Only two men were wounded, and although their horses died, the battle was celebrated. Captain was not heartless and without God; before any celebrating, the opposition had to be buried. The few horses they had left alive and not injured were unsaddled and released, and 150 unmarked graves were dug and filled. By dinnertime, everything was done. All the scouts had returned, and although the battle was over, everyone was too tired to celebrate. John did make a trip to the ocean and returned with more good news. It was only four miles to the shore, and several ships were at dock. Captain announced for everyone to get some rest. "Tomorrow we will start our long adventure. We will prepare and plan to leave this land behind." He announced, "A new life will be upon us soon!"

CHAPTER 4

FAMILY

Mikey had the grill going, and the sun was finally out. The slight breeze was swaying the leaves of the giant oak trees. More than three days have passed since we had left with our family and friends. The thought of our home, our fields, and our record crop was gone. Captain had led the men and all the families away from danger. We had been through tragedy, a fierce deadly battle, dense fog with only a trail to follow, and yet the attitude of the entire caravan seemed to be peaceful. Mikey was handing out pancakes and syrup; all was good. Captain and Mark were mounted and riding together, which was a dream Mark has talked about for years. As they rode away, Chris and John followed. Six others rode off to the east. I had slept with my dog, Strike, and my trusty horse, Flash. It seemed as if I had only slept for minutes, and yet the sun was up, and several of the men were already riding away.

Mikey recognized that I was finally awake and welcomed me to the breakfast table. He prepared a plate of blueberry pancakes especially for me special. Just as I began to eat, Doc sat down beside me. He sipped on his coffee with a look of happiness. He started to ask me questions, "How did you learn to ride so good at such a young age?" He asked, "Why do you call your dog Strike and your horse Flash?"

I had never thought of why, I guess, but I replied with a commonsense answer, "My horse is named Flash because he was born during a lightning storm, and the flashes of the lightning allowed me to see him being born. My dog Strike was named after a slight strike across his chest." Doc smiled and enjoyed our conversation. He complimented my riding and thanked me for insisting he come with us. Doc had seemed to have a new outlook on life and insisted "he will no longer be drinking." I don't imagine this will be an easy task for Doc to accomplish. We talked about the bear and the amazing ride through the rough terrain. We talked about most everything that morning—about my sisters and mother and about how Captain had led the battle and had his men prepared even after a long grueling ride.

I listened to Doc Schweitzer as he poured his story out. He talked about his wife who was a cousin to King Nicholas's wife, who also died of the plague. He tried to explain how he tried to save her as he did me and how his life had been changed because of her death. His tears came and went along with my smiles and grief. I think about our ride together and how the conversation this morning has created a bond, a family bond. I believe we are now friends. I thanked him for the talk several times as he was talking to me as an adult and a friend. Mikey was listening and was cleaning up while Doc and I finished up. We were the last to eat, and we sat and talked what seemed like hours. Doc Schweitzer hugged me and thanked me again as he walked away. Mikey was impressed and could not believe I had shot a bear to save Doc's life. As I was telling Mikey the entire story, I realized that almost no one knew what had happened, how I got Doc to ride with me through the rough terrain and through the maple trees.

Mikey could not believe I shot a bear in his camp and then just left it there. I shot a bear that had been spotted a few times, but not even Mikey could get a shot at him. Mikey and I sat for a while as I told him the entire story; then, I helped him finish cleaning up. We were about done when several of the others came over to the table. Even my sisters wanted to hear, so I announced, "This is my last time telling the story." By now, most of the other kids were attentively listening, and it made me feel pretty awesome. It made me feel like I was Captain. Doc watched from a distance, while talking to Mother. As he sipped his coffee, I could see him smile. He gave Mother a hug and walked away. Mother seemed to glow with pride and came and sat down. For the first time in several days, she seemed to be at peace, and yet her face still had great concern.

Mark and Captain were riding into camp with Mark riding with pride. His dreams of riding with Captain and his hopes of Captain trusting him as a soldier had come true. Mark was wearing a cavalry uniform, which was something I had never seen before. The girls watched him and Captain ride in too, and it was a rare sight for all of us. Even Mother did not seem to mind; she was happy to see them together. As Captain dismounted and I led his horse away, Mother and Captain hugged and kissed, which was something that none of us has ever seen very often. Captain sat down and enjoyed a cup of coffee with Mother at his side. All of us were just watching and listening as Captain explained the delay. "We are going to camp in this spot for another day, maybe more." He then began to assign chores to all of us. We were going to build a temporary cabin using the supply wagon and the trees, a place for shelter and to sleep. I was enjoying being outside, and I knew Mark did not mind either. Captain knew that Mother and the girls wanted something more.

As we began our project, Mark and I both got our horses ready for the day. I again noticed Mother with her arms around Captain watching with pride; her family was working together to build a shelter for the girls.

Amazingly, Mark and I had planned something like this many times. We had built many forts out of trees in the past. Our years of planning was paying off; except this time, we actually got to use a saw and rope. Mark and I knew what we needed, and I began cutting trees and using our horses to drag the bigger branches and trees to our building site. Mark was barking out direction to all the girls. "Get the rope and cut them like this. You two begin tying the ends like this." There was never a fight or even an argument. Captain had brought over the supply wagon and just let us build. It was not long before we had a nice two-room makeshift cabin built, and as we were sitting in our newly built castle, we decided we needed a better roof. We worked hard to support the roof with larger trees, and that had proved to be a much more difficult task than we remember doing. Diane actually helped a lot and had used her horse along with the block and tackle to raise the large tree to the roof.

It was amazing that after only a couple hours and the entire family working together, we had constructed a very livable shack. Janet made a table, and Linda and Carol were making chairs. Mother came into the cabin, not knowing what she would find. To her amazement, it was pretty decent. She immediately exclaimed, "This will work." Captain rode off and now was returning with what looked like a bail of grass. He brought it into the shack and spread it out in the sleeping area. He had gathered enough moss for at least three beds, and the entire family just sat in our new cabin smiling in silence.

After a few minutes Mark, spoke up. He wanted to hear the story of me shooting a bear. Captain wanted to know how I saved Dr. Schweitzer's life, and Mother had not heard any of this. For the first time in my life, everyone in the family was listening attentively as I told the story again. We laughed as Mother's eyes opened wide and her jaw seemed to drop. Captain had not heard me tell a story with such conviction. It still seemed as if we had a long journey ahead of us, but we have had several days of very difficult times, and this story was like a little glue to keep us together. It formed a bond like nothing before.

The day was coming to an end, dinner was being planned, and the scouts had returned with good news. There was no one looking for us. News of the Russian army had not been heard by anyone, and we were safe. Our food was packed away, and Mother talked about what we were going to eat. Mark and I asked Captain if we could use the rifles he gave us to try to hunt down a deer. He smiled and gave us the okay. Our horses were near ready, and both Mark and I agreed we must go immediately. We did not bother to saddle our horses. We grabbed our rifles, mounted our horses, and rode away into the trees. We had hunted together many times, and we knew each other well. Mark made sure the wind was right, as I rode outside the grove for nearly a mile. I tied Flash to a tree and began my stalk. I had spotted a nice buck and wanted to make the kill. Before I could get a shot off, I heard Mark shoot. I heard the cathump and knew he had made the kill. We made quick work to field dress that buck, and there were plenty of high fives and smiles as we quickly rode back to camp. As we rode in, Captain asked what we forgot. He then noticed we had a nice buck already, and his laughter alone was enough for us. Surprisingly to Mark and myself, the girls had built a tripod butcher stand. The deer was hanging and was completely skinned out when Mother came walking up; she was wondering what all the commotion was. When she saw that we had immediate success hunting and the girls were done skinning and were butchering, she knew then that our family had come together. Fresh venison was on the menu. It was a good day.

CHAPTER 5

The Announcements

Mikey had outdone himself this morning. The pancakes were accompanied by bacon and ham. The entire community had eaten, and Mikey was resting while enjoying a cup of coffee. The last of the kids got up and left, and some of the ladies started to clean up. Viola poured the remaining grease onto the deer carcass, and the pigs entertained the guys fighting over the deer carcass. Fresh conversation, smiles, and laughs made breakfast our best meal so far.

Captain had been thinking about something all morning, and it was weighing heavy on him. His restless posture was easy to recognize. I had mentioned to Captain about trying to catch some fish for supper, but he had something else on his mind. I don't think anyone but Mark and myself knew there was a fresh creek running into a lake only a mile from the oaks. I have learned to never pester Captain about fishing, but Mother and some of the others were also talking about washing and bathing. I did not realize I have been in the same clothes for a week, but I think everyone was. About as the families started to leave the eating area, Captain stood and asked to be heard. He suggested, "The creek for fresh water and bathing is only a mile away." He made it a point to remind everyone to fill their water containers and canteens. His last point was to separate the things you can carry. He did not go into detail, but I was certain Flash and I could carry my belongings and probably more. He announced that he and the three remaining officers will be gone until sundown. Then he sadly announced, "Lieutenant Martin had died from the bullet wound to his hip. His casket is almost ready, and his funeral will be tomorrow morning." It was visibly hard on Captain and Mother to hear of Martin's death. He was godfather to Diane and has been a close friend to Captain for many years. As everyone was now on their feet, Captain finally mentioned, "Tonight, after dinner, everyone interested in when and where we are going next should meet me at the fire."

Captain then gave Mark and me permission to try to fish for supper.

The girls were in the makeshift cabin and came out with only their underclothes on and clean dresses in hand. Diane asked the way to the lake, and so off all four of them went; within seconds, half the camp was following. It was late fall and rather cold for a swim in the lake, but I think the idea of bathing outweighed the thought of how cold it would be. I grabbed my fishing rods, and Mark grabbed the horses. We both knew the best spot to catch fish, and we were heading that way. Several of the men asked to join us, and of course, I immediately invited them all. I only had two fishing rods, and although I used them the most, they were Captain's; Mark had no thoughts about using the second rod.

We made quick work of the mile ride to the river. We both had been watching for frogs. The closer we got, the more there were. With a smile and enthusiasm, I spouted off, "We are going to kill 'em!" Mark agreed. I had learned a long time ago to hit the frogs with a stick before trying to catch them in the grass. I had three frogs in no time, and my line was in the water. Mark was not far behind, and as the men started to arrive along the river, our lines were in. No one else had even a pole. I was starting to whittle a makeshift second rod, and several of the men were doing the same thing. I did have enough line, and it wasn't long before eight frogs were dangling in the water. I found a few big rocks to sit on and to perch my pole on. A few of the guys were wading in the river, even washing themselves. I mentioned to Mark loudly enough for them to hear, "As long as they are near us in the water, we will probably not have much luck." They got the hint and strolled away. It was about then I had my first bite.

It struck hard and immediately dislodged my pole from the perch. It flew into the water faster than I could grab it, so I let out a Tarzan-like scream and jumped into the river after my pole. It must have been quite a leap, as before my feet hit the bottom of the river, I had my pole in hand, and the water was nearly drowning me. Mark and a few others let out an amazing laugh. I don't think I had heard the men laugh and enjoy themselves like that ever before. Mark was there to help me to shore, and as I got my footing, I turned my attention to my rod. The fish was still hooked and now was putting up quite a struggle. As I was landing my fish with Mark's help, I could not stop smiling. The men were still laughing, but I knew I had caught quite a fish and the attention of the men. "A few more fish like this and we would have enough fish to feed everyone," I exclaimed.

I was settling back into my spot when James came strolling back closer to us. He warned, "Stay away from the water as it will scare the fish away." Another laughter started, and I guess I deserved it. He walked over to me and laid five dead frogs next to me. He smiled again and said I can catch his share of the fish.

Mark, taking his turn with the jokes, said between breaths, "I guess you won't need a bath." The fishing was steady with more fish being caught than frogs. We began to cut the frogs into pieces so all the lines could stay baited. By early afternoon, we had thirty fish on shore, and the conversation turned to who was cleaning fish and how are we getting them back to camp. It was not my first time fishing and not the first time we had caught more fish than I could carry. Mark gave up his rod and started to clean the fish. He found a pretty flat stump and started in on filleting the fish. He would fillet the fish, and I would debone them. A few of the others tried to help but were wasting more meat than we liked, so we assigned them to rinse the meat thoroughly. "I have an empty game bag along for the fish fillets," I said. "But we must have a hundred pounds of fish, and it will not all fit in the bag."

I did not get close to having the room for our catch, and so Mark began to question the men. "Who of you has more than one shirt on?" he asked. The men knew right away what his plan was, and before we knew it, the men had tied their sleeves into knots, dipped them in the river, and filled the makeshift game bags with the fillets. We all walked together back to camp, and the horses carried the day's catch. We reminisced about the first catch and laughed again. We had a great day at the river, and as we approached camp, I reminded all the fishermen that we all were there and my first fish was still the biggest of the day. Once again, the guys' laughter filled the meadow with our day's fun.

As we returned to camp, I was showing Mikey our catch. Mother was quick to ask if I had bathed since we left the farm, and once again, Mark and I laughed. I began to tell the story of the biggest fish of the day, and that no, I don't need a bath. Most of the camp had gone to the lake and had returned long before we did. There were clothes hanging on a makeshift clothesline everywhere. A line normally used to tie our horses was now a clothesline. Mother and the girls had moved the horses off the line, and they were just grazing in the area. Captain had not returned, and Mother asked us if we had prepared a small bag to carry if we were to no longer have use of the wagon. I told Mother that I don't have much and that I would be able to carry my stuff and probably help her with anything she needed help with. I went on to tell her that my rifle and shotgun, my fishing rods, my bedroll, and my jacket would all fit easily on Flash. She then went on to say, "What if you don't have Flash, would you be able to carry what you needed?" I easily could but would not consider leaving the oaks without Flash. I could not believe it would be suggested to leave Flash behind. Mother in her calm motherly voice assured me that we would not leave Flash behind.

Our catch was more than plenty for the entire community to eat their fill. We all were done eating, and there were still plenty of leftovers. Captain and his officers had not returned, so the dinner table remained, and the fish and potatoes that were left over did not yet go to the pigs. The sun was all but gone, and the shadows of Captain and the men with the last of a beautiful sunset at their backs began to appear. There were now six men and no wagon riding into camp. Mother immediately started to heat up the coffee and the fish. There was more than enough, and the arrival of two extra did not cause a commotion, and two more plates were immediately ready. Captain and the three officers and the two new arrivals all sat down, ate, and sipped coffee with very little conversation. Captain again looked agitated. He did ask how fishing had gone; knowing the answer, he then asked if all the girls got to bathe. It was small talk, and it what was not actually what was on Captain's mind.

The entire camp had gathered at the fire. Everyone pitched in with firewood for the community fire. Wood was plentiful and mostly oak, so the fire was big and warm. There was a spot reserved for the six men coming to the fire, and everyone was anxious to hear the news. As Captain began to speak, a complete quietness was obvious. Only a slight crackle of a burning hot fire could be heard. Captain first introduced the two new men. "This is Ole and Captain Oxford." Ox was also a captain, and Ole was his first mate.

They were well-dressed men, very tall, and by the way, the girls were immediately smitten; they were handsome. Their physique and stand-tall posture gave the men away. They were not German and certainly not Russian, both with light blonde hair and big blue eyes. The two new men said only a few words, and it was not German. They spoke English, something Mother had taught us but not something I caught on to. Mark and Diane said hello in English. Captain announced that these two men would be teaching English to all of us. "We all must learn how to speak, read, and write in English." Captain's speech was short and to the point.

Captain traded a wagon for books, pencils, and paper, which was something no one had expected, and the families' murmurs had started. Captain barked in displeasure of the lack of attention he was now given. He talked of our journey and the sacrifices we all have made. He talked about the wounded men and the men that we had lost. We all bowed our head and said a prayer for Sally and the lost men. I thought he was done, and that is when he stood up onto the log. He announced, "We are leaving Russia! When the time is right, we will board a ship and sail for America. Now is the time to speak up if you do not want to go. We will have to board the ship at night and get everything boarded and ready to sail as the tides roll out." Captain was not sure exactly what day we were leaving, but it will be soon. The announcement of our departure would be sudden, and he urged everyone to be ready at a moment's notice. His final words were said with conviction and almost like an order, "We are German now, but in a few months, we will be Americans." A loud cheer filled the oaks. No one ever spoke up, and all of us were anxious but excited to get started on our journey. For the first time that I can remember, Captain remained at the fire as did the majority of the community. More wood was added to the fire, and we enjoyed each other's company late into the night. Ole and Captain Oxford were now the center of the attention. The story of my big fish was laughed at several more times, but talk of America and what our new life would be like dominated the conversations.

CHAPTER 6

The Departure

The trails to the river and the living area of the community were more than obvious with ninety-three people living in a small area. Fires every day and most nights have left a scar on a once uninhabited area. It was the third day Captain and five others were leaving the oaks with as many wagons. Our makeshift camp that had twenty-five wagons, and several cavalry tents were starting to shrink. This day, Captain took our entire supply wagon of food. I knew our departure from the oak grove was not far away. Chris and John have been riding patrol along with several others. Every morning and every evening, the men had been riding further and further to make sure our community was still safe. The worry of Russian soldiers searching for the lost Russian men that lie dead in the 150 unmarked graves has become the topic of many conversations. "These men had families and children," I heard Mother say. "There will be a search party, and the graves and blood will be noticed." There was also the concern that

Captain and his men's last battle against the Russian army was cause for King Nicolaus to send his army to find the AWOL cavalry.

Our time in the oaks is coming to an end. Our food and supply wagon is gone. Our second wagon, part of our makeshift cabin, and the cavalry tents were down. Mother gathered and packed any gear we had left in camp. In only the few days we had there, the friendships we made had become as good as friends can get. Our family and friends have been through a lot, and the thought of continuing our journey together was easier and not quite as strange. The people who were once not more than an acquaintance, now seemed like family. The girls made new friends, and both Mark and myself felt closer to being a cavalry soldier than we ever had. Our riding skills became as good as anyone's. Chris had given us many pointers on how to ride. He would say, "Ride low through trees. Keep your head down and your eyes open. Let the horse run. Move your bodies with the horse. When in the open and going at a full run, give the horse all the rein, and move your hips and learn how to direct your horse with only your legs."

Mark and I caught lots of fish and in return showed the cavalry men how to fish and have fun trying, how to clean and debone fish, and we have made some bows and arrows. We also began learning the skills of hunting a deer with a bow. We had many attempts on stalking deer with our bows, and we had Chris and John to thank for that. Our adventure, although not without tragedy, had been a lot of fun. We learned a lot of new skills and sharpened our skills that Captain had been teaching us since we were very young. Everyone in camp had been learning from Captain

Ox, and our English had been improving every day. Diane was hanging with Ox every day, and her English was getting really good. She was also now teaching others. Carol had been reading, writing, and teaching English to the boys and men. Everyone had been learning, and even Mark and I learned some English.

Learning English from my sisters was not for me. I am a horseman, riding faster and further than any other. I have become infatuated with Flash. He is my best friend. When I am on him, I am a cavalry soldier, and I feel like I can do anything. I have taught him to come to me on a whistle, he swims with me on his back, and when riding and running through the trees, we jump and swerve and dodge left or right. We know each other well and each of our moves before they happen; we ride as one, and I know we both are enjoying our rides together.

Captain and the men had once again returned to camp with only the horses. They returned long before sundown and announced that tonight is the night that we were leaving camp and would be setting sail for the New World—America. He once again made sure everyone knew that we could only take onto the ship what we could carry and no wagons would be loaded on the ship. Captain had arranged for every wagon and extra horses to be sold or traded for supplies. Extra blankets, books, ammunition, and winter clothing were all things that Captain mentioned that we would need. Winter was coming, and we would need to stay warm. Ole had been showing us a way to soak solid oak logs with grease and some shaving from ironwood. These logs outlasted and outperformed any other heat source and could be burned in a barrel for heat and for cooking, something no one has thought of. Ole assured us we would want to and needed as many of these logs as we could make and load.

Supplies needed for our trip across the Atlantic was a big concern, but Ole and Ox had made the trip before and were confident that they could safely lead us across the ocean. Several barrels were filled with fresh water. They were heavy, and my curiosity on how to load such things keep me asking questions. Once again, Ole has an answer that I could understand and make sense of. "Why were we leaving at night?" was still hard for me to understand, and "Why doesn't the ocean freeze? and "How can all this stuff fit in one boat and the boat not sink?" "How can we sail if there is no wind?" So many questions, and yet Ole and Ox had answers, not always answers I understood, but quality answers.

That evening after dark and as I looked around our now dismantled camp, I began to cry. Mother comforted me and tried to hide it from the others. I was not totally sure why I was crying. I guess it was that we were leaving an area where I was so happy being at. I was a soldier and accomplished rider in Captain's cavalry. I was the best fisherman in camp and had the best rods and all the gear. The cavalry men asked me for advice on how to fish and how to fillet fish. They asked me to ride point with my well-trained horse. I was not sure if I would ever get to do these things again. Mother was holding me tight as if she might not ever get to hold her youngest child again. I guess we were both a little bit scared. Holding each other was very comforting that evening.

We were all just about ready to start our four-mile ride to the Black Sea when we heard a mighty scream. "The Russian army is coming!" John and Chris were riding hard and heading our way. They had been riding guard that evening while watching for just such an event, and it was here. The Russian army had finally found its missing AWOL cavalry and were sure to find the unmarked graves. The trail they were on was leading them right to us. Captain had already hauled all the rifles and ammo to the ship, and we didn't have much left in camp. Captain was once again on his horse and barking out commands. The departure from our beautiful camp was swift and complete. We were gone within minutes, and Flash and I were at the shores quickly.

Captain and his men had stolen a Russian ship and had attached several wagons together to make a temporary but solid dock to load our entire supplies onto the *huge* ship. There were several strangers there to buy or just haul away what we couldn't load onto the ship, and Captain was not in the wheeling and dealing mood. What he said went, and there were no arguments. Captain was making quick decisions as he wanted us loaded and on our way before any Russian soldiers even knew that they had found us. The ship was loaded quickly, and by 2:00 a.m., we were sailing slowly away. It had become a bit windy, and snow was falling. We moved slowly through the water, and I could see the dock made from fifteen wagons was being dismantled.

We had loaded so much supplies and horses and people it seemed impossible for us to float, but yet the giant ship was moving further and further away. Captain did not count how many horses were loaded. He did not count how many barrels of fresh water or of Mikey's syrup were loaded. He filled the ship until he figured it was full, and the rest was left behind. Several horses and all the wagons were basically what was left. Every man, woman, and child were watching as we floated into the snow-filled darkness. I could hear gunfire from the shore. In my mind, we had loaded and left just in time. Captain was still very nervous, and so he ordered men onto the deck with their rifles. Ole and Ox were definitely experienced sailors, and Captain listened to Captain Ox.

We were sailing away in a stolen Russian ship with stolen Russian cavalry horses. We had killed an entire division of Russian soldiers, and King Nickolas and his men were now on the shore from where we just left. If we were to get caught, it would mean definite death to everyone. Ole and Ox knew the risk too and were making sure that all the sails were pointed in the right direction. Most of the cavalry men stayed on deck all night with their loaded rifles. The wind was roaring along with the waves. The snow was starting to let up, but the wind was not. The giant ship was swaying and dancing in the water. We no longer could see the shore, and the waves were bigger than I could imagine. The swells were huge, and as the front of the boat came down, huge waves pounded the ship; water was coming over the front. Ole quickly dropped the big sail down, and two little sails were raised. The efficiency and skill of how these two men kept the ship from sinking and moving forward was nothing short of a miracle. They sailed the ship and stayed on the wet deck all through the night. Wet, tired, and hungry, the two sailors and several cavalry men got us through the windstorm. By sunup, we were at sea.

The big sail was back up, and the little sails were pointed in another direction. We were moving slowly, and the water seemed to end where the sky began. We could not see shore from any direction, and a lot of the men and women were getting sick. As I watched the sun come up that morning, strange things went through my mind. One of my biggest concerns was what if the ship were to sink, which way would I direct Flash to swim, and could we swim enough hours to find shore? Captain Oxford was now speaking about balancing our load and how the horses were to be split. Half the horses were to move to one side and the other half to the other, front to back and side to side. Ole had made comment on the load size and made sure what Ox was telling the men was getting done correctly. We went from a beautiful huge camp with huge areas to ride and hunt in to a very small, contained area. I was concerned on how we would ride the horses. I was told that we would not ride any of the horses and their food intake was to shrink to nearly nothing. We had two months to ride on this ship, and we better get as comfortable as we could. I could not imagine not riding Flash for two months. The horses were separated evenly, and very small living spaces were announced to each family. It did not seem possible to live this way. Mikey has been settled in and now has pancakes ready for whoever wanted some. Many of the women and children were sick along with several of the men. The ones that could eat, ate, but Mark and I got all the leftovers. The rocking boat did not bother me, and if anything, I enjoyed it.

As the sun got higher and the wind once again picked up, I noticed how fast we were moving through the water.

We were creating a nice little wake, and I commented on how fun it would be to fish off the back deck of the boat. Ole just smiled and commented on how I was already becoming a pretty good sailor and how my fishing skills would come in handy. The sea air was cold. Without a winter jacket, it would be too cold to stay on the deck.

Mikey was keeping the galley and living area warm with his barrel-style oven. Diane was making a makeshift schoolroom and thought everyone should spend time in school. She insisted that she will teach us reading, writing, and arithmetic in English, and if she has any questions, she would ask Oxford. Diane and Ox were getting quite close, and it was obvious to me there was more than just learning going on. I was not impressed with Diane's makeshift school and her idea of being my teacher. Mark just laughed and said she would never teach him anything. We stuck together on the idea, but Diane was confident she was the right person for the job. Mother knew it too; Diane had always been the teacher type, and Mother was all right with Diane and Oxford being close. Captain, on the other hand, was not okay with it. He did not want any of his daughters mingling with the men for any reason, school or not.

The girls had been flirting with all the men and had "private talk" among just the single men. Dancing and laying with the girls were joked about a lot. Mark and I laughed too and gave permission to take our sisters and do whatever they wanted with them. Captain on the other hand did not like the talk and wanted to forbid the men to see any of the women on board; if caught, they would have to remain in the basement with the stock for the remaining of the trip. This rule of the Captain's was not followed and would be near impossible to enforce. The living quarters were small, so to keep the men from seeing women would just not be possible. There were forty-one men, which included Ole and Oxford, thirty women, and twenty-two teenagers of which fifteen were young ladies; all of which wanted to snuggle with someone during the cold nights at sea. We had been sailing for only seven nights, and they were already starting to pair up. Captain kept a close eye on all his family and made sure that every night before lights out, we prayed together for safety and that the good Lord would keep all the families together and safe.

Captain insisted that our entire family stay in one area and sleep together. He allowed me to stay with my horse from time to time, and that was only because I promised to clean the onboard corral. There was plenty of straw to bed down in, and both Flash and myself enjoyed each other's company. Strike did not ever come down to the double bottom to visit the horses. When I went below or stayed overnight with Flash, he stayed with Linda. She held Strike every night, and I did not mind. Even when I was with the family, I did not mind Strike sleeping with the girls. He was a gentle dog, and even though I thought of him as mine, he was our family dog, and I knew the girls were taking good care of him.

CHAPTER 7

PIRATES

The concern on Captain Ox's and Ole's faces said it all. The seven days and eight nights of sailing before we have finally made it to the Atlantic Ocean. The way the two were comparing notes, it was obvious we are not making good time. Whispering, I heard Ole say, "There are other Russian ships that might know that this ship is AWOL with the forty AWOL cavalry men."

I overheard Ox quietly talking to Ole, "We have made it. The Black Sea was okay, and the Mediterranean went fine, and now we are finally on the Atlantic. We must prepare for any and all attacks!"

Ole assured Ox, "We are traveling with fifty women and children, but we are also traveling with an experienced army." I don't think either knew that I was on the back deck fishing.

I spoke up, "Most of the teenagers are also experienced with a gun, and we will fight! Who will attack us at sea anyway?"

The Englishmen, quite startled that I was there and that I had heard them, responded, both at the same exact time, "Pirates!" Although most of the pirate attacks are more rumor than true, Ole made sure I knew that there was still a major threat. I asked him why they would attack us. His response was very scary. He said, "The women and children will be sold into slavery. All the men will be killed, and all the horses will be killed, and anything on board will be looted." He went on to tell the stories of the Red Bearded Brothers on the Mediterranean and then the Black Bearded Pirates off the coast of Africa. I was not sure if they were telling me the stories to scare me, as they knew I was one of the youngest on board, or that I needed to know that the threat of pirates is real. I could not believe what I was hearing, and any excitement I had left about this long ocean voyage was now squashed away. I was scared and didn't want to fish any longer. I tied up my lines, secured my poles, and went straight to Diane and Carol; I asked to see the map of where we were planning on going. Neither knew what our route was, but they did show me the maps of the Mediterranean and then the Atlantic. Ox showed Diane our trip on the maps and where we had been. He did not show her where we were going. I did not tell them what I had overheard, but I needed to find Captain and talk to him. He always has an answer. He always made me feel better, and I needed some convincing that we would make it to America.

I found Captain in the bottom cargo holds, feeding and watering the horses. I was barely able to talk, and I was shaking like an autumn leaf on a giant cottonwood; I finally began to speak. "Captain, did you know there are pirates?

Did you know they might capture us and sell Mother and the girls into slavery and kill everyone else?" I was almost yelling, and my voice was squeaking with fear and anxiousness. Captain calmed me down and began telling me that most of the pirates have been exterminated and the rumors are not true. He grabbed a few rifles and sat me down. He began talking to me in the calm way he does.

"Let's clean these rifles, and I will tell you a story." As I listened to him tell me a story and calmly clean his rifle, all the while he was watching me clean mine, I started to see why everyone, and I mean everyone, can trust the leadership of my father.

The very well-liked Captain and his well-trained men gave me more confidence. He asked me, "How many rifles do we have on board?"

I answered with a questionable, "One hundred?"

Then he answered, "One hundred army rifles and fifty muskets, well over one thousand rounds of ammunition and an entire barrel of musket balls." His response gave me more confidence, and I wanted to run to tell Ole that no pirates will be able to take our ship.

Captain kept me in that cargo cleaning rifles for two hours, all while he was taking inventory of the horses. We had a couple horses that are not doing well, and we talked a lot about how the horses were doing. I was happy Captain was talking to me about all the horses and asked questions on what my opinion was on how Flash was doing. I gave him my opinion and told him a story about Flash and how I thought he was the best horse on board. "Flash listens to me, and I can control him only with my legs. We ride as one." I explained, "I was riding hard and trying to ride as fast as I could through the thick part of the oaks. I had my shotgun in one hand and my fishing poles in the other." Captain smiled and insisted I tell him what made me think that this particular ride made him the best horse.

I told the story of retrieving Doc and how Chris showed me how to work with the horse while riding and ride as one, not a horse and a rider, as one moving part. Chris told me how, if you trust the horse, the horse will trust you. "And it's true!" I squeaked out. I went on to say, "After the ride to get Doc and then when I was riding in the oaks and it was thick, I trusted Flash. He would never throw me, and he will just go anywhere, no matter where I tell him to go, even if I direct him with only my legs." When I was running in the oaks and there was a steep hill with thick trees, and Flash could not see where the trail went, he trusted me as I sent him into a downhill blind run. I leaned back, and Flash just went for it. I trusted his amazing skills and he trusted me. I said again with pride, "I can outride anyone when I'm on Flash."

Captain listened with a smile or a smirk and commented, "I am glad you are proud of your riding, and it is a good thing, but there are more skills than being the fastest horse." As I looked a bit confused, he went on to say, "Many of the cavalry horses are very good and have been through many battles. They fought as tough as their amazing soldiers, and many of the horses have saved lives." I pondered a while and listened. Captain made it sound like there might be a chance that other horses are as good as Flash. I conceded that his horse might be as good. Captain laughed and agreed, but to my delight, he said, "*Maybe*, but Flash is faster." Captain really knew how to make me feel much better.

The next morning, as I was fishing on my morning perch off the back of the boat, Ole came to visit. We talked about the difference of fishing in rivers and lakes compared to the Atlantic Ocean. I did not have much luck in the ocean so far, and Ole gave me some ideas. I know that fishing close to the bottom was usually your best chance to catch fish, and I had almost all my line out and still no bites. Ole pulled out a large roll of really thick fishing line and explained, "I can use the thick line to get close to the bottom and then use this"—as he pointed to my line—"to catch the fish, near the bottom of the ocean, with the undetectable thin line." He showed me a new knot and how to tie the lines together and how to secure them together so they wouldn't come loose. I was very surprised, and his knot worked perfectly. He then explained, "You must fight the ocean fish by hand. Use your pole to identify you have a fish, and set the hook, but then use your gloves and pull the line, hand over hand."

We tied the lines and used some old fish guts for bait from several days ago and sunk our tackle one hundred feet to the bottom. We increased our weights, and within an hour, wouldn't you know it, I had a bite. I pulled it in hand over hand just like Ole explained. It was a huge fish that felt like a whale. It seemed like forever, fighting that first ocean fish, and Ole was watching. He retrieved a large gaffe with a smile. Ole was awesome on the deck and gaffed that huge fish, something I had never seen before. It must have weighted fifty pounds. I wasn't sure if we could eat this fish, but Ole assured me it is a very good eating fish and was very happy I caught it. I would not have caught it without Ole, but he gave me all the credit. I caught a few more that morning, but none that gave me the thrill of my first red snapper.

Ole and I talked about pirates a lot that morning. I told Ole, "We will *never* be taken over by pirates, and we have lots of rifles and muskets. We have a great army leader, and every man on board is a very good shot, and we will defeat any pirates." Ole talked to me that morning like a big brother and agreed that we have a better than average chance.

The next several days, I spent more time on the deck with Ole than I had ever before. Up until just a few days ago, I would fish an hour or two and then spend the rest of the day in school with Carol or with Flash. Mark and several others now take turns fishing, which gave me a lot of time with Ole. He taught all of us how to sail. We would take a sail down, then up, turn it left and right. He commented, I was becoming a good sailor and will need to help him during trying times. He explained to all of us that if we were under attack, we would have to manage the sails and the direction of the ship along with keeping all the fighting equipment and guns full with ammo. We would practice and even pretend we were shooting and fighting the pirates. This went on for days and days and days. It was somewhat cold but warmer than winter at the farm and not windy.

Ole said even though there was not much wind, we were drifting with a current that Ole called the Gulf Stream. He went on to explain that how sometimes it's better to drift than to fight big waves and wind. He assured us that the current was moving our giant ship nicely, and I agreed with him as I can tell by how my fishing lines were dragging on the bottom instead of a perfect vertical jig. Ole did concur and then chuckled and said, "Don't get a snag. You won't be able to swim to the bottom and unhook the snag or jump in and save your rod." Everyone got a laugh, and our anxious mood immediately turned to a much better one. Filled with laughter, our day was one to remember.

It was as if Ole had predicted the wind, and for several days following our fun day on deck, the wind blew. The ocean was rough with six-, seven-, and even ten-foot-tall swells. It was an amazing sight, and Ole's skills were nothing short of professional. Oxford would steer the wheel from the helm while keeping a close eye on the compass; the giant vessel stayed true. Ole would bark out directions to us, moving the sails as needed, raising them when needed, and lowering them as told. Ole was enjoying it, as were the rest of us, well most of us. These giant waves have caused several of the women to come to the deck and get sick again. There was a rule: you only throw up over board. After the first few days, everyone followed that rule as no one wanted to clean up last night's puked up fish and potatoes. Mikey wasn't far behind with a special concoction of dried toast with cinnamon and sea salt. He handed it out to the sick like candy. Everyone gobbled it down. It seemed to work pretty well, and most of the puking stopped. We "sailors" got what was left, and it wasn't bad. The weather looked ominous, and we were heading directly into what looked like quite a storm. We lowered the sails, slowed down the speed of *Blu Moon Escape*, a name we all agreed was a good name for our vessel, and prepared for a storm.

The storm passed rather quickly, but what was upon us was nothing short of a nightmare. Ox and Ole were blaring, "All hands on deck. Take your positions. Get your rifles and prepare for a battle!" Oz had spotted an unidentified vessel heading right for us and moving fast. It was the first time since we left the Mediterranean Sea that we had seen another boat, and the way Ox was screaming, it was not going to be a friendly encounter. "Ten men on the left, twenty on the right, the rest near the bow," he yelled. "Captain, direct the sharpshooters to the starboard, and the rest to the portside! We must defend at all cost or all will be lost!"

Captain and his men had been in many battles together, and Captain did not have to direct a man. Every man knew their position, and it was done as was said and as fast as any man could go. The rifles were lined up and loaded. The men were loading the muskets and attaching bayonets to every rifle and every musket. Every soldier was amazing and was on point. It was obvious that everyone has done this before, as they were very efficient. Our vessel, *The Blu Moon Escape*, was prepared in minutes. Captain Oxford was very serious and demanded, "Everyone get down. Hide and be prepared to fire your weapons, and fire everything we got until I say stop! Aim at anyone on board! Anyone you see! If you don't see anyone shoot at the gooseneck and the mast." He kept going. "If the mast falls, then take the muskets and put as many holes in the ship as possible. *Don't stop shooting until I stay stop!*"

All non-soldiers were directed below immediately and were told to be prepared to come on deck if reloading rifles and muskets were needed. "Stay low and don't get shot,"

Ole screamed. "We will surprise them, and we cannot let any of the oncoming vessels men on our boat. Shoot to kill!"

Captain Ox continued, "This is no time for mercy, and it could be bloody. Be prepared for war!" Every man on board was an experienced soldier and had fought valiantly and along each other's side many times. Captain did not comment. He knew it was good for the men to hear him. Doc and Marcella were preparing for the worst; both were demanding the women to their nurse positions. It was the first time I had ever heard anyone raise their voice to Mother. She was not Mother; she was Barbara, and I had never heard anyone call her by her first name. Preparations were intense. It was so much more intense than the battle in the trees with the Russian soldiers, but we were prepared.

Ox was looking rather calm standing at the helm while keeping a very close eye on the oncoming vessel. They were not flying a flag and neither were we, and by this, we at least knew it was not a Russian boat nor was it English. They knew we were not affiliated either, and that usually was the target pirates looked for. As the Buccaneer ship approached, Ox and Ole remained amazingly calm. They were the only two visible on the *Blu Moon Escape* deck, and that was by design. Captain Ox said quietly, "Let them come close, closer, closer." And then with a loud scream, he said, "*Fire!* Fire everything! Sharpshooters, take out the helmsman. Shoot anyone on board!"

The battle seemed to go on for quite some time. Every soldier including Captain and all his officers were shooting. Captain Oxford then turned our ship portside and began screaming, "We dropped their mast. Now sink the boat!

We must sink the boat!" As soon as he said it, and almost in unison, every soldier reached for the muskets and started firing.

Captain ordered Mark and others, "Reload everything, and keep reloading. I will tell you when to stop. Glen, get below and settle the horses."

Ole without hesitation ordered half the women, "Make plugs out of dresses soaked in lard. Wrap them over wood chunks. Do it now!"

Our ship had taken shots fired from the pirate ship, and although we had easily defeated the pirates, our vessel was not out of danger. Ole demanded rope on deck and was tying knots I had never seen before. He tied the rope to the *Blu Moon Escape* side and immediately prepared to fill any holes. Amazingly, our portside did not have one penetrating hole, and our starboard side had only taken half a dozen penetrating holes. The pirate ship was sinking fast. Once Captain Ox was certain we had defeated the pirates and their ship was near gone did he give the demand, "Cease fire."

The pirate ship sunk out of sight. Ox cheered, which caused an amazing cheer from everyone. Captain had retrieved the homemade ship plugs and was assisting Ox in the repair while I returned to the deck and was cheering along with every man on board. We had won another onslaught and come out victorious. I assured Captain that the horses were somewhat rattled with the gunfire, but I calmed them down, and all but the one sick horse were great. The sick one was lying down, and the other horses stomped him a bit. I told Captain, "In my opinion, he won't make it. We need to get him out of there before it gets worse." Captain only nodded and finished plugging the holes. His quick response and sharp voice commanded me to take Mark and two others and get him out of there. I asked, "How? We cannot lift a horse, even with a block and tackle."

He shouted almost in anger, "You and Mark know what to do. Get it done now!" I looked at Mark, grabbed my rifle, and headed to the basement of the ship.

Ox was quick to denounce the use of a rifle in the basement and announced, "No firing rifles near the hull or in any of the lower cargo holds!" As I returned the loaded rifle, I looked at Mark, and we both knew how this would go.

I turned to Captain one last time and asked, "Are we to save the good meat and the entrails, or should we throw it overboard?"

Before Captain could answer, Ox replied, "Drain all the all blood into an empty barrel, skin the animal, and debone the entire thing. Cover the good meat with the skin, and carry everything else to the back deck, where you fish, but do not throw anything overboard yet." Mark and I were now more confused but did what we were told. Captain and Ole finished the temporary plugs and quickly headed to check anything below the keel; no damage was noticed. All the shots that did penetrate were through the freeboard. Ole finished the patches from inside the boat. He knew what he was doing as if he had done this before. Captain was impressed, but Ole was not done. Ole was quick to help with the horse, all the time doing twice what any other one of us could do. He was explaining the many reasons to not throw anything overboard at this time. "We had just sunk a ship with at least twenty men on board." He explained that the sharks were surely to find the sunken vessel with many bloody corpses, and we did not want the sharks to follow us. "We do not even want horse blood in the water," he explained, and it made sense to all of us.

We removed the mortally wounded horse away from the other horses and arranged the block and tackle to raise the horse by its feet. Mark knew exactly what to do and cut a large knife hole in the horse's wind pipe. It died within minutes and without barely a sound. It took all of us to raise that horse. Once in the air, Mark cut the jugular right over an empty barrel. We have had to kill wounded horses before, but we never saved the blood of a horse. We were however experienced at saving blood, as back on the farm in Russia, Mother's blood sausage was pretty good. The blood nearly filled that barrel, and Mark commented on how much sausage that would make. "I never had horse blood sausage though," Mark said. Ole was impressed with our skills and what we knew.

I even smiled and explained to Ole, "It was our job to hang the animals and usually skin them, but it was the girl's job to butcher and cut up steaks." Ole laughed and laughed; he did not believe the girls we call sisters will butcher and cut up a horse.

We all pitched in and finished the job rather quickly as we took turns butchering and sharpening knives. Ole could not be anything but impressed with our efficiency and knowledge of what meat type we liked for steak and what was roast and what was jerky. Of course, in the past, we had never cut up a horse, but it was pretty similar to a cow, and we finished without incident. Mikey was already carrying several steaks to the fishing deck and washing them and was preparing a steak feast. Mikey gathered the steaks; he then gathered the roast meat and the jerky meat. After a thorough washing, he packed the meat in what was left of the snow and salted the jerky meat immediately.

We returned to the deck where Captain and Oxford pulled up the ropes temporarily and were talking about the men and the battle. Captain was impressed as he knew his men were fierce soldiers, and they both agreed; it was a good plan. Ox was also amazed at the accuracy of every soldier and how the men responded quickly with every command being followed to a tee. It was a one-sided battle, and not one person was hurt or even injured. Our ship was not permanently compromised. The sails were up, and we were sailing for America. Once again, Captain and his soldiers had saved the entire community with quick thinking, help from Captain Ox and Ole of course, and solid shooting from every man. Captain, my father, was truly an amazing man!

CHAPTER 8

A Month at Sea

Our journey was about halfway, as we had spent seven days sailing our way through the Black Sea and the Mediterranean Sea and now had been in the Atlantic Ocean for twelve days. The currents had been floating the *Blu Moon Escape* mostly as we haven't had a lot of wind. Captain Oxford and Captain must have talked many times about preparations and what would be needed to make the entire trip at sea safely or as safely as can be expected in 1896. Captain Ox had made this trip twice, and Ole has made it once. Of course, from England, but we were now on the same currents they had been on in the past, and Ox assured me we would be in America in less than two weeks.

Our provisions were doing well. Fishing was mostly good, and we had eaten most of a large horse. Mikey was more than an awesome cook, and what's left of the horse was made into breakfast sausage. Mikey said it was the best part of the horse. Horse meat, especially a twelve-year-old cavalry horse, did not taste very good, so Mikey might be on to something. Mikey had also strung out the ligament straight from the horse's backstraps. He said it will make for the best bowstring we have ever seen or made. I had made all of mine from deer but was looking forward to Mikey's idea. The wet bowstrings were stretching while drying in the ocean air on deck. Captain Ox did not like it, and Ole thought Mikey was crazy and agrees with Ox, "It smells!" It was stretched from bow to sternum. Mikey was on deck checking his new bowstring, and Ox was asking him how much longer he had to smell that dead horse. Mikey's reply brought laughter from every one that heard his next statement except from the two captains on board. They were not impressed. Mikey said to Ole, "I have Ox's girlfriend Diane cutting up steaks as we speak. Everyone gets fresh steak tonight, and I will make a pie for Ox and Diane to have on their date tonight. Fresh rib eye and apple turnovers. Ox is sure to get some tonight."

Without even a look, Oxford looked at Ole and said, "I have to see her cut up steak," and walked away.

Captain looked directly at me, and then stared down Mikey and asked, "What the hell is going on tonight?" Mikey was not laughing anymore as Captain was making a straight line toward Mikey.

Mikey looked at me and asked me, "What do I say?"

My quick as I could think of answer was to tell Captain the truth. He has never spanked or disciplined anyone I know for telling the truth, so I yelled, "Tell the truth. At least he won't kill you!" Everyone was laughing again except Mikey, and Captain did not break a smile.

Captain got right in Mikey's face, and Mikey blurted the truth, "It's Diane's eighteenth birthday, and they are in love. Ox cannot find the nerve nor the words to ask your permission to marry her."

Captain looked right at me and said, "Great advice you gave Mikey, and what he said. Is it true?"

I was not sure what to say, so I mustered enough words together to say, "It is her eighteenth birthday, I know that. I'm not sure about all the love stuff!" My crackling voice continued, "I heard Janet teased Diane jealously, and Carol commented she is in love with Ole, but I was not supposed to hear all that."

Captain sat down, looked at all of us with a look I have never seen before, and said, "This boat ride better be over pretty damn soon," and words like feex-a-dunlevettle-knuckle-mood and several *shits* and *damns* and a lot more as he walked away looking for Mother.

I looked around, looked at Mark, and said, "Steaks tonight come with entertainment!" Once again, everyone busted out laughing. Even Mikey was laughing, still shaking a bit but laughing.

Captain did not have dinner with the rest of the family that night, but neither did Diane, and Ox was nowhere to be seen. Mother knew everything, and even though she is the only person I know that can speak to Captain right now, she said nothing. The evening came and went without distraction.

The next morning, Captain showed up in the makeshift school and asked Linda for her journal. "I have heard you have kept a journal of our entire trip, and I would like to see it." Captain asked quietly. Linda explained there is not much in it.

"My journal is of my trip, not yours, and war scares me to death. I am not brave like Mark and even Glen. I stay below and stay with Mother as much as I can." She continued, "Diane has Ox. Janet is smitten with every single soldier on the ship, and Carol is in love with Ole. I have no one but Mother," and began to cry. Captain asked if he could still read it, and she complied. Captain disappeared to the horses, as that was his place to think lately. Linda looked at me, and her only comment was, "*Thanks.*"

I commented, "It's not my fault. I am the youngest, and the only thing I'm in love with is my horse and maybe my dog!"

Linda threw me a dirty look and said, "It's my dog now." That was the last time I spent any time in the classroom.

I left that room and headed straight to my horse, and that is where I found Captain, with his horse. He asked me why I didn't say anything to him, "I didn't know what to say." And for the first time, I said, "Father, you are the greatest cavalry leader and captain there is, but to me, you are officially not a captain. You are my father." My eyes filled with tears as he did not say a word. He walked over to me, and with tears in his eyes too, he hugged me for a long time. He then turned and walked back to his horse. It was a long time of silence. Both of us just brushed our horses completely. I think I brushed Flash twice.

I began to make a straw bed and finally broke silence. "Captain," I said. "Can I spend the night down here with my horse?"

He never looked at me, just stared at his horse, and said, "You would have made a great cavalry man. You and Flash will do something great in America, and you will make me proud." He paused for a long time and then said, "I will need a horseman and cowboy on my ranch. You see I am no longer going to be a captain. I am building another farm, and this time, I will be there every day. I am done being a soldier."

There was another long pause, and I replied, "I will be your horseman, Captain. Flash and I can still do great things. America has lots of horse races, and some of them pay lots of money. I was reading in one of Carol's books. If I am the best, I can win thousands of dollars on Flash, and I can have a ranch beside you. We will have a huge farm, the best horses ever, enough cows to feed everyone, and plenty of farmland. It says in Carol's books, America is giving away land for free. That is my dream, Captain. A ranch, farmland, family, and lots of horses. That is my dream!"

Captain finally looked at me and said, "You will make that happen, and yes, you can sleep down here tonight."

I said, "I have one more question. Can I still call you Captain?"

He half smiled and replied with a head nod, "Sure you can," and walked away.

The next several days seemed to drag on, and the thirty days on a boat was now not seeming like fun anymore. I was still fishing a lot, but alone mostly. Mark would join me once in a while. Ole could not understand why I liked to fish so much, but he too joined me once in a while, and we talked a lot. Ole and I had become good friends, and I asked him a lot about America. He had been there once before. I know it wasn't for long, but my curiosity about America was always on my mind. He did not know any more than I did about America except what Carol has told him what she had read about. We both talked about a ranch, free land, a family, and friends. I teased him about Carol, "She is only sixteen, and you are nearly thirty, almost twice her age!" Ole always remained silent if Carol's name was talked about. Ole and Ox have only been sailors. Yes, very accomplished men at their craft, but Captain was still convinced the Englishmen were not the best men for his daughters.

Captain Ox finally got the nerve to ask Captain for his first daughter's hand in marriage. He gave Captain Oxford and Diane his blessing under one condition, "They cannot sleep together until we all get to America, and they have to be married by a priest and in a church." All parties agreed to Captain's terms, and Mother was elated with joy. Diane and Oxford seemed very happy and a good match.

Mother tried to explain it to Captain many times, "Ox is an educated man and was a captain in the English navy. He is single and in love with your daughter." She would argue, but Captain still never liked the match.

As the days passed, Captain Ox figured only another two or three days, and we will be sailing into Ellis Island, a common port where immigrants came into New York, and it would not be a day too soon. I was fishing with Mark, Captain Ox was at the helm like always, and Captain and Ole were working on their English. Mother made a rare appearance on deck and announced that pneumonia was spreading throughout the ship, and Linda had it. "Her fever is well over 100, and Doc does not have the proper medicine to treat her." She went on to say, "Stay away from the schoolroom, as Doc has turned that into a makeshift hospital, and Marcella and I have both been exposed. There are now ten people on board with pneumonia, and we have no more room. Three soldiers and their entire families, along with Linda, are in the new clinic. All are sick with pneumonia. Stay away."

Mother turned and walked away and was obviously very upset. Before she went back down to the makeshift hospital, she turned around one last time. Her words had never been as firm and clear. In English, she looked directly at Captain Oxford, then to Ole, and then back to Oxford, "Get us to New York as soon as possible. We don't have much time, and your timetable is up. Get us there now!"

Captain looked at Ole, then Oxford, and said, "You heard her. Get us there as soon as possible, and if there is anything I can do to speed up the process, consider it done." Ox and Ole knew there was not a port that would allow us in with sick people, especially with ten sick Russians where the plague is bad. No one wanted it anywhere near a heavily populated area, and even if it's pneumonia and not the plague and with a doctor to confirm it.

"We are sailing a stolen Russian ship and two wanted Englishmen are at the helm. We have fifty Russian horses and an AWOL cavalry," Captain Oxford exclaimed. Ole and Captain still discussed the options. None sound very safe or good but were options.

"We have killed an entire Russian division, sunk a ship that we have no idea where it was from, and are being chased by King Nickolas's army. We are not getting this ship into the harbor in daylight safely." As he was continuing to cuss and swear, Captain spoke up with his idea, "We will enter at the furthest away entry during the middle of night. I will get off the ship with four men, including Dr. Schweitzer, get the medicine needed. I will arrange to buy fifteen wagons, more supplies, and get back on the ship, and we will sail away before anyone knows we are here. We will sail until everyone is healthy and then return again under darkness, unload everything we have left, and head west." Captain sounded confident that it may work.

But Ole and Oxford questioned it over and over, "How will we sail in there at night and then turn around and then somehow sail out to sea unseen and in the dark?"

Captain looked at the two and said, "You two are the sailors. You have about two days to figure it out. Me and my men will take Doc in there and get what we need. That's our plan. If you have a better one, let's hear it!"

For the next two days, Ole and Oxford concocted a plan. Captain rolled the plan out to Dr. Schweitzer and Mother; neither were impressed or confident it would work, but both were very adamant about not losing any of their patients, including Linda.

Two days had passed, and Captain had gathered plenty of Russian money but was not sure he could buy what he needed at night with only Russian money. Captain Oxford explained that he might know where to go, as he has been there twice, and remembered several people willing to take anyone's cash, from any country, just not at a dollar-for-dollar exchange, and didn't care where to find them in the middle of the night.

Captain Oxford looked at Captain and finally said, "I have several thousand English dollars, and almost everyone still accepts English currency." Captain did not know what to say.

He thanked Oxford and said, "Well let's do it!" Oxford was sure it was enough to buy fifteen wagons and medical supplies, but it was his entire life savings, and this was money for a ring and a ranch for him and Diane to start their new life together.

He offered anyway and did not explain it to Captain; he just gave all of it to him and exclaimed, "Try not to spend it all, please. We may need it to get out west." Nothing else was said.

Ole knew the harbormaster from his childhood while living on the docks in London, and now he lives here and runs the harbor. "We will have to bribe him, but he will do it." As Ole smiled, he remembered the time he stayed with the harbormaster for one night on his last trip here and thought he could work it out. "I can get this ship in and out in one night," he said, "but I'll need some help."

Captain said, "Manpower we have on board. How many men do you need?"

Ole knew it would take at least ten men, and so he said, "I need at least ten of your strongest men, some rope, and a whole lot of luck, but I can get it done." Captain volunteered ten of the men without even asking. He knew they would do it, and the plan was set.

The two days went by slowly. The entire ship was worried. Dissention and sickness continued to get worse. Five more of Carol's students were now sick. The entire Wangler family died, a very well-liked sergeant, his wife and daughter were now gone. Doc was afraid it will get worse, not better, and unless we got some medicine very soon, the entire ship's population would be sick or dead. He suggested that we have a burial at sea and burn everything they had. Their beds, cloths, everything. That night, only one day away from New York, we set them afloat with everything they had in this world. Ole started them on fire, said a final prayer, and sent them to the deep. It was my first at-sea burial, and it was very sad. Everyone was crying as they were muttering prayers, and the women were carrying rosaries wrapped in their hands. Ole had seen it before and knew details on how to make a raft and how to send them out with the current. My fishing deck was the launching pad for the Wangler's at-sea burial.

There was a full moon that night. It was cold, and as the clouds began to cover the moon, a light snow began to fall. It was almost Christmas, and the Wanglers were nearly out of sight. Several prayers were said and stories of Sergeant Wangler were told. All the girls were holding hands, and Carol was reading scripture from the Bible. Captain began to speak, "He saved several of our lives including mine. He was like a brother." Captain was quite choked up and could not talk clearly. The girls began to sing Christmas carols, and the songs continued until we all went to our beds. Mine with my horse. Doc, Mother, and Marcella returned to the schoolroom.

Mother wept as she walked away, and if she was still praying, she whispered, "It is so much emptier in our hospital. I hope no one else needs the space."

CHAPTER 9

NEW YORK

Two days went by, and we still had not seen any land. Oxford assured Captain as soon as the storm passes, he would adjust our path and the *Blu Moon Escape* would set sail into port. Since the night of the funeral, it had been snowing hard, and the wind had been blowing steady. Drifts of snow had built up on deck, and the men were taking turns shoveling it over board. All the sails were rolled and wrapped, and every rope was secured tightly. Below deck was about the same, except for the sick were not seen. Mikey would leave food outside the door, and every couple hours, Doc would ask, "Has anyone seen land? How much longer until we set out for medicine?" He was now looking very scared, and he too was starting to feel like he was sick. Doc would never say it, but his look was easy to define. "Get medicine now or expect many more deaths!"

As if it seemed our trip was coming to an end that no one expected, the sun came up, and the wind was still. The calm eeriness of this cold December morning seemed nothing but lonely. I started up to the deck when I found Captain. I was talking about the horses. I was worried and was adamant to Captain that the horses need something to eat. "They are out of hay, their straw is all but spoiled, and several of them are sick." I squeaked loud again, "Captain, we must do something, and it must be soon!" While Captain and I worked our way to the helm, Captain gave me instructions to keep all the horses with water.

He said, "The horses can live a long time without eating, but they must drink water." And just about then, Oxford and Ole stood up. They were both sitting leaning against the helm, something no one had seen before, and until they stood up, neither of us could see them. Ole looked at me and said with confidence, "No way we let anyone die, *no way*!" He looked at Oxford and he screamed, "It is time we go ashore. We have forty capable men, Captain. It is only a few miles!" Oxford looked at Ole and made sure he heard him.

He made sure everyone heard, "Make it happen, Ole, make it happen!"

Captain looked at six men and gave the command, "Make it happen!" For the first time in several days, there was action like only a division of German soldiers could make. Just below deck and almost permanently attached to the ceiling were eight huge paddles. The *Blu Moon Escape* was equipped to paddle.

Oxford mentioned it to Captain over a month ago that such thing could happen if needed, but he also said, "These paddles have never touched the water, and it would take some powerful men to move this ship." The water was full of snow, not ice, and Ole assured us, "Eight men can move this vessel." And then he looked directly at me and said, "It is time for the men to get this vessel moving. Captain Oxford will need your help near the helm. Let's go." And he pointed to the helm. With Oxford at the helm, me at his side, and Mark, Chris, and John all on deck just waiting for commands, the ship began to move.

It was slow going, and slushing through the snowy Atlantic, The *Blu Moon Escape* was once again moving. Ox had adjusted the wheel, and we were heading directly west. The men were taking turns rowing, with two men per paddle and eight paddles. To my surprise, we were moving pretty steadily, and as the sun got a little higher in the sky, there was finally some optimism. Captain asked me to accompany him to the double bottom to help with the horses. I didn't mind at all, but I was wondering why Captain wanted me with the horses at such a time. Mark and the guys were working the small sails on Oxford's command while I set out for the double bottom with my father.

I got there. Captain had his saddle ready, but the rest remained in storage. Captain announced my presence with a nod. "Find five other saddles. Put them on horses, and make sure one of the saddles was Doc Schweitzer's. Make sure that his saddle goes on his horse." He was quick to add that I was not allowed to saddle Flash, and I was not going with. Before I could even say anything, Captain knew. He said again, "Flash and you are to stay on the ship until we unload, and that is all I'm going to say. You are staying here!" I stayed and saddled the horses. I pretty much knew whose saddle was whose, and so I saddled the horses. I made sure and made double sure that I had done everything right. I did not want Captain or anyone mad at me because I didn't saddle their horse correctly.

I returned to the deck, and I was coming up from the double bottom. I could hear the excitement. "Land ahoy!" Ole yelled, and everyone began to cheer. Captain Oxford once again began demanding the sails be set for a landing, and as the sails made a swing around, the ship was sailing. A perfect whistle of a breeze picked up, and the ship began to drift southwest with the wind. Captain was marking our spots on his map; he was watching shore and watching his compass very close. As the ship neared shore, Ox, Ole, Captain, and our men were all around the helm discussing how the landing would go and that we are ten miles away from New York City. They were discussing a shore landing.

Although a lot more dangerous for Captain and his men, it might be the best way in, especially considering the sick, the stolen ship, and the safety of everyone remaining on the ship. Ox informed the men and Captain that they would have to jump in the freezing cold water with their horses and swim to shore. The ship needed at least twenty-five feet of depth, and they would have a half mile or more to swim. Captain announced, "Once in the water and the horses are swimming, the men can hang onto the horse tails. The horses can swim a long way dragging the men. We will make it to shore. The horses and men have done this before."

Oxford and Ole looked at each other, looked at the men, and began to speak, "The water is very cold, and you may go into shock. Keep a pair of dry clothes in a separate bag, and as soon as you get to shore, start a fire and put on dry clothes. Keep the horses near the fire as they will be very cold as well."

As Ox was talking to the men, Ole was cutting slices of rope. He said, "I have cut a piece of rope for each of you. Tie yourself to your horse, and if you lose the tail, this rope will keep you near your horse, but you will still have to keep your head above water. Once on shore and fire started, remove the saddle and dry the horses. Dry the horse blankets while the horses graze. They have not eaten in a couple days and need food to get warm." Captain and the men looked to shore. Almost everything was white, and it looked as if there was not much to graze on.

"Jumping in and swimming in this cold water will be tough on the horses. These horses have been through a lot, and we are pushing them to the limit!" Captain went on to say, "Let's stay together, and if any one of us gets in trouble, we must help him. If we lose a horse, be sure to cut your rope immediately and swim for shore. We have to do this. The health of the entire ship depends on us." Captain was repeating himself, and the men knew he was not sure that what they were about to do was the best idea, but time was not on their side, and no other plan made sense.

"The horses are saddled and ready to go. I did feed them what we had, and I gave each of them some sugar and carrots. They have all had plenty to drink." I then looked at Captain and the men and continued, "I have Doc's horse, Captain's horse, and four others ready. They might not be the right horses for these men, but they are the horses I think will make it to shore!"

Ole looked at me and exclaimed, "Let's go! I will help you get the horses to the deck. The lower door will lead the horses to the back deck, and the horses and men will enter the water from there." As we were heading to the double bottom where the horses were waiting, Ole began to ask me about the horses and if they really could swim. He wondered if Flash could actually swim with me on his back.

I told him, "I have practiced with Flash many times in the lake. At first, he did not like it, but he caught on, and after a few tries, it seemed harder for me to stay on him than it was for him to swim. From what I read in Carol's book, it is easier to swim in the ocean than a fresh water lake. I just sit in my saddle, hang onto his mane, and I squeeze tight with my legs. Flash swims wherever I tell him to." Ole then asked about the other horses. I went on to tell him the story Chris told me. "The entire division was trapped and had to cross the Rhine River, and it was in the spring. It was cold, and the water was really moving. There were ice chunks floating, logs and debris everywhere, and all fifty horses and men crossed without any problems. They each held onto their own horse tail, and across they went. Once on the other side, they didn't even dry off. They mounted their horses and rode away. The story seemed a bit far-fetched for me to believe at first, but Captain confirmed it, so it must be true. That is how I got the idea to train Flash to swim with me on his back." I continued, "That's how I know every horse can swim, except Doc's horse. I don't know that horse very well. Chris just brought him when we went to get the Doc that day I shot the bear." I was talking away, and Ole was listening, and as we were bringing the horses to the fishing deck, Ole changed his opinion and had now a better outlook and was now more confident that the men will make it to shore.

We arrived on the back deck with six horses, all saddled and ready to go, and although the four men and Captain were ready, no one has seen Doc. Captain said, "I will go get Doc and get him ready. You men double-check everything, I will be right back." Captain scuffled away quickly and returned with a white sheepish-looking Doc. All the men welcomed him and assured him that this is very doable and that each one of them will help him at first sign of any problems.

The Doc still did not look very confident but mounted his horse, tied the rope securely from the saddle horn to his wrist, and said, "God help us!" He spurred the horse, and in the water he went. The men all laughed and cheered and immediately joined him in the water. The horses struggled a bit at first, and as the men grabbed their tails and were floating behind each horse, it began to look almost like it was an everyday thing. It did not take long, and the horses were walking and then the men were walking, and before long, they were all riding toward shore. It took several more minutes to make it to dry land, and once safely on shore, I could see a slight glimmer of a fire. It took twenty minutes or so, but the fire grew until it was clearly visible. The men and horses gathered around the fire, and clearly everyone had made it. A big sigh of relief came from all of us on the ship.

Captain Oxford said with confidence and a smile, "Let's get these sails up and move north to the rally point. We must not wait. Captain will be ready with supplies in no time, and we must be prepared!" He barked out commands, and the big sail was in the air within minutes. The small sails were also up, and we were sailing east, away from shore. I watched Captain and the men until all I could see was the fire.

As I was watching, Ole came over to me with the binoculars and handed them to me. He said, "Watch them as long as you want. They should be riding off soon, and you should see them on top the ridge with the horizon as a backdrop." I watched for as long as I could. I wished I was with them and prayed they would be able to get the medicine and supplies needed and get back to the ship as soon as possible. I did see them ride away, and as they disappeared, my eyes watered up; I did not want this to be the last time I see Captain. I had watched him ride away before, but this time, it felt different. Captain was in a new world. He was no longer a cavalry captain, and the task at hand seemed harder to comprehend. I guess I was worried.

We sailed east and then headed north. We sailed most of the day and could not see the shore. As the sun started to set, Ox again barked out commands, and the ship turned east. The wind was straight out of the west, so we were moving at a pretty good clip. Just as the sun went down, Captain Oxford announced, "Lower the sails, wrap them tight, and prepare the oars. We are going to oar the rest of the way." The men did as he said, and the *Blu Moon Escape* was ready for anything. The night came and went, and we still had not moved. For the first time, we had our anchor down while we were in twenty-five feet off water and holding. With the binoculars, I could see land. It was way off in the distance, but Captain Oxford pointed out the lighthouse. He pointed out the ridge and the dock where we were heading. The Atlantic Ocean was really blue and barely a wave. The giant ship sat quietly in the water, and for the first time, I took particular notice its beauty. The entire crew on the ship deck sat quietly and watched the water and the birds that had started to fly around as if we were going to feed them. A few seagulls were squawking, and one landed on the far end of the ship. I was going to say something but couldn't find any words to describe it. We had sailed across the Atlantic Ocean and now were anchored waiting our time before heading to the dock to retrieve Captain, Doc, and the men that accompanied them.

Mikey had cooked the remaining beef and pork with some vegetables and had brought it to the deck for us to eat. I stayed on deck at the helm with Captain Ox. Ole and the men were standing along the rails waiting for Ox to give the command to start oaring when Mikey showed up. The food was a welcomed smell, and we all began to eat and compliment Mikey on what a fine job he has done. He has kept the entire crew fed and had prepared daily soup for the sick. He was always ready for whatever he needed to do next. Mikey has fed us well and was now feeding the horses the remains. He was very valuable, and everyone agrees that without him, the trip would have been much worse.

As the daylight once again began to slowly disappear, Ox ordered the anchor up. He was explaining the plans and once again began announcing upcoming duties. We were going to oar as close as we could and then spin the giant ship around to have the ship facing outward as we approach the dock. We were going to do this quietly in the dark and hopefully not be detected by anyone. I did not understand the how or why, but Ole certainly did, and the men just followed orders.

Everything was going as planned, and the men that were oaring began to spin the giant ship. I was watching Ox work the wheel. About the time we were completely turned around and were near where we needed to enter the dock, the ship began to hit bottom. Captain Ox immediately insisted we stop and yelled for Ole, "We must wait for the tides to come in, and even then, I'm not sure it will be enough for us to continue!" Ole was checking depths on all sides and agreed with Ox that this was as close as we could get. The two Englishmen knew they were in trouble and were quietly discussing their options when a welcomed voice out of the darkness was heard. "It is Captain and Doc," I yelled. "They are in a skiff with two men oaring and are heading directly for us!"

As quickly as I could, I headed to the fishing deck with a lantern in hand screaming in delight, "You made it! You made it!" I kept screaming.

Their boat was loaded as full as a boat could be without sinking, and as they stood up, Captain handed me a rope. "Tie this off, and let's get this thing unloaded." Captain said, "We have medicine for the sick and supplies for the horses. We found everything we needed." Captain and the men looked tired but happy to be back on board. Captain grabbed a large bag, and he headed straight for Mother. Doc, although quite worn and looking very peeked and white, followed quickly. The remaining men tied off the skiff securely and started unloading the supplies. They had hay bales for the horses, what looked like two halves of beef, and several other bags that I did not ask about. After everything was unloaded, the skiff tied off and lifted out of the water, Captain Oxford was once again demanding the men to oar. "Oar harder," he said, and within a few minutes, we could not feel the bottom and were heading out to sea. The *Blu Moon Escape* was back at sea, and as the sails went up, I looked back with the binoculars. I could see lights blinking in the lighthouse as if to confirm the men had made it.

Captain remained below with Mother and Doc. The makeshift hospital needed to be thoroughly cleaned. The smell was a horrible rancid sewer smell; it was very disturbing. After administering the medicine, Mother and Doc immediately started scrubbing and washing everything. Captain was bringing the dirty clothes to the deck and would grab another bag on his way back to the makeshift hospital. This went on for hours, and even though Captain had not slept since jumping into the ice-cold water, he would not leave Mother and Doc. He was relentlessly cleaning the dirty linens, hanging them to dry on a makeshift clothesline, and then would immediately return to Mother. This went on all night and into the next morning.

Captain and Doc, along with Mother and Marcella, were determined that all the sick must survive. Their will and determination were obvious to every person on that ship. Oxford and Ole had not seen such dedication in anyone; even the men were commenting on how Captain, even when they have known him for years and seen him do things most other men could not, continued for three days now with virtually no sleep. The adoration toward Captain and Doc went on and on. Neither of the adored knew what was being said and didn't have to; what was talked about was simply a miracle from God.

The two men explained and told us the story of their two days in New York and how Doc found the medicine needed and how if it wasn't for Captain keeping them out of trouble and out of jail, none of them would have made it or even be alive. "Mike and Tony are looking for quality covered wagons," Josh said, "and are arranging a spot for us to live until we head west. They are also researching where the free land is and how we will get there." Mike and Tony were the other two men left behind. They were both sergeants in the cavalry and were both trusted by every person on board. Josh was one of the youngest in the cavalry but a very talented sniper and well-liked by everyone. His big blue eyes shined brightly. As the moon seemed to glow off him that night, he told story after story, and once finished, he would tell it again. I could not stop listening and dreaming about if I would have been there and wanted to ask so many questions. I just listened with pride knowing that these men are my friends and Captain, our leader, is my father.

It has been several days since Captain and Doc had returned, and I was told it would be at least ten days, and everyone has to be healthy before we returned to New York. I was fishing off the back deck, perched in my spot and dreaming of riding Flash when I heard a voice I have not heard in weeks. Linda appeared and was feeling much better. She wanted to know if she could fish with me. I demanded, "Sit down and let me show you how to fish." The fish hadn't been biting, and I was thinking about trying some new bait anyway. I handed Linda a fishing rod and said, "Reel it in, lets redo that bait. Maybe you can bring me some good luck." She smiled as to agree but wasn't even sure what I meant. I did most of the talking, and she watched and listened. I asked her if she knew how to tie a good fishing knot.

"I can tie a knot. Of course I can," she squeaked. I had her tie a knot and like the smart-ass that I am. I pulled and broke the hook free.

I explained, "Fishing lines have to be tied perfectly and just this way or they come untied." I explained to her, "Put the line through the hook, wrap it around the hook five times, take the end and put it through the loop, and pull it tight. Then cut off the excess line, attach a weight, and sink it to the bottom." I gave her the advice I give everyone, "Ninety percent of the fish are caught in ten percent of the water, the bottom ten percent." We laughed and talked for several hours. I asked about her journal and if she wrote in it when she was sick. I asked if I'm in it.

Linda just smiled and said quietly, "A little."

The next few days were sunny and cold, but the patients in the schoolroom all have recovered or were nearly recovered. They are all up and around. Mother was so happy, and Doc had slept for an entire day. The mood had definitely changed, and everyone was ready to get off this boat to see New York. The girls were singing Christmas carols, and many of the men were joining in. I asked Mother if we were going to have Christmas this year. Her response was perfect as always, "Of course we will have Christmas. It's Jesus's birthday!" I meant were we going to be on the ship or in New York. Of course, she knew that but did not want to overstep her boundaries, as Captain has not yet announced our plans. Mother explained that Captain will tell everyone the plan that evening after supper, and as always, Captain spoke up after the last plate was clean.

"We have come a long way, and our dreams of owning our own land in our new country is getting closer." Everyone cheered as he continued, "Tomorrow we will head into the harbor. We will head in as fast as we can and as far as we can. Captain Oxford and Ole will get us right up to a dock, and we will unload everything. *Do not* leave anything behind. The ship must be empty. We are leaving this Russian vessel right where we dock it, and we do not want any identification left on board." Everyone knew the plan already, but saying it out loud to everyone at once was Captain's way of praising the men and women aboard and thanking them for everything. "We will not need this ship any longer, but we will never forget it." As Captain spoke up, "Tomorrow we will be Americans. We will spend Christmas in New York as Germans from Russia, Americans!" Once again, everyone cheered.

The sails were set, and it was a cold, breezy day. The *Blu Moon Escape* was heading straight west into the harbor. We passed several other boats and ships. Captain Ox and Ole were on point and docked us in a perfect spot like Captain said. Everyone immediately started to unload. The horses were very skinny and spooked to be back on land. Mike and Tony were waiting and had arranged a spot for us to go to. Ten wagons were waiting for us to hook up our horses to and fro. It was a perfect landing. The unloading went without a hitch, and even though the horses looked very skinny and generally unhealthy, ten teams were hooked up, wagons loaded full, and we were making our way through

New York City. It was huge, and there were people everywhere. There were hotels bigger than our ship, and everybody was so busy. All of us on horseback, ten teams of two, and all of us looking quite amazed or confused; we went ten miles unnoticed. Our camp was awesome and was in a grove of tall cottonwoods. There were ten little cabins and an indoor bathroom and shower for us to share. Mike and Tony had found us an old military camp that now was used just for this, migrants staging up before they head west.

CHAPTER 10

THE WEDDING

Captain and the soldiers had been going into the city on a regular basis, and every day the men come home with more wagons, more supplies, and more information on where we would be moving to next. Mother, Diane, and the rest of the women were planning a wedding, and between all the new sights to see and all the commotion, our community was very excited and always on the move. Mark and I, along with the other non-cavalry guys, were not allowed to go to New York City unless we were with Captain or one of the sergeants. I was okay with riding Flash around the fort and the countryside, and Mark and the others were okay with riding, roping, and shooting too. We were finally back on our horses with Captain insisting we practice riding, roping, and shooting every day. Even a lot of the girls were riding. I'm not sure if the girls were riding along with the others because they liked to ride or they just want to be around us guys; either way, it was fun to ride Flash, and I liked showing off my horse and my skills. Diane and Janet called me a showoff all the time, but I think it was because they cannot do what I can do. I practiced lots of new tricks that I read about in one of Carol's books. I fell down a lot, but the ground is either white with snow or soft and muddy. It looked like I've been rolling in the mud most of the time, but it did not bother me. I loved riding and was getting pretty good at roping too.

Mother asked Mark and me to prepare the wagon and a team of horses one morning and wanted us to accompany her and the girls into the city. Her exact words were something like, "Wash up and stay out of the mud puddles. You are getting fit for a new suit, and you don't need to be smelling like horse crap all the time." Of course, I laughed but did what Mother asked; no need to upset Mother. We did hook up a team of horses, saddled our horses, and I tied on my rope and scabbard with rifle to the saddle just in case, and along with several others, we set off to New York City.

As we rode the ten miles to the edge of the city, I was working my rope and throwing it at anything I could. If anyone of the girls gave me a chance, I would rope them around their body. Mother seemed annoyed, and it wasn't until I had Linda roped and got her dress dirty that Mother put a stop to it. We were just coming to the city limits of New York, and I was very interested watching all the people and horses. Mother gave strict directions that we were all to stay together at all times. She looked right at me and said, "Do not wander off! It is a big city, and you could get lost or worse. Stay together!" She gave a list of things we were to do, and nothing else would be tolerated. "We all are going to the tailor to get fitted for some new suits, and the girls will get new dresses. Then we will go to the general store and get a few things and then back to the fort. I do not want to say it again. Stay together!" Once again, she looked directly at me and then at Mark as if he were to keep an eye on me. I did not understand why I needed a new suit but was told everyone needs new clothes for the wedding.

I was forced to watch as Mark was fitted first. Mother made sure I knew that *no* horseplay would be tolerated. The tailor fitted both Mark then me, and it went fine. I was allowed to get back on Flash, and Mark got on Bootleg, his horse, and we were to watch over the wagon while the girls picked out their new dress colors and had a dressmaker measure the girls. I was watching everything in the city as horses and wagons went steadily by. So many people were doing all their own thing. I noticed just down the road a bit that there was a large horse stable with lots of cowboys going in and out with their horses. There was a farrier next to the stable who was constantly being interrupted as he was working on the horses. I wondered how he ever gets anything done with so many distractions.

With my mind racing and my imagination dreaming of me working at such a place, the time went by quickly and Mother and the girls were ready to go. They all loaded into the wagon, with Mother driving. She let out a short command and snapped the reins. The horses started toward the general store. It was a busy place, and Mother once again insisted, "Everyone stay together." The store was only a few lots past the stables, and as we rode by, several of the cowboys were eyeing up the girls. Mark was on one side of the wagon, and I was on the other. We rode by quickly, but as much interest as the strange cowboys gave the girls, the girls gave back. They were smiling and waving as if they were in a parade. Mother did not like it and even seemed nervous as if the cowboys might be a threat. We went by without incident, and we were at the store in only a moment's time.

We tied off right in front of the store, and as we were tying off, the owner greeted us with a big, friendly smile. "I am Charles Olson, and I own this store. My friends call me Charlie, and I hope we can be friends too. How may I help you and your beautiful family?" He was very welcoming and eager to help Mother with supplies and information. He was also very chatty, so for every question Mother had, he had two. Mother asked about all kinds of wedding stuff, where to get this or that. Charlie had an answer and a question and matched Mother, question-for-question. Mother was polite but did not tell Charlie a lot.

I had a question for Charlie and could hardly get a word in. Finally, I blurted rudely, "Charlie, I have read about horse racing. Do you know where the races are?"

He was courteous but firm as he looked at me and said, "I will help you when I have all your mother's needs taken care of." I guess it made sense, and Mother immediately smiled at Charlie and continued to ask questions. He pointed at a banner in the window, and as I looked to where he was pointing, Mark was heading that way. The poster read "New Year's Day Celebration" and listed all the events of the day. In bold print, there it was "Horse Racing" to include: one-mile, ten-mile, and fifty-mile races, all on New Year's Day. My eyes got huge, and my immediate smile was evidence to Charlie that I was more than interested in the horse races.

Mother had gathered most of what she needed, and Charlie had answered all her questions. Mother began to look around as Charlie turned his attention to me and the poster. In my excitement, I inadvertently removed it from the window and was reading it out loud over and over again. "You can have that poster. I have more," Charlie said. Mother noticed that I had removed the poster and was embarrassed. Charlie eased her embarrassment by quickly reaching for a couple more posters. He handed Janet a poster and taped the other to the window. He then looked at Mother and said, "I can see your son likes his horse and wants to race?"

Mother complied, "He rides every day and all day if he could. He sleeps with it most nights. Those two are inseparable," talking as if Flash was part of the family. Mother talking like that alone made my day, but New Year's Day horse racing would be my dream come true. That would make the day my best day ever.

Charlie looked at the girls and spoke up, "There are girls' events too. The girls horse race is two miles this year. They have a rifle shoot just like the boys. There's also a pickle contest. My wife got second place last year. There is salsa, sewing, and all kinds of things to do. It's all right there on the poster."

Every one of us had our favorite of course. Mark loved to shoot his rifle, and Diane can really ride and would probably win the women's division, I thought, but she will be married, so she won't even try. Janet was great in the kitchen, and we all loved her pickles. Carol liked her books and was writing silly poems all the time. Me, I loved to ride. I liked to shoot and rope too, but I figure I better concentrate on riding. Linda was always knitting or sewing, patching shirts or jeans. Between Mother and Linda, I think everything we were wearing that day Linda had made, she has even made her own saddle. I could hardly contain myself and wanted to tell Charlie about Flash and how we won our county horse race and how I saved Doc and how Captain trusts me to ride with the cavalry, but Mother immediately gave me a look that said, "*Be quiet!*" I knew what that meant, and out the door I went.

We all left orderly and quiet. Mother gave Charlie an honest thank you. He walked Mother out and helped her on to the wagon. The supplies were paid for and firmly packed. We were all ready to go. I rode up next to the wagon where Charlie was standing. I did not say anything at first but gave Charlie a wave. I let Mother give the command, and on the snap of the reins, the wagon was rolling. I stalled for a few seconds. Charlie looked at me and Flash. "That *is* quite a nice horse. Pretty thin but tall and beautiful," he said. "Is that your horse you want to race?" he asked.

I replied, "This is the horse I want to win every race with. See you on New Year's Day." And with a quick squeeze, Flash instantly took off running to catch up to the wagon.

I could not stop talking about the horse races. Mark was quite supportive and also talked about Flash and how we might win the race. The rifle shooting contest is what Mark was interested in. Mark knew that Captain's snipers will be entering the contest as well, but he also knew he can shoot better than any of them on the right day. We both assured each other that we could win and that we had only a couple of more weeks to practice. "We will practice together and help each other to get better. Captain will be so proud," Mark yelled.

"Yeehaw!" we both yelled and road away. Mother did not mind since we were halfway home, and she loved to see her boys ride together and be happy. Mother was happy to drive the team home without us, as it gave her some private time with all her girls. Diane was mostly talking about her upcoming wedding, but everyone was excited. I couldn't figure out why Mother and the girls were so excited about a wedding. There was, after all, a huge horse race to prepare for; New Year's Day was only a couple weeks away.

The girls quickly unloaded the wagon into our family cabin, and Mother instructed me to unhook the team and return them to the barn. Our fort, as Captain calls it, had a nice barn and corral—a place for all our horses. I was leading the horses into the barn, and I noticed Captain riding in with four cows. The was one big Holstein, black and white, and three black heifers. He led them right to the barn, and as I opened the door, he led the cattle in. Mark closed the door behind our horses and began to ask Captain about the stock. Captain always put business first. He put the cows in their own stall, and then he helped me with the team, and then he began to answer questions. "Yes, these are our cows. Yes, one is for milk and the other two are pregnant. No, we are not butchering any cows while at the fort." Captain saw my excitement, and he knew it was not because of the cows. He finally looked at me, and before I could even speak, he chuckled and asked, "What's got your spurs twisted?" We laughed a bit, and I immediately started telling Captain about the races.

"Three races, all on the same day, and I want to win them all! Charlie said Flash is skinny, but I know we can win the races."

Captain looked at me, and holding back a smile, he said, "The races are for adults only. You must be eighteen to race and win money." The wind had been knocked out of my sails. I was almost crying when Captain pulled the same poster I had out of his saddlebag. Looking at the poster, Captain began to talk very monotoned as to try not to upset me anymore. "I talked to the horse race community, and they said it is mostly up to Charlie, but Charlie agreed to let you race if I give permission." It took me a couple seconds to realize Captain was teasing me and that he would for sure give me the permission I needed.

I squeaked out loud, "Please, Father, can I race? Can I race in all three races? Can I, Father, please?" Captain got a bit teary eyed and gave me his approval with his familiar head nod. I think it was that I asked my father for permission and not Captain.

He did say, "You had better practice and get Flash in a little better shape. He has been doing nearly nothing, and now you want him to race against the fastest horses in all New York. Flash will need work every day and extra food and extra attention." Captain knew that there wasn't more attention possible to give to a horse. Captain talked a bit about the quality of horses that will be running and that I am not to get my hopes to high, "There will be hundreds of horses competing, and even though Flash is our fastest horse, there are a lot of good quality horses that will be racing." I understood what Captain was trying to say. Mark said the same thing, but I did not care. I was going to win!

My dream of horse racing was going to happen. I could not wait!

Mother and the girls were all giddy about the wedding and explained to Captain that everyone was fitted for new clothes but him. Captain said, "I will wear my military dress uniform." Mother went on to explain why she thought he should wear civilian clothes and that his Captain days were over. Captain did not respond and sat quietly and drank his coffee. After supper, Captain started to ask some questions, "Did you find a church and a priest? Where is the celebration going to be held? When is it going to happen?" Mother had all the answers but so did Diane.

She explained before Mother could say a word, "The pastor agreed to have a ceremony in the church and that the celebration would be here in the fort." Mother looked happy and agreed to everything Diane said.

Captain did not smile once and just asked again, "When is this going to happen?"

Diane looked at Mother and then looked back at Captain. "December 29, I can't wait!" she screamed and gave Captain a big hug as to thank him for approval before Captain could say anything.

He then asked, "Does Captain Oxford know all this, and does he agree?"

The girls got a big laugh out of that, and Janet said, "Ox will do anything Diane says. He's in *love*." And they laughed even more.

It was about then that Captain Oxford knocked on the door, walked in, looked around with a weird look on his face, and said, "What is going on?" Everyone began laughing again, and even Captain was laughing. Diane told Ox about the laughter, and even Ox began to laugh.

Captain was hooking the team together and was planning a trip to town. Mother was going along to gather final wedding supplies, and Captain agreed to drive the wagon to town since he had a surprise for her. Mother was making the plans to whom they should see first and so on. Captain let her talk, and when she was done, he just calmly said, "I will drop you off at Charlie's. He will have everything there waiting for you to look at. I will run my errands and be back before you and Charlie are done chatting." Captain knew his measurements and had a new suit for himself already made up. All the kids' suits and dresses were done, and to Mother's surprise, Captain had Mother's beautiful white wedding dress adjusted to fit Diane perfectly and ready for a wedding. Captain has managed to get Mother's wedding dress from Russia to America, into town for a professional cleaning and adjusted perfectly while Diane was measured, without anyone knowing. Captain was waiting and loaded with all the new clothes, and a big smirk on his face for sure.

As Mother came out of Charlie's place, they both noticed Captain was acting as if he was the cat that ate the canary. Charlie immediately began talking to Captain asking about the family and generally just being Charlie. He was just a very nice elderly man that owns our favorite store. He asked, "Is your youngest getting his horse ready to ride in the New Year's celebration." Captain nodded and did not lose his devilish smirk.

Mother could not take it and finally asked him, "Okay, what is the surprise?" Captain announced that he had picked up the kids' wedding stuff, but Mother knew that was not it. She began to look through Mark's and my bag and noticed that Captain has a suit to match ours perfectly. She was happy to see it but knew that was not what the surprise was. As she opened the girls' dress box, she began to cry. She found her lost wedding dress that was thought to have been left in Russia. She immediately gave Captain a kiss and hug and hopped onto the wagon like a kid on a Ferris wheel. "Diane is going to be so happy. I can't wait to tell her!" Charlie waved and wished us a merry Christmas. Folks replied the same, and off they went. As the ride got closer to the fort, Mother noticed that she had not looked in all the boxes, and there were a few more boxes almost hidden. Mother did not ask but looked at Captain a few times, then the boxes, then back to him. Captain did not waiver and drove right up to our cabin. As Mother was unloading the dresses and suits, Captain walked over to the dinner area with all the boxes in hand. Mikey had set up a large Christmas tree, and Captain emptied the boxes and set everything under the tree. He had an envelope with every man's name who was in his cavalry on each one and a few other small packages as well. Each of his kids, Mikey, Marcella, Ole, and Oxford all had gifts as well.

It wasn't long, and the girls had the tree decorated. They had been making decorations for the wedding and a few more for our tree was perfect. It wasn't long, and everyone in the community had gifts from one another under the tree. Diane had a small box perched in the tree. Its label read, "Di, I love you." Everyone knew what it meant and what it was. The rest of us had to wait to receive our gifts from Captain. We all knew what she was getting, but none of us knew anything else.

Christmas morning was a bright, sunny morning; it was cold but not bad. I ran Flash ten miles while sprinting the first two and trying to time myself, which was something I had been doing since I heard about the races. We were getting faster, and the excitement of Christmas was not on my mind. Diane's wedding was just a distraction. I was training for race day, and nothing else really mattered to me. Mikey was up early and had several snacks and food ready to eat. He had even made Christmas cookies, gingerbread, my favorite. The community gathered, and Father Moore was saying mass right in our community center. He stayed after mass for a long time. He ate with us, sang songs with us, and even watched as everyone opened the gifts. The entire room stood still as Diane reached for her box. Oxford had made his way to the tree, and as Diane opened the box, Oxford was on one knee. He put the diamond ring on her finger. She said with a crackling of tears in her voice, "Yes, I will marry you, Captain Oxford." She shouted, "I love you!" Everyone cheered, Mother cried, and Captain held her tight with a smile. He looked at Mother.

He too was teared up and said, "Our family is growing again." Mother's smile and Captain's posture was the Christmas miracle for Diane.

Mark and I got new riding boots, and Santa Claus brought new riding boots for Captain too. We all three had new black boots and new suits for the wedding, and the girls all had the same colorful dresses. Captain also got the girls matching necklaces and Mother a diamond necklace. Every envelope to his men had contents and papers for each man to become official American citizens. It also included all the information needed to homestead land in the Louisiana purchase along the Missouri River and $100. Captain had sold the stolen Russian vessel and wanted to share it with every man. They all helped get it the *Blu Moon Escape* here, and now they all got part of it. No one ever asked how much or to whom did he sell it to; they were just happy to have part of it. Captain also returned the five thousand dollars to Oxford he borrowed weeks ago when they first arrived. Captain included an additional thousand-dollar envelope to Diane as a wedding gift to Ox and Diane.

Captain Oxford and Diane got married at 10:00 a.m. on the 29th of December 1896. Father Moore presided over the vows and had a nice but short wedding ceremony. We were all in his church, and the girls sang songs. The wagons were decorated with homemade paper flowers, and a few of the men attached horseshoes and cans to Oxford and Diane's wagon. Ole drove Oxford's wagon as the two newlyweds drank champagne and kissed all the way back to the fort. We all rode back to the fort in single file except I rode Flash and Mark rode Bootleg. The girls rode with Captain and Mother. Carol wanted to ride with Ole in the wagon, but Captain would have no part of that. We all rode into the fort together, one following the other and went straight to the community center. Mikey had prepared a turkey feast with all the fixings, and after we were done eating, a band with accordion and bagpipes blared away all day and into the night. Everyone danced, and several of the men got drunk, and even Doc had a few shots to celebrate. Captain Oxford and Diane were now married. Mother was very happy, and even Captain had fun and celebrated his first daughter's nuptials with pride.

CHAPTER 11

NEW YEAR'S DAY

The days were going by slower than ever. All I wanted to do was ride and race my beautiful horse Flash. There were two days until race day. I was out riding and training Flash. I saw Chris on his horse and working him pretty hard too. I rode over to Chris, and we talked a lot about our trip and how we sure missed riding our horses. Chris said, "I am twenty-seven years old, and pretty sure that was the longest I have gone without riding a horse since I was seven years old."

I agreed and also commented, "Probably the same for me, but I am almost fourteen."

Chris smiled and asked, "When is your birthday? Do you have any special plans?"

I quickly remarked back, "January 10, and all I want for my birthday is to win the races!"

Chris laughed and commented, "The short race is not for us. The ten- and fifty-mile races, those are for us."

I looked a bit confused and asked, "Why?"

Chris just replied, "We are not horse jockeys, and for the one-mile race, they use a different saddle and start in a corral."

I finally asked Chris, "Are you racing in the races with Stirrup?" Stirrup was Chris's horse and was the only horse I know that could keep up with Flash.

He gave me a military nod like Captain gives and said, "I will race the ten-mile race, but the fifty-mile is the one you can win." It was the first time I had actually considered Chris and Stirrup as someone who could beat me and Flash, but I knew they were good.

I thought to myself and then asked Chris, "Why not race both races, like me?"

He said, "Fifty miles is too long, and I want to compete in a few other things too. Plus a ten-mile race and a fifty-mile race is a lot of riding in one day." I was glad he wasn't racing in both, but at the same time, racing side by side with Chris would be fun. Mark had mentioned that if I race all day, I would miss the shooting competition. I didn't care. I wanted to win the horse races!

Chris and I didn't see each other after that until race day. John was also entered into the ten-mile race; I had seen him and a few others riding a lot these last few days. I don't think any of the other horses but Stirrup and Chris would have a chance. Mark could really ride and would be stiff competition on Bootleg, but he wanted to win the shooting competition and so is not racing at all. I don't know of any other horses that could keep up to me and Flash, but there were fifty horses preregistered. I watched every horse every time we went to town, and every time we rode past the stables, I watched as closely as I could. As far as I could see, no horse I saw will be able to keep up. Charlie was very pleasant and complimented Flash every time he saw us after that day, I mentioned that I was going to win the race.

There was a big celebration in town on New Year's Eve, and nearly the entire community attended. There were fireworks and dancing and drinking, and all kinds of entertainment, things I had never seen before and never imagined. One guy juggled anything; he even juggled fire sticks. There was a magic show and ladies modeling all kinds of coats and furs. The horses looked like they were dancing and doing high-wire acts going over the streets. One guy walking around had stilts and was ten feet tall. New York City was sure full of a lot of people. It did take my mind off the races for a while, and the entire family watched the midnight fireworks before heading back to the fort. Oxford and Diane sat by us but in their own wagon and stayed later than we did. They were staying later to watch the bands and were dancing, and none of that really interested me. I did not ride Flash into town that night, as I wanted him good and rested before the big day. It was past 1:00 a.m., and Captain was quick to point out I had the big races. "The ten-mile race starts at ten o'clock tomorrow morning, and you better get to sleep. You have a lot of riding to do."

I nodded at Captain and Mother, and as I headed off to bed, I commented, "I won't sleep much tonight anyway."

I was up early and was in the barn saddling Flash when Captain came into the barn. "You're up early," he said as he sipped his coffee. Captain knew I was in the barn and only came over to the barn to talk to me. He gave me twenty dollars and said, "Ten-dollar entry per race, good luck. I know you have been waiting for this for a long time, but it's not the end of the world if Chris or someone else beats you." He was watching me saddle Flash with pride but also knew although Flash was fast, I was only a thirteen-year-old who was competing against grown men. "You know, Chris is one of the best riders I have ever seen, and he is racing today," Captain finally said.

I did nod and commented, "He is only racing the ten-mile race. He will be fast, and if he beats me, it will be close," I continued, "I want to win the ten-mile race, but I really want to win the fifty-mile race. It's the biggest purse and the tallest trophy!" As I mounted Flash, Captain again wished me good luck. He gave me his assuring nod, and off I went. I had a ten-mile ride into town and wanted to walk most of the way. Flash really wanted to run, but I held him back. The race started at Charlie's. It ran mostly through town and finished at Charlie's store as well. Thirty horses would start and then twenty more horses would start exactly one minute later, but all the horses would be timed. As I rode to town, Chris and John rode with me. They both were teasing me that without Captain at the start, Charlie wouldn't let me race, but I knew Charlie and Captain had already talked. I just smiled and joked back and forth with confidence. Chris and John knew Flash was fast and I have raced before. The teasing was just in fun, but they also knew that Flash and I would be hard to beat.

The names were drawn out of a hat as to who would go in the first thirty and who would go in the second. I was in the first thirty and so was John, but Chris was in the second start, something I did not want. I wanted to see Chris race, and if he beat me, I wanted to see him and

Stirrup ride. It was nearly ten o'clock, and all fifty horses were ready to go. Flash was nervous and was very jumpy. I was too but tried to stay calm as I could. It was announced with a countdown, and thirty horses including Flash were ready to go. Three, two, one, and *bang!* A gun went off, and away we went.

Some of the riders talked about letting me get out ahead of them, and then in the last mile, they would catch up. I did not say anything but knew Flash could run full speed for ten miles, and I would be pushing him, knowing ten miles is only warm up for a day riding Flash. The route was easy to follow, and the roads were nicely groomed, and from the start, I was in the lead. I rarely looked back or even faltered for a second. When I did look back, all I saw were two horses behind me, but neither was John. As I went by the sign "One Mile," I gave Flash a spur, let the reins loose, and remembered what Chris said to me, "Ride as one. Let the horse run with as little as resistance as possible." Flash stretched out that last mile and really ran. As we crossed the finish line, I knew we had a good race. I watched as the other horses come in. John was the tenth horse to cross the finish line, but out of fifty horses and a minute behind on the start, Chris was riding hard and came across the finish line just behind John. He had past almost all the other horses and was swinging his hat as he crossed the finish line knowing he had run a good, clean race.

All the horses finished, and the times were not announced until the last rider crossed the line. Chris rode directly over to Flash and me and asked how we did. "I won the race, but I don't know my time," I said. Chris asked if I felt good and if I let Flash run wide open the entire way. I answered, "Pretty much wide open. I was in first by quite a bit, so we didn't go wide open until the last mile."

Chris smiled and said, "I went wide open the entire race. It seemed like I passed all fifty horses." We gave each other high fives and rode back to the finish line together to hear the announcement on who won. Charlie came outside by the finish line and announced third, then second, and then the winner. Chris had beat me by one second. I was disappointed of course, but Chris was really cool and raised my hand next to him while the crowd cheered. Our horses knew each other, so it was pretty cool. He congratulated me, and I did the same. Captain gave us both a congratulation head nod as we rode by together. He set the trophy on the wagon by Mother and asked if she would bring it back to the fort. Mother and Linda were both sitting on the wagon. They congratulated Chris and agreed to bring his trophy home.

The fifty-mile race was to start at noon, and Chris quickly reminded me to get prepared. He said, "Make sure Flash gets some water, but not too much. Take the saddle off him and brush him a bit." He was sure helping me a lot, and it almost seemed like he felt bad for beating me in the ten-mile race. He told me he had bet on me to win the fifty-mile race, and if I win, he will share the cash with me. I asked him how much did he bet, and his comment was, "All of it." He had won $100 and now has bet it all on me to win.

"Why would you bet on me to win it all?" I asked.

He replied, "I've seen you run that horse fifty miles, and that was through rough terrain and trees. This will be a piece of cake, and plus I have ten-to-one odds. No way you'll lose! See you at the finish line. And don't let up, you run Flash as hard as you can. Remember to ride him as light as you can and be part of his movements. Don't resist him at all. He knows how to run!" As Chris unsaddled Stirrup, he grabbed his rifle, and with a smile, he said, "Now let's see if I can beat Mark." And as he walked away, I knew he was a great friend and was proud of me. He acknowledged beating Flash and me was tough, and if I were riding side by side with him and Stirrup, the outcome might have been different.

I thanked him for his confidence in me and said, "I won't let you down."

The fifty-mile race started in the same spot as the ten, but all forty horses left at the same time. It finished in front of the courthouse where the grandstands and all the people would be. The street between the courthouse and Charlie's was lined with people and would be cheering the leaders as they headed to the finish line. The fifty miles did leave the city and had some hills and trees to navigate through before a five-mile stretch leading back into the city and to the finish line. We were all lined up, and once again, three, two, one, and *bang!* The gun fired to start the race.

There were quite a few guys in front of me and would not let me near the front row, so as the forty horses ran through the city, I was in the middle of the pack. All the horses pretty much stayed together until we left the city, and as soon as I could, I opened Flash up. I was passing horse after horse, rider after rider, and did not look back. I heard, as I rode by, a few guys say, "Better pace yourself. It's a long race." I did not care and pushed harder. I was in front by the twenty-mile marker. I did not look back after that and concentrated on being light. I let Flash run with ease with no resistance. I passed the forty-mile marker and knew I had only ten miles to go. I remembered riding on Mikey's trails when I had ten miles to the farm. I was running faster now, and Flash was showing no signs of getting tired.

As I raced into the city as fast as I could get Flash to run, I could see the streets were lined with people. I remember thinking, "This is more people than I have ever seen. I hope no one runs in front of me." I finally sat up, looked back, and realized I had outpaced the entire field of racers. I thought for a second, "Did I take a wrong turn. There is not another rider in sight," but the cheers of the crowd quickly changed that thought, and as I rode to the finish line, I knew I had won the race. The band was playing, and Chris, John, Mark, and even Captain were waiting for me just past the finish line. They all seemed happier than I was. He had just won a thousand dollars. Chris was trying to give me a hug and pulled me almost out of the saddle. I watched as the other riders ride in, and the crowds cheered. I sat with Flash with pride at the finish line when I heard a rider had fallen and his horse is loose and he cannot finish. I signaled to Chris and John, and away we went. We rode ten miles with Chris and John at my side, and we found the downed rider. I gave him a boost up, and John caught his horse. We rode double back to town, and about halfway, Chris had the downed rider jump onto his horse. His horse had blown a shoe, but as we got closer, I suggested he ride his horse past the finish line. He complied, and as we rode by the finish line together, the crowd cheered even louder.

After the trophy presentation and all the congratulations were done, I asked how Mark did in the shooting competition. He finished third out of 150 shooters. Captain's sniper took first place, and some retired buffalo hunter took second. It was very close, and the three had to have a final shoot off. Mark went first and missed one bull's-eye, and that was enough for him to get third. He still won twenty-five dollars and a small trophy. We were all heading back to the fort when Chris rode up to me and handed me $500. I had already won 150, but Chris insisted on sharing his winnings from the bet with me. I took it with pride and thanked him again. He reminded me if I would have won the ten-mile race, I would be going home with a lot less money. I hadn't thought of it that way, and it did ease the pain of my first loss. Chris was such a good guy to make all of it happen; I even wonder if Chris had it planned this way all along. We laughed and talked and cheered all the way back to the fort—a ride that seemed only to take minutes, but a ride I will never forget.

CHAPTER 12

THE SNOWSTORM

The days seemed so short and the nights became long and cold. I spent most days with Flash riding on trails and roads. Captain and the men were in hold mode, and as Captain would say, "As soon as the snowstorm passes, we will head west." All the paperwork has been summited to the US officials, and anxiety was at an all-time high. The men were staying to themselves. Families were separated and not getting along. Most of the men had committed to homestead land in the Dakotas. A few had decided to leave the community, but Captain had asked all not to announce their intentions until they leave the fort. The fort was rented until January 15, and after that date, all the men would be expected to provide for themselves.

Captain had announced that we had acquired twenty-five new covered wagons that were all equipped with private water tanks, and he also will provide oxen or mules to pull the wagons. Once to our destination in the Dakotas was final, it was a gift, each cavalry man, of course, gets his own horse, saddle, and tack. Every man gets a brand-new Russian rifle and uniform and a picture of choice, which Captain encouraged. He said, "This is our heritage. This is where we came from. Our sacrifices earned these things." He continued to say, "My final gift to every man that sacrificed their life to save me and my family is an assignment." The men shook their head, and "It figures" with laughter was commonly heard. "Your final gift from me to you is I will do any possible chore or favor for you before you or I die or we separate." Captain went on, and many questions were asked. He answered every question with amazing skill and professionalism. Every man agreed that it would take some thinking, and Captain made sure they knew there was no expiration date on this gift. As the snow started coming down and the men were finally relaxed, Captain said that there is one exception. "I will not help any of you marry my daughters!" A big laugh filled the center, and a few more logs were added to the fire.

It snowed all night long, all day, and all night again. The piles are at least twenty-four inches tall, and the temperatures were dropping fast. The barn was completely full. We had sixty horses, ten mules, ten oxen, two milk cows, and three bred black heifers. There were twenty-five wagons, and the tack shop is completely full. The remaining hay for the stock was outside, but everything was tarped. The men had strung ropes from the barn to the cabins and from the cabins to the center. The rope was to help guide us during whiteouts. Going outside became very dangerous very fast, and getting to the barn or the outhouse or the center was not easy. No one could even see each other's cabin, and the wind was bitterly cold. Captain was not happy, and Mother was worried. Out of four of their daughters, Linda was the only one with us. Diane was, of course, with Oxford, and no one has seen them except to get some food. Janet has made the rounds but spent most of the time in the center with any guy or guys that would spend time with her. It seemed like every night, she was kissing a different guy, and she danced with everyone that asks, but she mostly dances with her friends. I did not know and neither did Captain or Mother where she had slept the last three nights. Carol spent most of the time with Ole or Doc. She had been teaching English every day, and the school and the hospital had become one in the same. Doc Schweitzer was very smart and helped Carol with the school. He also taught her lots of nursing skills. She spent her nights in the school with Ole and Doc, who were both single men, and both have showed interest in Carol.

I was with Flash every day, but a girl who was in the barn every day was beginning to be very nice to me. She liked riding and had been around every time I raced Flash. Even back in Russia, she was at the county horse race finish line. When she talked to me, I felt nervous, and my voice squeaked. Talk about embarrassing, but she has been in the barn every day since the storm started. Her name was Laurie. Today she asked me, "Glen, will you help me get to the center? We can have lunch together if you don't mind?" She was flirting, but I didn't mind. I was smitten, so I smiled and granted her wish. We followed the ropes and made it actually pretty easily; the men had made pretty good trails. As we ate lunch, we watched as the men were shoveling the snow out of the wagons. Mark was shoveling snow alongside Captain and pointed at me having lunch with Laurie.

Captain did not mind since I had been in the barn feeding and cleaning stalls almost steady since the storm started and so was Laurie; Captain was aware of that. Captain seemed to know everything except where his daughters were, and that bothered him. Linda was mostly with Mother but has been spending a lot of time with Mikey. It's like the storm was driving Captain crazy. He needs to be doing something, planning something, or helping someone out just to keep himself from worrying about his family.

After almost three full days had past, three cold windy nights, the storm had finally let up, and planning and loading wagons had now taken precedence. Captain, Mark, and I were all preparing the horses and stock for the trip. Trails are starting to form, and Captain and most of the men were planning a trip into the city hoping for news on the land. Mark was nineteen and has also applied for land grants and homestead land. He went into town with every man; not one woman made the trip. Captain told me to stay behind and finish loading the tack into our wagon.

I was the only guy who didn't go to town, but Laurie stayed in the barn and helped me load the wagon, so I didn't mind. The two of us finished and decided to go for a ride. The snow was deep, but we stayed mostly on what were trails and roads. We rode all the way to the river where we stopped in a secluded spot—made only by wind and snow—and had a sandwich. Laurie was so much more prepared than I was; all I brought with was a few dried pieces of jerky and some water. She had sandwiches, cookies, and even a piece of fudge, and it was along that river I got my first kiss. That was another day I will never forget, and even though I thought, up to this point, Laurie and I were just friends, I think something else was starting, and it made me nervous but excited. We talked about if the ice was thick enough to cross on our horses, and as we mounted our horses and rode up to the ice edge, I spotted a beaver house. I knew that ice was thin around the giant beaver house, so I stayed away from it. I did ride out onto the ice; Laurie followed me and crossed easily and gave me a shout, "Let's go. The wind has blown a cool trail. Let's run for a while." That was all I needed, and away we went.

Flash was more than willing to run, so we ran for at least five miles. I did not run Flash to hard because I wanted to stay close to Laurie. I even let her run in front of me for a while. Flash did not like running behind another horse, but I gave him a slight squeeze and tightened the reins. I did not mind watching her ride. We turned back, and when we got to the river, we slowed down and walked the rest of the way. We talked all the way back to the barn, and Laurie asked a lot of questions, mostly about the races and if I want to race again. The men were not back from town yet, so we went right to the center where most the women and all the girls were there preparing a nice meal for all the men. They all are praying that the land deals paperwork come through so we can head west. It almost like they are preparing a party or celebration and excitement filled the air.

Diane hung out with Carol in the school and talked about what Oxford and Diane were going to do. Oxford has applied for homestead land not far from where Captain planned on making his farm. Carol had plans for her and Ole too, but Carol was only sixteen, and Diane was sure to point that out. Janet and a few of her friends were with

Mother and Linda working in the kitchen. There was a lot more giggling coming from the kitchen, and I wasn't sure if they were laughing at me and Laurie hanging out or were they just giggling about all the guys they have been kissing.

Captain and all the men were returning, and although none of them were back yet, we could hear them from a ways away. They must have been drinking, which means celebrating, which means there was good news from the courthouse and the land deals. The snow was still deep, but every man was mounted, and the trail had been padded down pretty well. As I made my way to the barn to help with the horses, Laurie followed right behind me and was planning to help with the horses as well. I asked her, "Why are you following me?"

She smiled almost embarrassed-like and commented, "I love horses and want to have a big horse ranch too. My father has applied for land along with my uncles, and we plan on having a large farm and ranch too." I had never thought of that up until this point. I blushed and smiled, and with an approving nod to her, we walked to the barn together. Just as we shoveled the doors out again and shoveled a spot to put the loaded wagon out of the way, but still able to get at it, the men started to arrive in the barn. All the men worked together, and before long, all the horses were in their corrals. A solid line was formed, and hay bales were loaded into the barn like a well-oiled conveyer belt was passing them along.

Laurie and I worked the haystack together, and to my surprise, she could really haul hay. One of the guys was watching her haul hay and was impressed as well. He teased and was flirting with her and gave her a nickname "Hay

Hauler," and although she didn't like the nickname at first, it immediately stuck, and from that point on, Laurie was called Hay Hauler. She was teased, and "Hey, hey, Hay Hauler" was shouted out by every one of Mark's buddies and most of the men. She did not mind as she worked hard, and every person there knew she could hold her own while hauling hay or any task in the barn. I just smiled and tried to keep up. She kissed me, and I was really dying to tell someone.

The horses and barn settled a lot faster than I had hoped, and everyone cleaned up and headed straight to the center. I was the last one in the barn, but I watched Laurie leave the barn with her father. She did smile and give me a wave. Captain closed the doors to the barn with me, and as we walked over to the center, he asked me how my day was. I was so excited to tell someone, but I decided Captain was not the one to tell. I told him, "I went for a ride all the way to the river. I crossed it riding Flash and rode all the way to the trees where the wind made a huge snow pile and riding could not go on." I tried not to lead on that I was not alone, but Captain knew my story was not the complete story. I continued to tell him, "The wagon is completely full. I moved it away from the tack shop and covered it up."

Captain commented, "That's a lot of work by yourself and still have time for at least a ten-mile ride!"

His comment was almost question like, so I told him, "Laurie helped me load the tack shop into the wagon." Captain still knew I was not telling him the entire story. As quickly as I could, I switched the subject to his trip into the city. Captain was in a very good mood, as all the men were, and I knew the news was good.

Captain only commented, "Everything but the ride into town went perfect. You are lucky you stayed here." He smiled and gave me his famous head nod and went into the center. The men did not wait for Captain, and as we walked into the center, it was a buzz, and everyone was happy. Every man that applied for homestead land got it, and every grant to buy farmland was accepted. Even Mark was accepted for a homestead and a farmland grant.

I didn't know whom to talk to or know if I should tell anyone about my day. I kept a close eye on Laurie that night, and even though we did not talk, Mother saw the glances and waves. She knew we had spent all day together alone in the barn and riding our horses together. She even knew Laurie had packed lunch and was planning this for quite some time. Mother walked over to me and asked, "How was your day?" with a smile.

I smiled back and answered as inconspicuously as I could, "Everything was fine. Captain said I got a lot done, and then I went for a ride." Mother smiled knowing everything that had happened, well almost everything, but she just walked away and headed straight for Laurie's mother. I was a little bit worried; Mother might say something. As she was walking straight over to talk to Laurie's Mother, I looked at Laurie with a bit of a worried look. She looked back and just waved. From that point on, I knew that the ladies knew I liked Laurie and she liked me. I did not tell my secret to anyone that night.

Everyone was very happy, and since the night was almost over, Captain began to speak. He asked for everyone's attention. "We have had a good day. We have all been granted land and areas for our farms and ranches. Our dreams are in our hands," he said. All the families cheered, but all I could think of was my first kiss. I watched Laurie, and she watched me as Captain continued, "Every man now has a choice to make. Are you going to the Dakotas with me? Do you want to give up the cavalry life and become full-time farmers and ranchers? Are you willing to leave New York and follow me to our dreams?" Everyone cheered again. Captain really knew how to fire up the men. He then announced, "Tomorrow we prepare our entire community and all our horses and stock to make the trip, and on January 10, day after next, we will start our wagon train of horses, men, women, and all our kids, with our wagons full, to the Dakotas, where we will be free men, free German men and women to live out our lives and dreams!" Cheers once again filled the center; more wood was added to the fireplace, and although some of the women and children left, every man stayed late into the night.

CHAPTER 13

FORT HARRIMAN

Mike and Tony found this fort a month ago, and it has been a perfect place for our community to live. It was so much better than the *Blu Moon Escape*, but in my opinion not near as cool as the oak grove. It was shelter for all of us, and it almost felt better than home to many of the men. The officers had nice homes, and the bunkhouses for the enlisted men made a great living area. The center and kitchen were a better facility than any fort in Russia and better than most of the homes that any of them grew up in. When Mike and Tony first got here, they only had to make small repairs and do some cleaning. All the work was done before any of us got here. A few things came up as it was old and had been used hard by the military, and the last regiment that was here did not clean up after themselves. Captain insisted we were going to do everything in our power to clean it completely and leave it better than we got there.

It was January 10, my fourteenth birthday, and I wasn't sure anyone knew but me. I told Chris, but not sure he would remember. I was hoping Mother told Laurie or Laurie's mother about my birthday, but again, I was just dreaming. I had not told anyone about my kiss but sure was hoping for one on my birthday. I was up early as nearly every man and woman in camp was. I went straight to the barn and was going to ride Flash around one last time before we left this place. Captain was saddling his horse and was planning a trip heading to back New York. He said it was going to be a quick trip, and he was going to ride hard. He asked, with a serious look but knew I would never turn down a ride with Captain and ride next to Captain's horse, "You want to ride along with me?"

I smiled. "I will be ready whenever you are," I exclaimed.

Captain said, "Okay then, tighten your rig. It's muddy as hell, and we are going to try to be back by ten. That means we're not stopping for anything."

I commented, "Good, I love riding hard, and it will give me a good look at your mount. She is twelve years old and has some miles on her. Think she can keep up to Flash?" I challenged. Captain gave me a smile and looked pretty confident when he nodded his hat.

"Let's ride, see if you can keep up!" was the last things I heard as Captain took off. He was riding fast and hard, and it did take me until we were halfway to town to catch up to him, but I think he slowed down a little. We rode hard side by side all the way to town. The snow had mostly melted, but the road was frozen from the overnight freeze, and surprisingly, the horses had no problem running all the way to town. As we slowed down through town and were coming up to Charlie's store, Captain looked directly at me and said, "I bet you forgot your own birthday?" I looked right at Captain and nodded my hat, something I have watched him do for years.

"I knew it was my birthday, but wasn't sure you did or anyone else for that matter."

Captain responded with a short answer, "Charlie told me." I looked at his horse.

"Your horse ran pretty good, Captain. Do you think she can make it back at the same speed?"

He smiled and said, "We will see." We tied up the horses in front of Charlie's, and as Captain was walking away, he said, "Go talk to Charlie. He has something for you." I hustled into Charlie's store like a dog with a bone. He was with a customer but obviously was expecting me.

The rich-looking man looked at me and said, "Is this him?"

Charlie immediately spoke up in his friendly voice, "Yes, it is, and he's here early." He looked out the window and asked, "Did you ride Flash into town today?"

"Of course, I ride him everywhere and every day."

Charlie looked at the rich man and said, "Glen, this is Dave. Dave, this is Glen Gross, the fastest man I've ever seen ride, and he is only thirteen."

I smiled. "Fourteen today!" I shouted.

Dave smiled and walked right over to me. "Happy Birthday Glen. Your father wants me to give you this." And he handed me a schedule of horse races. "I want to be your best friend," he said. "I want to sponsor you and your horse to race in every one of these races. Charlie has told me all about your horse, and I would like to see it." He looked out the front window of Charlie's place. I was so happy I didn't know even what to say. I walked toward the door.

"He is right out here, come look." We both went outside, and he immediately commented that Flash is kind of skinny. All I said was, "Built for speed," and I went back into Charlie's store feeling a little hurt, but only a little. I went over to Charlie and asked, "Captain says you have something for me?"

Charlie said, "Yes, I do," as he reached for a map of New York, Pennsylvania, Ohio, Kentucky, and even a few more of the little states listed. "It has trails, towns, country water holes, taverns, and eight horse races listed on the map," Charlie said. I must have had quite a look on my face when I looked at Charlie. "Are you okay?" Charlie asked and looked toward Dave. "This is the first time I have ever seen Glen speechless about his horse." As he looked at Dave and then at me again, he asked, "So, are you interested?"

"Of course, I'm interested, but do you think Captain will really allow this? He needs me to help get to Pittsburg. It's his first planned stop on our way to the Dakotas?" I asked.

Charlie smiled and said, "Son, this is Captain's birthday gift to you. Do you think Dave was here coincidently?"

I looked at Dave and said, "I guess not." I paused for a minute, looked at Dave, and said, "So why would I need you to sponsor me? I can go race in all these races and keep all the purse to myself!"

Dave looked at me and said, "I hope you can win every race, and if that's the case, with me as a sponsor, you will win a lot more than the purse. I will pay you thousands. You will have fame and fortune."

I looked out the window again, and I saw Captain come walking up with another tall kind-of-goofy-looking man. He walked right into Charlie's and looked at Charlie and then Dave. "So, did you tell him about the race in Pittsburg?"

As he looked back at Charlie, Charlie just handed Captain a list of all eight horse races listed and said, "Yes, and then some. Dave already has enough sponsor money that Glen won't even need to win. He finishes in the top ten in Pittsburg, and he will bring home over a thousand dollars, and if he wins, he will get paid five thousand. If he wins in Kentucky, he could make ten thousand or more."

Captain looked at me, looked at Dave very seriously, and before Captain said anything, Dave spoke up. He was talking fast like a salesman, not smooth like he talked to me. "I will guarantee his safety, and here is five hundred dollars, in advance, to show I am serious."

He handed it directly to Captain, Captain handed it directly to me, and while looking directly at me, he said, "Good luck, you better save it. You might have to pay it back. Let's go. We have a lot to do." And as he looked at Dave, he said, "We will see you in Pittsburg in three weeks." Dave looked at Captain, then Charlie, then me. "The race is in two weeks, guys."

I looked at Dave and said, "I will be there!"

We all walked out the door with no other words except for Darren, Captain's follower, he said, "So, you're the one that won the fifty-mile race, and your only thirteen?"

I mounted my horse and said, "Fourteen today."

He said, "Happy birthday. I will see you around six. Congratulations on your New Year's Day win. New York usually has the fastest horses anywhere. I will be betting on you in Pitt."

I smiled and nodded. "Thank you." I looked at Captain, and we rode off, never looking back. Before we got to the end of town, I asked Captain who Darren is.

Captain said, "I hired him to take pictures tonight. Happy birthday!"

I smiled at Captain and asked, "Do you think you can keep up? I won't hold Flash back. If the roads are good, I will show you why I will win in Pittsburg."

Captain just nodded and said, "Let me see him run. I will keep up." And just like that, we both took off on a dead run.

Flash seemed to be holding back for some reason, and as we were side by side, I told Captain, "Flash won't open up. The roads are perfect."

As I said that, Captain swayed about ten feet over, as far over as he could to stay on the road, and spoke, "Try now." It was like Captain knew. I gave Flash the reins. I tightened my hat and gave Flash quite a spur. It was like he hit another gear. Faster than when I won the big race. Captain did not fall too far behind, and as we entered the fort, I slowed down. Captain rode up next to me and looked at Flash. "He really can run. Not too many horses have ever outrun this horse, and just so you know, I wasn't holding back. He can really move."

We rode up to the barn together, and there stood Laurie. I didn't know what to say. I smiled as I went by her and said quietly, "Hi, Hay Hauler."

Captain looked directly at me and just said, "That's something we need to discuss too."

We both went to the same stall, and Laurie walked right up to Captain and said, "We will take care of your horse and gear, sir. Looks like you guys ran them pretty hard. Who won the race?" Captain was as eager to get out of there as I was for him to leave.

He looked at her, nodded his hat, and said, "Thank you," and walked away.

She turned to me and said, "You must have won, and oh yeah, happy birthday." She walked up right in front of me and laid another big, juicy kiss right on my mouth, dirt and all, and said, "Did he ask you about me?" My response was honest as could be.

I said, "No, we didn't have time. We ran all the way there. He gave me a birthday present, and we raced all the way back, and yes, I won. The only thing he said was, after I said, 'Hi, Hay Hauler,' he said, 'Another thing I need to talk to you about.'"

Laurie walked really close to me again. I thought maybe she would kiss me again and said, "What did you get for your birthday?"

I pulled out a map with all the states and races on it, and she said, "You got a map for your birthday?"

I started laughing and said, "I guess I did, but I also made a deal to race in a horse race in Pittsburg in two weeks." I pulled out five hundred dollars and said, "Dave gave me five hundred in advance, and if I finish in the top ten, I get another five hundred, and another five thousand if I win!" Laurie was in disbelief.

She was speechless for almost a minute and then looked at my horse. I had the saddle removed, and she said, "He is pretty skinny, but he sure can run." She walked over to me again, looked me directly in my eyes, and said, "I will never miss a race of yours." Kissed me again, and started to remove Captain's saddle. We brushed and bathed both horses for over an hour and just talked about horses. When Mark came into the barn and told us lunch was still in the center, but everyone was about done.

All three of us headed straight to the center, and all Mark said was, "I heard you beat Captain in a race?" I acknowledged. He gave me a high five and said, "Nice work," and walked up to the center door. Holding the door open for Laurie and then me, he just smiled. He quietly said to me just as I passed him, directly in my ear, "We need to talk." All of us went and sat by Captain and Mother. All the girls were there; even Laurie's two sisters were sitting there. I could not wait to tell Mother and the girls about the upcoming races, but I figured we should eat first since we were the last ones.

I started to eat, and immediately, Carol chimed in, "Some guy gave you five hundred dollars just to show up and finish the race in Pittsburg?" I was so relieved. I thought she was going to ask about Laurie, and I didn't know what to say. I had thought about what to say to the girls and even Mark, but not with Captain, Mother, and Laurie's sisters sitting there. I did not have an answer. Carol then poked at me, "What's up, cat got your tongue?"

I then answered, "Yes, Dave, my new best friend, is giving me one thousand dollars cash just to finish the race in Pittsburg. I get five hundred in advance and the other five hundred on race day. I get an additional five thousand dollars if I win. Charlie gave me a map." I pulled out the map and the advance of $500 and said, "If I win every race of these eight, I can win forty thousand dollars, maybe more." Mark could not believe his ears and grabbed the map.

He immediately said, "It is only $150 purse per race. It says it right here on your map, and how are you going to get to all these races?" I looked at Mark and then the girls and then to Laurie as almost to give away our newly founded relationship. "Dave has sponsors, and the sponsors are paying me to race. The purse is just bonus."

Mother looked directly at Captain with a very serious look and said, "He is only thirteen!"

Captain looked at me then Mother and said, "Fourteen today." She did not bring the race up again the rest of the day, and I know it wasn't the races she was concerned about; it was my new best friend Dave that she was needing to talk to Captain about. Mikey had made birthday cake, and Captain announced that at six o'clock or so, a photographer will be here and will be taking pictures of everyone. He asked that the soldiers please put on their uniform and take a picture either standing or sitting on their horse.

The night finished early, and after the pictures and supper, everyone went to bed. Tomorrow was a big day, and we would be pulling out of the fort and onto a trail that had not been tested since the snow. Everyone was loaded and planned on rolling out of the fort early, before sunrise. Captain was keeping all of us back and made sure Mother, Marcella, and Mikey all got out to the road and were heading west before returning to the fort. Captain assigned us to sweep every house, every cabin, barn, and the entire center for any remnants that we were there. It didn't take long as every person in camp knew Captain wanted it clean. All of us were on our own horse, so Captain knew we could easily catch the wagons. The fort was spotless, better—way better than when we arrived. Captain was satisfied and said he would show us the way to the road. Mark and I knew the way, so Mark told Captain that we would catch up; we needed to do one more thing, and then we would soon be on our way. Captain trusted us completely and gave us his nod. "See you soon," he said and rode off with the girls.

I was not sure what Mark had planned, but we rode behind the barn and found a solid piece of wood, like a sign with no writing. We rode back to the entry of the fort, and Mark stopped. He got off his horse and instructed me to do the same. I acknowledged, and as I reached to tie off the horses, I saw him grab a hammer and wood chisel out of his already overstuffed saddlebags. He looked at me and said, "Let's make a sign that shows we were here." He reached into the snow and pulled out an old cruddy sign that read, "Fort Harriman, 1840–1888." Mark broke that sign in half and said, "I can fix it if we need to. Let's get busy." We worked on the new sign, and in about sixty minutes, we had made a sign that read, "Fort MG and family, 1896–1897." MG stood for Mathias Gross. We did not want it to be too obvious, but we hung the sign and took off. We rode slowly at first, and I told Mark about Hay Hauler and how we have kissed three times. I told him what she said, "She will never miss a race of mine, and that she likes me and then kissed me on the mouth again. She kissed me first. Three times."

Mark laughed. "Yeah, you said that. Three times." He took off running and said, "Catch me if you can." His horse was very fast too, but I was not going to let him beat me in a race, even if he did get the jump on me.

The roads were filled with wagon wheel tracks but was still pretty frozen-perfect again, and I let Flash go, again. He did not have a problem finding his gear, and as I started to pass Mark, he was running fast and smooth. I could see the wagons already, and they had an hour head start. Mark gave me a yell as I was passing, so we slowed down. We walked slowly the rest of the way, and before long, we were caught up to the girls and Captain. Janet immediately noticed the broken sign sticking out of Mark's stuffed saddlebags.

She asked. "What is that?" Mark pulled it out and showed the girls. Captain asked where we found it, and Mark told him. He did not tell him what we replaced it with, and Captain never asked again.

Mark went on to tell Janet and Carol, "I will refinish it one day. I will paint Oxford and Diane's wedding date on there and give it to them on their first anniversary."

They thought it to be a great idea, and without even taking a third breath, Janet asked, "Did Glen tell you about Laurie? What did they do? Are they boyfriend and girlfriend now?"

Mark smiled, and just as he rode away, he said, "Ask Glen. He's the lover boy." All three the girls looked at me and were almost getting Captain's attention as they pestered and pestered. Finally, I did what Mark did.

"A gentleman never tells," I said as I rode past the girls. "Catch me if you can." Just about then, Mark went down the ditch and really gave it to his horse. I did the same, and we were riding in the snow in the field, and it was smooth, and we were cruising.

We quickly caught up to Laurie and her mother as they were both in the fourth covered wagon being pulled by two oxen. They were barely moving it seemed, but Laurie's sisters were walking next to the wagon, so Mark slowed way down as to say hello. As I rode up the ditch to get closer, Laurie smiled and politely said hello and asked, "How's your ride?"

As politely as I could, I responded, "Well, up until this point, pretty fun. Mark and I stayed back an extra hour and took care of a few things. We rode fast and had fun and caught up real fast."

Laurie's mother, Della, looked at Flash and said, "So that is your fast horse, looks skinny to me."

I looked at Laurie and winked. "He is built for speed. See you later." And away I went. Down the ditch and back out into the field. Mark was waiting for me, and he followed.

I took off as fast as I could, and it didn't take long before we could no longer see the wagons. I commented to Mark, "Maybe we should turn back for a while." He stopped, had a drink of water, and looked right at me.

"She kissed you three times, and she kissed you first? She is pretty cute. How old is she?" he asked.

"She is sixteen," I replied.

He smiled again. "Older women always make the first move." And he took another big swig from his canteen. About then, we saw Chris and John riding right for us, so we waited to see what they had to say.

As they rode up, they stopped and gave us the all clear ahead and then John asked, "What is that wood you are carrying?"

Mark pulled it out and read it to the two men, "Fort Harriman 1840–1888." Mark went on to say, "I found this old sign in the grass, and I'm going to redo it and give it to Ox and Di on their anniversary. Put their wedding date on there of course."

John just looked at Mark. "You are carrying that all the way to North Dakota?" He then looked at Chris and said, "I knew that fort had to have a name. Fort Harriman. I wonder who he was?"

CHAPTER 14

PENNSYLVANIA

Zeus and Apollo have been pulling hard for ten hours a day, and we seemed to be barely gaining ground; we had been gone from Fort Harriman for five days, and we had only traveled two hundred miles. "Captain, at the pace we are going, we will never make it to Pittsburgh in time for the race, and Dave has prepaid me to place in the top ten," I said as I rode next to Captain.

"Zeus and Apollo are working hard pulling the lead wagon. They are the best mules we have and are breaking a trail through the snow and ice and pulling a big wagon," he replied. "If the race day gets near and the wagons are still too far to make it, you will have to ride ahead and race on your own. There is nothing I can do. We cannot hurry the entire wagon train because you have a race," said Captain. We rode side by side for a long time after that, not saying a word. I would look at him, and he would just keep his head straight forward as not to see me. I could see he was thinking up a plan but was not willing to share with me.

I finally broke the silence and asked, "If I am to ride ahead of the wagons and race, will it be okay for Mark or some of the other guys to ride with me?"

Captain gave me a nod and said, "You will have to ask him, but I believe he wants to race too. I believe he is already entered into the shooting events and the ten-mile race. He thinks he has a chance to beat you in the ten-mile race and will definitely challenge you in the fifty-mile race." I did not respond, as I figured there is no way anyone will beat me in a fifty-mile race.

As I rode up to Mark and Chris, they were talking about the races as well and were discussing how they can make the most money possible. "I am betting on Flash and Glen to win the fifty-mile race, and I'm betting every penny I have," I heard Chris say. "I won't be sharing the winnings this time, and if he wins, I will have enough to buy some cows for my new ranch."

As I rode up next to Chris, I commented, "Thanks for your confidence. I will not let you down." Mark did not have as much confidence in Flash and me as I did, and he made sure I knew.

He did not come out and say he was going to win, but he did say, "I am racing this time so he will have more competition than in New York."

I gave Mark a big "yeah right" and proceeded to ask, "If the wagons are not to Pittsburgh by race day, will you guys ride with me the day before and help me find the racing grounds? Captain said I have to ask you, so, will you?"

Chris answered with a smile, "Of course."

But Mark was not so friendly and said, "Well, if you can't find the race, how are you going to race?" They both got a chuckle and were harassing me a bit knowing that I would find the race.

"Your friend Dave will be waiting for you at the outskirts of town I'm sure," said Chris. "That guy sure has a lot of confidence in you and your skinny horse. I hope he's right."

As we slowly rode past the slow rolling wagons, I pondered the same thoughts, but mostly, I was thinking on what I would do with my winnings. Since I was confident that I would win and would have thousands of dollars to spend. I asked Mark, "If you win the shooting events, are you going to ask Dave to sponsor you in the next tournaments?"

Mark just shook his head and said, "For some reason, he only likes you, and there are not enough guys and interest to win big money in shooting. I can't even find guys to bet me."

Chris smiled and said, "No one is dumb enough to bet against you two. You have been riding and shooting since you could walk. Captain has provided you with the best horses and the best guns, and you both shoot and ride every day. You are two lucky guys, and you better not ever forget it." Chris rode away and almost seemed upset. As I looked at Mark and he looked at me, we shrugged our shoulders at each other as to agree, but also as to say, there is nothing we can do about it. Captain has been a great father to us.

The wagons rolled on and into the dark before Captain announced to stop and set up a mini camp on the bank of a small river. Captain did not want any wagons to try to cross the river in the dark, and John has not reported back to Captain as to where there is a good crossing. Every river we crossed, there were anxieties and worries. Our community has traveled a long way, and to lose someone or some of our things was becoming more important every time we crossed a river. Twenty-five wagons lined up along the river instead of in our traditional circle, and tonight there were several fires, almost like we were traveling separately. Our wagons were fourth and fifth in line today, followed by Mikey with the food and dinner supplies.

I rode along the riverbank quite a ways looking for a place to cross but did not find a thing. The banks were steep, and the edges had ice with fast-moving open water in the middle. It was dark and looked dangerous. So, as I rode back to our wagons, I spotted Laurie and her family. I rode over to their mini camp, and I helped Willie, Laurie's father, gather some wood to start a fire. He knew his three daughters were being courted by several of the men, but he also knew that Laurie would not even talk to the other guys unless I was around. We had gathered a good amount of wood when Laurie walked around the corner with some old paper and matches. She started the fire and asked me to stay and have dinner with them, but I got a feeling that although Laurie and I thought it a good idea, Willie did not, and so I pleasantly declined the invitation and commented, "I will take a rain check, and next time I will ask Captain first." I had not talked to Laurie in a few days now and really wanted to. I knew she wanted to ask me something, but I wasn't sure what she wanted.

I rode Flash quietly back to our wagons and unsaddled him, brushed him down, and sat down by the fire. Mikey has supper nearly ready, and Mother and Janet were already calling everyone for supper. It was a good hot dish, and I was hungry, but I remained seated next to the fire wondering what Laurie wanted to ask me. I was thinking about the day and the conversation I had with Chris and why he thinks we are spoiled but mostly about the race and if I would win. Since Dave had sponsored me and given me an advance, I have begun to worry more and more.

Mother sat down next to me and handed me a plate and fork. She asked me what was wrong and if I was feeling okay. I responded, "Oh yes, Mother. I am fine, just kind of a long, slow day, and I am just thinking about stuff." Mother did not like me racing for money and did not like the idea of her baby, the youngest in the family, riding off to a city where none of us had ever been. Mother insisted I go get some food and made sure I knew that once everyone is done with supper; she would make apple turnovers using the fire. Mother knew it was my favorite, and she knew it would cheer me up. I ate quickly and grabbed a bucket and went to the river for water as to show I am helping with the dishes. I walked out onto the ice and reached as far as I could. About the time the bucket was full of water, the ice gave way. *Splash!* Into the water I went.

It was cold and scared the crap out of me. I tried to get my footings, but the fast-moving water knocked me to my butt. There I sat in the middle of the river freezing cold with a bucket of water. I thought, *An end to another day, and I'm spoiled!* No one really even saw me or heard me, so I stood up and realized the river is only three feet deep. I dunked my head and washed my face as I set the bucket of water next to me on the ice edge. I hadn't washed in fresh river water in probably a week and figured, what the heck, I'm wet anyway. I headed straight to the fire, and as I got close, I set the bucket down and immediately added a lot more wood to the fire.

Mother was by the wagons preparing the apples and saw that I had the fire roaring, and she said with a smile, "I can't make apple turnovers with that big of fire." It was at about that time that Linda spoke up and realized what Mother was doing and headed right to Mother to help. Apple turnovers were not only my favorite, but everyone loved them, and now that Mother announced dessert, everyone gathered around the fire. Diane and Ox joined us every evening for supper since we have been on the wagon train, and it wasn't until Oxford sat down next to me that he noticed that I was soaking wet.

He asked, "How did you get so wet?"

And then Diane noticed too. "Where did you get enough water to bath?"

As calmly as I could and still shaking, I answered, "In the river. It is not very deep, and I needed a bath." I was looking away. Oxford knew I was not being honest because he knew I wouldn't bath but once a month if Mother didn't insist.

As Mother walked up to the fire with her hands full, she looked at me more closely now and just smiled. "Now I know why you made such a big fire."

Linda followed Mother to the fire with supplies, saw me soaked, and said, "That's a first. You take a bath without Mother insisting."

And that's when Ox spoke up, "No way you took a bath voluntarily. That water is freezing. What is going on?"

I still did not say anything, and then Janet spoke up, "He has a girlfriend now. He doesn't want to smell like a horse all the time."

Captain didn't like the sound of that, so he looked right at me and then with a fire glistening off his rough face, looked right at Mother and said, "He fell in the river retrieving water, and that is why he is so wet."

He looked at me for approval, and I immediately thought, *How does he know everything*. Then I answered, "Yes, I went out onto the ice because I figured it's thick enough to walk on. I got close to the edge so I could get water, and the weight of the full bucket caused me to break through. Yes, it was cold, but I figured I am wet so might as well wash off." Everyone immediately looked to the river and then back at me, and all at the same time gave out a huge laugh. I also said, "Laurie is not my girlfriend. We only kissed three times." The laughs continued, and I was the butt of the jokes that evening. Mother calmed the crowd to a silence as she handed out apple turnovers. She gave me mine last and smiled as she gave me the leftover apples. It was time for bed, and Mother was gathering the dessert plates when she whispered in my ear as she handed me her extras. She always left half her dessert.

"She really kissed you three times?"

I was up before dawn and had already had Flash to the other side of the river and back a few times before I saw Captain. He was sipping on coffee and did not seem like he was in a hurry, like normal. I rode up next to him. "Good morning, Captain. Are you almost ready to get rolling?" He confirmed that he was a little slow this morning and asked if I had found a crossing. I replied, "The river is not very deep and is mostly sand and gravel bottom. I have crossed several times and made a trail for the wagons to cross, not far from where I fell in last night." He kind of chuckled as he gave a big stretch.

"Well, you might as well hitch up Apollo and Zeus. You're the only one ready to go." I did look around, and Captain was right again. Besides Chris, John, and a few other guys saddling their horses, I was the only one up.

By the time I had the team hooked up, Mother said the wagon is ready to go. I didn't know she meant for me to drive the team across, but she grabbed Flash, jumped into my saddle, and said, "Come on! Let's be the first across."

And as I jumped into the wagon, I noticed nearly every eye in the entire wagon train was watching. I said, "Come *on*!" and snapped the reins like I have seen Mother do several times. The team headed right where I directed them, and the wagon followed behind. I crossed the river with ease, and on the other bank, as the team pulled it straight up without even slipping, I noticed I was having fun, laughing, and even hollering, "Yeehaw!" I yelled looking back at Mother, "That was fun!"

She rode Flash right up to me, smiled, looked at me, and said, "I think I will ride Flash today, and you drive the team. You will be first in line today, so don't go too fast." She pointed toward the trail heading west. "Go ahead. Get started. I will catch up." And just like that, she gave Flash a spur, and back into the water she went. I did like what she said and headed west. It wasn't long after I was rolling west that other wagons followed, and the westward wagon train through central Pennsylvania was rolling again. I pushed the team hard, and the snow was deep. No one has used the trail since the snowstorm, and there were spots that were deep and slushy. I knew then why Captain insisted on naming the team Zeus and Apollo. The two as a team were amazing, pulling through drifts and slush that I never thought could be done. The pulling gods of the world were with the team while I drove the team fifty miles, which was farthest we made in one day since we started. I stopped just before sundown. Captain and Mother rode together and stopped next to me and the wagon. Mother smiled, and Captain gave me his approval nod.

"Did you have fun today?"

I smiled back, and as best as I could to repeat Captain's exact nod, I nodded back and said, "This team can really pull!"

The next few days went more slowly than ever; we were only traveling thirty to thirty-five miles a day. The snow was deep, and the wind was blowing, and so everything was slower; even Flash huddled up to the wagons, and we just slowly moved west. It was only two days until the race, and we were still nearly one hundred miles from Pittsburgh. We all were sitting around after supper; Chris and John were there too. Before I could ask Captain about where and how to get to the race, he spoke up looking at me, "Mark and you"—nodding toward me—"John and Chris, you four ride into Pittsburgh and get a couple hotel rooms. Glen, you pay." And without even a hesitation, he added, "You can leave anytime you want. John, once in Pittsburgh, help the boys get the horses into the livery in a comfortable spot. Then all I ask is that you eat your meals at the hotel and charge everything to your rooms. Glen has volunteered to pay." It was never discussed who would pay for what, but I had more money than I had ever had, so I did not argue a word. I knew we could get there in less than a day, and that would give us plenty of time to see Pittsburgh.

Chris spoke up, "Captain, if you don't mind, there are quite a few men that want to go to Pittsburgh with us, and I think everyone wants to see the races." Captain immediately referred to the safety and well-being of the wagon train.

"The women and children, the stock. We have everything riding on this, and I don't think abandoning the wagons for a race is a good idea," he said with a tone that all of us knew that meant not everyone will see the race. He thought for only a second and said, "We will draw straws on who gets to go and who is staying. Shortest straws stay. Long straws get their choice. Anyone with a wagon or stock that needs a driver will have to find a driver if they are going to watch the race. I will stay behind and try to keep the wagon trail rolling west." Captain immediately had straws ready to go. Ten out of the twenty families wanted to go. Everyone had their own mount. It made it easy, and everyone seemed okay with the outcome. Captain gave us the okay to head to Pittsburgh a day early, but the plan was for everyone else to ride in on race day. I had money in my pocket, riding with my best friends, and heading to Pittsburgh, Pennsylvania, USA.

We got to Pittsburgh in what seemed like only an hour, but the ride took nearly all day. We did not run hard, but we never walked the horses. We stopped once for water, but the horses did not seem thirsty. The snow was light, the temperature was an even 40, and as we rode through town, the road was muddy, and there was horse crap everywhere. I noticed a nice livery next to the William Penne Hotel, but that looked packed, and now I was questioning if we would even find a place. We rode around town until we found the starting spot of the races and the details of the shooting events. The fifty-mile race was once again at the same times as the shooting events, and Mark has again chosen to shoot.

We stopped to preregister at the general store. A small man with a strong German accent met us at the door. "You must be the Gross boys?" he asked with a smile. "Dave has you boys registered and is waiting for you at the hotel."

I looked at him and asked, "Are we staying at the William Penne Hotel?" The small man just smiled and shook his head yes; he looked out at our muddy horses, then looked at me.

"That must be your skinny horse out there? I heard it was skinny. I thought it would be skinnier than that," he said.

I shook my head in disgust. "Why does everyone think he's so skinny. He is built for speed!"

The small man then handed me a poster and asked, "Can I have your autograph?" At first, I thought the poster was mine to keep, but he wanted my name written on that poster. Chris actually explained it to me, and then I was embarrassed. As I signed my name, Gary, the store owner, reached for a couple more posters and handed them to Mark. "You guys can have these. All the events are listed." As I looked at my signature, I realized the poster had my name and Flash's name written on it. It read, "Come watch the NEW fastest kid heading west, Glen Gross, and his horse Flash! NY State Champion and fastest fifty miles ever recorded!" That's about all I read, but I did grab a poster for myself, knowing Mark would use his for fire starting paper if he got a chance.

We headed straight out the door and right over to the livery stable, and we were met there by several guys that wanted to talk but mostly wanted to see Flash. The livery guys wanted to take care of Flash, but I insisted I take care of him. Dave had hooked up several stables for us, and Flash got his own stable. Once I had him settled in and I was comfortable leaving, we headed over to the hotel. I went up to the hotel desk, but everyone else went straight to the bar. Dave had the hotel rooms lined up, and as the desk clerk handed me the keys, Dave appeared in the bar and bought everyone a round. It was the first time I had seen Mark drink; I had water.

The hotel was amazing, and everyone was being over-friendly. A few strangers harassed me for not drinking whiskey or beer, but I didn't care. It was my first time in a hotel. The dancing girls were smiling at me and even wanted me to dance, so I did. Mark and I have a hotel room with two beds, and it had water and a fancy chair and fresh towels, and fancy pillows and blankets. It was amazing! I don't remember ever a better night's sleep. I mean, after all the drinking and dancing was over, I slept with a smile on my face all night. Mark was in the bathroom half the night; he said the room was spinning, and he had to throw up. I knew it is from the whiskey he drank, but I didn't care; we had a blast.

I was up early and over to the stables. I checked on the horses, fed them, watered them, and then I went back to the hotel for breakfast. As I walked into the hotel, Chris and John were just coming to breakfast. I told them I fed and watered the horses, and they just smiled. As we sat down to eat, Dave came into the hotel and sat with us. He explained that the livery will feed and water the horses, so we don't have to worry. He paid the guys over there to take extra good care of all your horses. I told him I already took care of that. "I was over there before breakfast. No one was there, so I just helped myself. I found everything I needed. It didn't take long."

Dave just smiled, looked at the others, and asked, "Was he in the hotel lounge with you guys last night?" And as he looked around, he said, "I know Mark was. Where is he?" I told Dave that Mark was sick and wanted to sleep in for a while. Chris and John got a chuckle, and as we were just finishing breakfast, Mark showed up. He normally would eat a good breakfast, but this day, he only had toast with a little cinnamon sprinkled on it—the way Mikey made on the ship when the girls were sick. I knew he had drunk too much whiskey.

We visited all over Pittsburgh that day, with Dave as our guide. He kept saying that I'm his good luck charm and he is mine. Chris wagered $1,000 for me to win—not top ten—to win. As the day went along, everywhere I went, people would ask me about Flash or about the race. The day went by pretty fast, and the guys were really cool to me even though I was only fourteen. They were in their twenties, and Mark was nineteen. They almost always were really cool toward me, and rarely did they tease me, but I have never just hung out with two cavalry scouts and Mark for a day; it was pretty awesome.

The next morning was race day, and I was up and ready. My horse was saddled, fed, and watered; I was riding by nine. The ten-mile race was to start at ten, and it never left the streets, basically, a full out ten-mile sprint. The fifty left town and went through some hills and some rocky terrain. It was wet and slushy, so I knew I needed to be on my game. There were two hundred riders in the ten-mile race. I drew the third start time. Every minute, another fifty riders would start. As we were all getting lined up, I heard a ready, set, and the starter's pistol fire; the first fifty men were off and running. There was only one minute apart and another, "Ready, set, *bang*," and I was next. I was not near the front, but as the minute ran down, I neared the front.

"Ready, set, and *bang*! And away I went, and Flash was ready to run. He never did like running behind any other horse, and it seemed like there was always another horse to pass. Mud was flying everywhere. I had mud in my mouth, my hair, my ears, everywhere, and as I approached the one-mile-to-go marker, there were only a couple horses in front of me. The last mile was a straight shot through town, and the finish line was just in front of the hotel. I gave Flash all the rein, and away he went. We had finally passed enough riders to have a nearly perfect, for being wet and muddy, road to ride on. Flash stretched it out and ran as hard as he could. The streets were lined with people cheering, and as we passed one of the remaining horses, going side by side down the street, I could hear Little Willie cheer. Everything else was a blur, but I could hear him scream all the way to the finish line. As I crossed the finish line, Laurie was waving to me. The times were announced, and Flash and I had set a new Pittsburgh time for fastest ten-mile race ever run on this track. Everyone cheered! Dave handed me a trophy, and it was filled with money. Everyone cheered again, but all I could think of was weeks ago when Laurie said she will always be at the finish line waiting for me, and there she was.

The fifty-mile race starting time has been moved up and was now going to start at three o'clock—two hours before originally planned. It has started snowing. The clouds looked heavy, and the temperature had dropped to ten degrees. As three o'clock approached and the horses were lining up for the fifty, it started snowing a little more heavily, and the wind was starting to blow. There were 140 horses signed up, but less than a hundred were ready to go, and just like that *ready, set,* and *boom!* The fifty was started, and Flash was running hard through the city.

There were still lots and lots of people standing along the roadside in town, but once we hit the outskirts, there was no one around. The trail was marked, and I rode through most of it yesterday, but it was blowing so hard; I didn't see the signs until I was right on them. Flash did most of the work and never missed a beat, and by the forty-mile mark, we were well in the lead. It was storming pretty bad, but I was in front, and I could not see any other riders. As I rode into town, I passed a sign that said "One Mile to Go." I couldn't believe I had gone forty-nine miles already and that I was on the same one-mile stretch to the finish line. There were people cheering but not near as many as the earlier race, and right where earlier I had noticed Willie, Laurie's father, and lieutenant from Captain's cavalry, there was Little Willie cheering me on. Chris was mounted, and even though it was not supposed to be allowed, he ran next to me on his horse, stride for stride, cheering Flash on, screaming like a schoolyard cheerleader.

As we crossed the finish line and the cheers were loud and confetti everywhere, I looked right over to where Laurie was this morning, and there she was, at the finish line, again. Dave was handing me another trophy filled with money, again, and everyone at the race was crowded around. A single rider rode up to me and reached for my hand. As I shook his hand, he commented, "You really like to ride, and ride fast."

I smiled and nodded. "I do, and Flash can really run!"

The single rider handed Chris an envelope full of money and said one last thing, "I hope I get a chance to race you again. There is a one-hundred-mile race next weekend and another fifty in a month in Kentucky. The Kentucky race is the biggest race of the year. It's the day before the derby. I hope to see you again." He started to ride away.

I waved and smiled. "See you in Kentucky!"

CHAPTER 15

DEDICATION

The storm continued to get worse, and no way were any of us getting back to the wagon train. Willie and John were experienced riders and assured us that they could make it back. I insisted that they wait until morning since the wagon train was one hundred miles away, and no one would make it back until nearly morning. Traveling at night in a storm was not a safe or good idea. Mark chimed up and said, "Captain is always saying, 'Make good decisions!'"

I then insisted, "We have a hotel room. We all can stay in there. Plenty of room." I continued, "Let's all have dinner at our hotel. We will have breakfast in the morning, and we will travel back together *in daylight*. We will travel much safer and faster that way."

Chris and John looked at each other and commented with a smile, "We won't be needing a place to sleep. We will be in the lounge all night." As we rode our horses back to the barn, we stopped a few times to talk and shake hands.

The snowstorm was getting worse, but we got to the barn without too much delay, and there was Laurie and Willie. She must have told Willie what was going on, because once I got off my horse, she walked right over and kissed me for the fourth time, right on mouth. I was still very dirty and even a little sweaty, but she didn't care one bit, and she didn't care who saw it. I kissed back, but Mark was pretty quick to point out that I was blushing, and although I wanted to kiss longer, I stopped and said, "It was a congratulatory kiss. What's the big deal?" I thought I was in the moment. I reached for another kiss, and for the first time, I started the kiss. I made sure I put my arms around her and kissed her again. It lasted for more than two seconds, and once I stopped, I said, "And that's how an American cowboy kisses his girlfriend!" For the first time, Laurie was embarrassed about kissing me, but she did not deny it and had her arms around me too.

Chris and John were heading to the lounge and said under their breath, "Maybe we should sleep in their room tonight."

Willie and Laurie were taking care of the horses by now, and I was pretty much talking to some of the other cowboys in the barn. A few of them were staying in the barn during the storm and had made a makeshift table out of few bales and a few pieces of wood. They were planning on sleeping in the loft, but it was pretty cold. When I asked about it, they pointed to a big fuel heater and commented, "That will keep it warm enough to sleep." Sean, a cowboy I recognize that had raced the last two races, kind of a smaller guy and has been in the top five in every race, walked over to me and handed me a bottle. He insists on me taking a shot of whiskey. "A celebratory shot, my lad. You have best me in four races, and I must know who you are?" Sean was Irish and had quite an interesting accent. Half the time I couldn't understand what he was trying to say, but he was full of laughter. He was very happy to place second in today's fifty-mile race, and so we hit it off right away.

For the first time, I took a shot of whiskey; it was cinnamon flavor, and it sure warmed my stomach. I also accepted a sarsaparilla and was sipping on that when Willie and Laurie came over to the table. Laurie walked right over to me and put her arms around me like I was her man and asked, "Who are your new friends, honey?" Willie was right there, and he did not say a thing. I kind of stumbled through my words, but I introduced Lieutenant Little Willie Mayer as a dear friend of our family, and I introduced Laurie as his daughter.

Sean was quick to point out, "She's a lot more than an acquaintance, unless in Russia all acquaintances kiss like that!" Even Willie got quite a laugh out of that as Sean shared the whiskey bottle with Willie.

I did then say, "She is my girlfriend and has never missed a race of mine."

Willie just lifted his glass and said "cheers" in Russian, and we all cheered again.

Mac, another cowboy who was a bit older, then handed Willie a sarsaparilla and said, "I have two daughters. Neither of them ever had a boyfriend who can ride like he does or has as much money as he does." And they cheered again and started singing songs as we all joined in. I didn't know what they were singing, but there sure was a lot of cheering and drinking. I invited our new friends to join us at the hotel for dinner and a few drinks, but they declined.

"We are here to race and then go home. We have no money to eat and drink there, and we must watch the horses."

I told him, "I have two guys watching our horses. What's a couple more." I was already feeling the alcohol affects and insisted "I'm buying" with a cocky, half-drunk smile. They said they will think about it and we should go ahead and have dinner. They might stop by later.

I ordered the largest rib eye steak on the menu; we all did. While having my new girlfriend at me side, I thought to myself, *If only Captain and Mother were here.* The hotel had a grand table for the champion and his family that included all the trimmings—the fanciest dining I had ever had. We ate and drank and laughed and even kissed a little more. There was dancing and hooting and hollering and champagne for everyone. Dave and his family were there, and they were having a great time too. Laurie knew there was something on my mind. Mark, John, Willie, and Chris had more than the dancing girls on their mind as well.

Willie stood up, gave a whistle, and said, "Here is a cheer to the friends and families that cannot be here with us tonight, but mostly to the man that made it possible. To Captain Gross, the man who made it all possible. Hip, hip, hooray!" Willie stumbled through the words repeating himself over and over, and we all cheered to Captain. This was the first time I had seen Willie this drunk, and he was a blast. We all knew in the back of our minds, we all were thinking of Captain and the wagon train one hundred miles away stuck in a horrible snowstorm.

We stayed up late into the morning, and Sean and Mac did join us, and we talked and danced all night long. Sean and Mac loved horses, so they fit right in, and man could they drink. Willie talked a lot to Mac, and for the first time I found out that Willie's horse was sire to Flash and Mark's horse. It explained why they were so fast and why Willie had quite an interest in how they finished and why Laurie thought Willie's horse was almost as fast. Although I watched Flash get born, I did not know that Willie's horse was sire to our horses or that Willie also owned the mare that bore them. Willie gave me and Mark our horses as a favor to Captain. He did not say what Captain did for him or what the favor was, but Captain liked giving and taking favors instead of money or gifts. All Willie said was, "I am dedicated to Captain for life, and a couple horses cannot repay him for what he has done for me and my family. I will spend the rest of my life trying to repay Captain Gross, and I have only one wish left for him, and when the time is right, I will ask. *Cheers!*"

The sun was coming up, and everyone was pretty full. We started to head up to our rooms, and our new friends headed back to the barn. The blizzard was still raging, bad, and finding the barn might have been bad, but several others had left the hotel and were also staying in the barn. The trail was easy to find, even in a snow-white blizzard. I told the hotel owner, who served us all night, anything we wanted, I want to pay our tab. He responded, "Dave has paid for everything. The livery stable fees, the dinner and drinks, and the hotel rooms. He even paid for an extra room for Willie and his daughter." He yelled half-drunk himself, "You may have made a lot of money, son, but Dave had a lot of money riding on you and won *big*! He made five times what you made."

Dave was gone already, but the skinny old hotel man was very happy and said, "He even gave the biggest tip I have ever had. Bigger than the Earp boys back in '65." I couldn't believe my ears. I had won well over $5,000. Chris won at least that much. Willie mentioned he did really well too, and we all got to keep all of it. Willie was pretty happy. He and Laurie got their own room, and he had already asked Laurie if she was ready to go back to their room. I knew it was going to happen soon, so I walked around the corner where no one could see us. I gave her a big, long kiss, and as she looked me in the eyes, she said the words "I love you." Before I could say anything back, Willie came around the corner stumbling a bit and gave me a hardy handshake good night. We stared at each other a bit, but they were up the stairs and out of sight in just a few seconds. I followed behind, and as I looked out the window, the storm was blowing, I could not see a thing but white, and I thought to myself, *What a great night. This is how Oxford and Diane must have felt on their wedding day. It is too bad it has to end.*

When I got to my room, Mark was already passed out with his boots on, and Chris was in my bed. John was on the floor with a blanket. Chris looked at me and laughed. "You are champion rider, but I am sleeping in your bed."

I laughed and laid down next to Mark. "We are brothers and have slept in the same bed more than we have alone." He was passed out, so I pulled off his boots, kicked off mine, and turned out the last mantle. I laid down with a smile. "Good night, boys," I said, and as I looked around, a bit of light shone in the window. "Get some sleep. Morning will be here quick." And within seconds, we all were snoring away.

I think we only slept about three hours, and by nine o'clock the next morning, Chris and John were up and ready to go. I convinced them to have some breakfast before they head to the barn. Mark was hung over again but accompanied me to breakfast as well. On our way down, Mark put his arm around me and congratulated me. He looked me in the eye and, with his horrible whiskey breath, told me, "I wagered every penny I won shooting on you to win, and you did." He went on and said, "If Captain were here, that wouldn't have happened, but Chris talked me into it, and we all won *big*! Thanks, little brother." I asked him how much they each won, and Mark answered, "I won $8,000. That's more than enough to buy lots of cows and horses in North Dakota! And Chris won more than that. Brother, you may have won a lot of money racing, but we cleaned out everyone that was betting. We are heading out of town a very rich gang. Even Willie made a lot of money, enough to pay for your wedding!"

Mark gave me a little slug and said, "Good morning, guys, how did you sleep?" as we arrived at breakfast table. Everyone else was nearly done but didn't seem in a hurry. I was in no hurry but kind of had a plan, so I ate quietly and somewhat quickly, and as I finished, I asked Laurie if she would help me with something. Willie gave her the nod, and we all headed out, the boys out to the barn and me and Laurie to the general store.

The snow had stopped, but the wind was still blowing, so our walk was quick and cold. We did stop once out of sight and kissed again; then she asked, "What is your plan?"

I went on and told her, as we ran through the snow, "I am buying everyone a new extra warm winter jacket and a warm hat and gloves, and that includes you and me too." We arrived at the general store about the time the owner did, and he knew who I was. He welcomed me in. He asked what I needed, and besides sizes I had a list in my head, Laurie helped pick out the right sizes, and it didn't look like we could carry it all. About then, Charlie offered to have them delivered to the livery. I did tell him that we plan on leaving right away. He replied, "If you're walking, you might as well ride with me over to the livery. Let's load this gear into my wagon right there, and let's go." We helped him, and it didn't take long before we were in the livery.

All our horses were saddled, watered, fed, and ready to go, and Mac and Sean were already gone. As I handed Willie a warm jacket, Chris commented, "We better get going. Captain was expecting us quite a while ago and probably is planning a search party for us." I gave everyone their coats and hats and stuff, thanked them for getting our horses ready, put on my gear, and agreed that it was time to go. I gave the livery guys ten dollars and thanked them. They said they were paid already. I thanked them again for their hospitality again and said, "You had several non-paying guests in your loft last night, and I know everyone appreciates it and not everyone won $250 yesterday."

They smiled and thanked me again. The older bigger man then spoke up, "I know every one of you won a lot more money than that. This is not the safest town, and lots of cowboys don't like getting beat and hustled by a bunch of strangers. Be careful leaving town. I'm not the only one that knows you all have a pile of money."

Chris led us out the barn, looked around, and said, "There are no women and children on the streets. Let's get the hell out of here in a hurry. They can't beat us in a race, they can't outshoot us, and they damn sure can't outfight us. Let's ride!"

Chris took off, and we all followed, fast and hard. There were several drifts, and the wind was cold, but at the pace we were setting, he was right. No way enough guys could keep up or catch up to us, and no way could they know where we were going—to set up an ambush. We rode near fifty miles before we even took a break. The wind was still blowing, but it blew so hard all night that most of the road was uncovered. We stopped for only a few seconds to let our horses rest, and Chris asked Laurie how she was doing. She just smiled, looked at me, and said, "Maybe you should bet me some of your money that Glen and I can find the wagons before you."

"Our two horses against your two horses with fifty miles to go?"

Willie put a squash to our bet immediately and said, "Captain would never approve of you guys betting. Let's just get there. I'm sure they need our help digging out and are worried about us."

I looked at Laurie, looked back at Chris and said, "Agreed, no bet. Let's just ride!" Laurie and I took off fast and side by side. Surprisingly, Willie was right behind us and almost pushing us to go faster. I can't remember really ever riding like that, fast and free, smiling and happy; it was an awesome ride. It was cold on my face, so when I arrived at the wagons, it must have looked like my smile was frozen to my face. Laurie and I arrived first with Willie and the guys right behind us. We all enjoyed the ride.

Willie and Laurie went over to their wagon, and Della and Laurie's sisters had the wagon almost unstuck and near the road. The team of oxen were struggling while pulling through a heavy bank of snow. Mother and the girls had our team of mules on the road and had teamed up four horses to pull our other wagon. Oxford and Diane were working on their wagon as well. Captain came over to me and Mark and commented, "Nice of you to join us. How far was your ride from Pittsburg to here?"

Mark answered, "About one hundred miles, but the first fifty, there were pretty heavy drifts across the road. The wagons will struggle. It was one hell of a storm, Captain. How is everyone here doing?"

He answered with a stern, unhappy voice, "We all are alive, we lost no stock, and we are nearly back on the road." Chris and John immediately grabbed the shovels from the girls and, in just a short time, had our second wagon on the road. They went on to help dig out everyone else's too.

Captain looked at me and said, "You look like you have a smile frozen on your face. You must have done well at the race yesterday?"

"Yes, sir, I did! We all did. I won both races. Mark won both shooting contests. The boys bet on me to win, and we all have pockets full of money." I exclaimed, "Let's get this wagon train rolling west, and I will tell you all about it."

Captain scowled, "I hope you had a great time. We did not, so yes, let's get rolling."

We had the entire wagon train rolling west; it was windy and cold, but we were on the move. John rode up next to Captain, and as I was telling Captain about what the guys in the livery stable said about not everyone was happy about all the money we won, John just said, "Maybe we should find a different route, bypass Pitt and head straight for Cambridge, Ohio."

Captain looked at John and said, "Do you know the way, and how are the roads?"

John said, "I think I know the way. I looked at the map, and it is actually closer than Pittsburg. I will ride ahead and make sure the road is good, Captain. I think it the safest and actually fastest route, sir."

Captain responded, "Okay, take three others with you and report back as soon as possible, and put your money in a safe place. We don't need you getting hijacked!" John nodded, something Captain could understand, and asked a few of the others if they would join him. Within five minutes, he was riding away with a few others.

Captain and I rode side by side, and I told him about everything except Laurie. He seemed to have something really bothering him but would not say. I told him, "I have won several thousand dollars and Mark did too. We have enough to start our ranch in North Dakota, Captain. Horses and cattle, Captain. We have enough now."

Captain looked at me and nodded once again. "I'm glad you did well. I'm glad Mark and the men did well. That is not my biggest problem. My men have always been dedicated to me, and me to them, but I think one or more will be leaving our wagon train." I did not ask, knowing he would tell me if he wanted me to know. He asked about

Willie, Laurie, and even her sisters, something I was surprised to hear, and a little nervous. I thought maybe he already heard about Laurie and me and was pissed off or something. He finally did tell me, but I really didn't know what he was talking about. He asked, "Do you think Laurie and her sisters can find out who Janet's boyfriend is and get back to me without Janet and Mother finding out?"

I looked at Captain and said, "Captain, every man here is loyal to you. No way has anyone crossed you. They are all 100 percent dedicated to you and our trip to North Dakota! Why are you asking?"

He looked at me and said, "Can you find out what I want to know?"

I knew I could get Laurie to do anything, and I figured I could count on her to keep it quiet, so I just said, "Yes, Captain, I will do anything for you, so will Laurie, but why, sir? Is there a problem?"

Captain looked at me and said, "Janet has been sick for several days, mostly in the morning. Find out and report back to me!" And he rode away.

I was eager to see Laurie, and when I rode up to her, she galloped away as if for me to follow her. Once away from the crowd, she said she had some juicy news, but it must stay quiet. Of course, and before I asked her any questions that Captain wanted answers for, she told me, "Kathy told me that she thinks Janet is pregnant, and if Captain finds out, he will kill or at least kick Mike and Francis out of the wagon train."

When I asked why both guys, she just commented, "Janet doesn't know who the father is!"

I asked, "How do you know?"

She said, "Well, Janet has been sick every morning, and Janet was with Mike several times on the ship and now has been with Francis since we got to New York. Captain saw her out puking in the snow this morning before we got here."

I commented, "That's what Captain meant by that. I didn't know." And then I went on to tell Laurie about Captain and my conversation just before I rode up to talk to her. "I must tell Captain. I won't even mention to him how I found out. He is going to be pissed off!" Laurie wasn't sure I should be the one telling Captain that kind of news, and she was right, I wasn't sure I want to be the one telling him either. I asked Laurie, "Do you think Mother knows?"

She just looked at me and said, "If Captain knows, your mother surely knows and just hasn't told Captain about it yet. She might not know the both guys thing. I'm not sure about that, but she knows that Janet is pregnant." I held her hand for a few seconds, and as we slowed down to maybe sneak another kiss, I saw the men riding hard and fast. They were returning with news about the road and path already and heading for Captain. I smiled and said goodbye without a kiss, but I said quietly, "I love you," and rode away with the men. She smiled and blew me a kiss.

As I joined the men, they were talking about a possible ambush and how they thought Captain would want to handle this. They rode up to Captain and began talking fast but in a calm voice. Chris said, "At the junction just ahead, there are ten men, heavily armed, waiting for us with bad intentions and are hunkered in pretty good. They will have a good chance of killing quite a few of us, and I'm not sure if we should just ride in there?" Captain almost looked relieved. He needed something to think about besides his pregnant daughter.

He immediately yelled out very loud, "Stop the wagons!" Everyone had had a long day already. We were all cold and hungry and ready for a break, so every wagon came to an immediate stop. He rode up and down the snow-filled road and yelled, "Grab your rifles and come with me. Ladies, circle the wagons right here and prepare and protect your family." He continued, "Once the wagons are circled, put all the stock in the center. We will camp here tonight." Every man followed Captain including Mark and myself. He looked at me and demanded, "Stay with the wagons, you too, Mark. Get on top of the tallest spot and shoot anyone that gets close. Use your best rifles. Let's see if you can hit more than targets."

Captain was back in fighting mode and was in the mood to kick some ass. They rode up to about a mile from the ambush spot, and Captain sent more than half the men around behind where the ambush spot was set up. John led most of the others behind the ambush spot, and Chris and Captain waited with only six others. After Captain figured John was ready, he slowly rode right up to where the roads met. He looked at Chris and asked, "Where are they?"

Chris pointed to the rocky, snowy hills and said, "Right in there. I don't see any of them now, but they were there."

About then, Captain spotted John coming up from behind. He immediately yelled for John, "Come on! They must have known we were coming this way. Let's get back to the wagons." And he took off like he was in a race to get back. As he got closer, he could hear gunfire and knew it was me and Mark holding off ten banditos trying to rob our wagons. Captain and his loyal men rode in fast and hard, shooting every guy they could see. Mark had already shot several men from long distance, and the rest of the banditos were now close to the wagons. Captain was irate; he did not think of this and ordered every man charge and demanded a fight.

Captain and all the men took heavy fire and finally killed every bandito, but not without loss. Five men, including Francis, were wounded and two were dead. It was a horrific loss, and Captain was totally distraught. It was not their first time losing men, but it was the first time in America, and Captain blamed himself for not leaving more men with the wagons. None of the women or girls were injured, but we did lose three horses as well as the men.

Doc and Marcella had a makeshift emergency area and were tending to the wounded. The two dead men laid covered up nearby, and the banditos were spread out. Some were not completely dead and were moaning out loud. They were definitely shot and not going anywhere. Captain ordered Chris and John to immediately circle the area to make sure no one got away and to gather their horses. "We will replace our dead horses with theirs and set free any others." He then asked Willie and the others to prepare the dead for burial and to start a big fire. They did not question, and every man was immediately busy. Captain checked on the girls and asked Mikey to prepare two markers for graves.

As Doc heard Captain ask Mikey, he interrupted and said, "Prepare three, Anthony W. just died."

It was a horrible tragedy. No one said a word, and every man, woman, and child listened as Captain announced the plan, "We will keep this fire burning all night, and come morning, the ground should be thawed, and we will have a decent grave site to bury our lost men." He went on to say, "I blame myself for the loss, and I promise, this will never happen again." He talked about the lost men, and almost like a eulogy, nearly every man had a story to tell about the lost and wounded. When the women and everyone else started to retire to their tents that night, Captain assigned men to keep the fire going all night to honor of the lost and wounded and to have a thawed burial spot. Everyone was very somber.

Although Captain never figured on this, not one man left the fire. They all stayed dedicated to their fallen friends and to Captain. Several stories and even some prayers were spoken that night, and every man there tried to console their dedicated leader. Lieutenant Willie came up to Captain, gave him a hug, and said, "If not for Mark and Glen, it surely would have been much worse. You should be very proud. Those two saved the wagons and the women from disaster."

Captain just shook his head. "Yes, I am proud," he cried out loud and thanked Willie for his kind words. "I will never forget this. It was a sad day," he said. The word "dedicated" is all I could think of; that is when I went to bed.

Mikey had three nice metal crosses with the lost men's names carved into a piece of attached wood on each cross. No one knew where the material came from, but Mikey was up most of the night constructing them. He had also made a nice breakfast and had it on hold for after the funeral. By morning, the graves were dug, fires surrounded each spot, and the deceased men were in their graves. Captain waited until everyone was around before he started to read from the Bible. He read in Russian, but his last words were in English, "These men died free American men, and we will honor them with an English goodbye." Willie, Mike, John, and Russ all had a shovel and were filling the graves with dirt. The women sang a few songs, and Doc was praying in Latin. The steal markers were pounded into in front of the graves, and it was over. We returned to the wagons where Mikey had prepared a good breakfast. Everyone ate quickly and began gathering the stock and hooked up the teams. Once the wagon train was back on the road, Captain ordered a few men to go back and pile the dead banditos in a pile and try to make the pile away from the grave site in the rocks where no one could find them.

John and Chris had been riding point and reported back to Captain that the road was clear and in good shape all the way to Cambridge, Ohio. They said, "If we ride hard, Captain, we can make it by just after dark. It is only twenty miles." Captain agreed that we would ride to Cambridge and spend the night. My private thoughts, however sad and inappropriate, were, *Will I make it to the Kentucky race?*

CHAPTER 16

THE ANNOUNCEMENT

John had found a perfect spot just a half mile from the new railroad station and knew Captain would agree to camp there. We set up our camp safely in the dark, and everyone knew, from this point on, safety was his top concern. As we stopped and started to set up camp, Captain announced, "Anyone wanting to get fresh water to wash up and sleep in a bed, John has rented the hotel in town, and all but ten men are welcome to sleep there tonight and tomorrow night. We will leave at daybreak day after tomorrow." It was a shock to most, but not to Doc or Mother. Doc had already relayed to Captain that the two wounded men would need more medical attention than he had available and had asked Captain to try to make time for them to go to the hospital. Mother knew he was going to get the answers he was looking for regarding Janet and also realized a pregnant seventeen-year-old girl would not be able to continue. Captain announced, "The further west we travel, the wilder territory we will travel through, including several dangerous rivers to cross and who knows how many Indians are left." He continued, "Anyone needing medical attention should join Doc as he will be taking the wounded men into the hospital tomorrow afternoon. Barbara, Marcella, and Janet will accompany any women or girls that need to see a doctor or need medical attention as well."

Doc then said, "The hotel is only one block from the hospital, and they will be expecting you. If you need immediate attention, go as soon as you want. I believe they even have a doctor on duty tomorrow by eight o'clock."

Captain asked Mark and me to stay with the wagons. Captain was surprised that several other men volunteered to stay with the wagons as well. Chris, John, Willie, and both Mark and I had stayed in a hotel and washed up just a few days ago; six others and their families stayed with the wagons. It was so close from our camp to the hotel that everyone just walked over to the hotel. Captain accompanied Mother and the girls but returned after a few hours. Captain had every room in the hotel booked, and every woman and every girl stayed in a warm bed for two nights, something that no one expected but maybe Mother.

Captain had ways to get his answers, and it didn't always have to come from Mother or me. Mother knew his intentions, but his plan kind of backfired. Captain rode in and talked to the doctors who were working the hospital that next day. He asked about everyone and if there were any pregnant women that he should know about. The doctor then announced to Captain, "You must be running quite a wagon train. You have five pregnant teenagers and five pregnant mothers, all between two and three months pregnant." Captain asked for the names, but the doctor would not give up their names. He said, "I have advised every pregnant woman to talk to you about continuing this journey. All the way to North Dakota. This is not a journey for pregnant women." Captain left with only a thank you and a big mess to straighten out.

He went directly to Doc and Mother and asked to talk to them in private. They discussed the problems that could arise with pregnant women on this trip, and he asked Doc if he can deliver babies. Doc then said, "Captain, this might be a blessing in disguise. This means at least ten women who won't need monthly supplies, and these young girls make a huge mess. They don't know their bodies like the older women." He looked directly at Mother and stated, "No offense, but you have had eight births. You know what I mean."

Mother said right back, "No offense taken, and you are exactly right. It helps me a lot. I'm down to only two girls with messy cycle. Two of the five teenagers pregnant are my girls." She looked directly at Captain and said, "You would have found out sooner or later. I will get you a list of everyone who is pregnant, and you can make an announcement on what you want to do." Mother turned to Doc and said, "What do you think?"

Doc looked at Captain and said, "I have delivered twenty-two babies, two breech, and I have never lost one yet." He then said, "Most of all of these women are all in the first three months of pregnancy. The all have at least six or even seven months to deliver, and if we stay on schedule, we will be in North Dakota before any of them are born."

I think Captain felt some sort of relief after he saw the list—at least it was not only his girls pregnant. Diane is married after all. Janet is seventeen, and Mark was born when Mother was only seventeen. His voice was firm but not as crazy mad at the announcement, and he sounded okay to every person there, even the pregnant women. He gave the option to everyone and made it clear, "If you do not want to go to North Dakota, now is the time to speak up. I will buy your land and keep your homestead for five years." The first hand up was Ole. He stood up and said, "There are several English families here in Chamberlin, and I for one am staying here until spring. Once I know it's safe for travel, I will be riding the rail to California and then sail a ship to Alaska. I have heard that experienced sailors are needed to bring people to Alaska and then bring others back. The Alaskan gold rush is in full swing."

Captain said, "Does anyone else want to go with Ole?"

No one answered, but Ole spoke again, "I want to ask you my one wish Captain."

Captain looked intrigued and answered, "What is your wish?"

Ole said, "I have fallen in love with your daughter Carol, but she is so young and fragile to go with me. My wish is for you to take her safely to North Dakota, and if and when I join you in North Dakota, I want you to promise me I can began to court her properly."

Captain did not hesitate and said, "I grant you your wish, but have you talked to Carol about this?"

Carol stood up beside Ole, gave Ole a big kiss, and then answered, "We have talked about this, sir. I want to stay with Ole. I love him, but I do not want to be a sailor's wife. When he returns to North Dakota, he will become a farmer. Oxford and Diane will help me to prepare our land while Ole is living his dream." Carol's last words were choked out through her tears. "When he returns to me, we will be married." She sat down and cried.

Captain's voice overtook the community once again. "Anyone else have anything to tell me or ask for my wish?" No answers, so Captain continued, "I have one more thing to say, congratulations to all of you who are expecting babies! They will be first generation Americans. I also want everyone to know, I will be a grandfather! And I look forward to watch everyone's family grow as will mine."

The two wounded men stayed in the hospital but promised Captain they would catch up once they were able to travel on horseback and not in pain. Captain agreed and set up livery stable arrangements for the men's horses. The next morning as planned, at daybreak, the wagon train headed west. There was a good road that was maintained, and as the snow was not melted, our next day was a good day to travel. It was still below freezing, so the wagons pulled easily on a well-maintained road. The sun was soon shining brightly, so we were all on the road; warm weather was imminent. Mother was in front driving Apollo and Zeus, so we were making good time.

While traveling through the hills and trees of Ohio that evening, Mark and I were riding a ways ahead of the caravan when we decided to try kill a deer. We found a trail heading north, and in no time, we were in good white-tailed deer country. It must have been my lucky day because Mark started his stalk on a huge buck, and it must have smelled Mark; it ran right by me. I made a perfect fifty-yard shot, and the buck hit the ground. Mark was not done hunting and was kind of mad I shot his buck. We still had daylight, and we knew the wagons were traveling on a well-maintained road, so we decided to try get another. I field dressed my deer and got him ready for travel. Mark rode over the hill, and before I was even done, I heard another shot fired; I knew he had killed something. He rode up dragging a buck and laughed. "You are all bloody! Gut mine to will ya?" Of course, I did, and after a practice run, I made quick work of field dressing Mark's deer, and we were headed back to the wagons.

Chris rode up to us about a mile from the wagons and said, "If Captain found out you two left the road to hunt, he may be mad. You're supposed to be riding point."

Mark and I both said at the same time, "We are."

Then Mark said, "We had to check those hills over there for Indians."

Chris looked at the deer trails and shook his head. "You two sure are lucky. Pretty sure the wagons will pass this spot, but not by much. I found a nice spot down by the river to camp at, two miles up. You two start skinning and preparing those deer. I want fresh venison tonight."

We both just smiled and nodded politely. "We want venison too. I will make sure to save you a good piece." I said, "I will give it to Mikey as he goes past so it's ready for supper. We will leave these carcasses out in the tall grass. It will be a surprise for everyone, so keep it under wraps until supper." Chris just rode away, shaking his little blonde head.

We had the deer completely ready to go before the wagons even showed up. I was a little bloody even after I washed up with what was left of my canteen. Mother and the team of mules were first by me, and I was able to wash up without anyone seeing too much blood. Mark and I just laid in the grass and watched the wagons roll by. Mikey was always near the end, so I even got a chance to invite Laurie to dinner before Mikey got close. I told her, "Fresh steak dinner for everyone." Mikey finally rolled by, and we gave him the meat. I told him, "Chris gets a nice piece of meat for keeping our secret and of course the Mayers and all of us get the chops, all of them."

Mark looked at me. "You think Laurie's sisters are coming to supper?"

"I invited them, and even Della confirmed that she would talk to Mother about it. So yeah, I'm pretty sure they will be there."

He jumped up, grabbed his horse, and said, "We better get going. We were hunting. You know Mother always wants us washed up after hunting." And away he went. I wasn't far behind since I did get my shirt dirty field dressing the deer. I jumped onto Flash, and away I went. We still passed every wagon; Mother and the team were almost to the river. Chris had picked a nice spot, and we assured Mother we will have a great supper that night. I did mention to Mother, "I invited the Mayer family over for supper. Della said she will bring dessert. We are having fresh venison and potatoes and onions on the grill. Mikey already has the meat. I got to get in the river and wash up. If you need anything let me know." And away I went. Mark was already in the river with his horse and even had some soap, so I jumped in next to him. The water was cold, so I didn't stay in there long. I removed my boots as to not soak them, but I did a quick washing of everything else, even used soap. Mark was smart enough to get a somewhat fire going, and so once the wagons arrived, we could dry off and get dressed before the girls came up to the fire.

His plan worked perfectly, and even Mother knew what the plan had been. Our fire was blazing, and we were still pretty wet when Mother announced, "Here come the girls." We were both quick to get dressed, only to find out it was Diane and Janet, our two sisters, and only our two sisters. Mother got quite a chuckle and said, "I will let you know when the Mayer girls get here."

About then, Captain rode up to the fire and asked, "Did you two go hunting today?"

I quickly answered, "It was my idea, and both Mark and Chris told me not to, but I couldn't resist. The deer trails were better than some of the cow trails back home."

Mark said, "I went with. We both got nice bucks, and we had them completely butchered, and we were back on point before the wagons got to where we killed these deer, and Chris was in front of us. We were safe."

Captain shook his head. "Next time tell me. We always need at least two men on point from now on. We must stay safe."

As Captain was removing his saddle and was tying his horse with the others, the Mayer family showed up. Lieutenant Willie and his wife, Della, and all three girls walked up to the fire where we had pulled up several logs to sit on. Laurie sat down right next to me, and the other girls sat across from Mark. Willie and Della walked over to Mother and handed her some freshly made apple turnovers and said, "Laurie made them all, but we have to cook them."

Mother just grinned. "That Laurie sure is handy to have around. She is always making food for the boys."

Della came right out and said it, "She is in love with Glen and plans on marring him you know?"

Mother answered, "So I hear. We would be glad to have her in the family, but they are pretty young."

Della answered again, "She will wait. She is not the boy-crazy type, like the other girls, but she sure has it out for your youngest."

Mother just smiled and pointed at Captain. "He might not be ready for his young prodigy to be paired off, at least not yet."

We had an amazing supper of fresh venison chops with potatoes and onions on the grill. We had delicious apple turnovers for dessert, and we all enjoyed one another, and even with Mark making immature remarks about Laurie and me. Captain knew a long time ago that we liked each other and never even cracked a smile to Mark's remarks. For the first time, we all talked about our horses together.

Father confirmed that our horses were gifts from Willie, and he rides the stud that sired his mare. He kind of chuckled. "My horse is eighteen, and the mare sixteen, and I think she is pregnant too, from my stud again." They sure have been prolific, and they produce awesome foals." No one talked about anyone being pregnant anymore that night. Diane, Janet, and Carol left camp after supper, and Linda just went into the tent. Mark was showing his trophies to the Mayer girls.

Captain was nearly sleeping along with Willie, and Mother and Della were tiring out when Captain announced that he is going to bed. Willie spoke up and said, "Captain, I know Janet is pregnant, but I also know from solid info that Francis is the father. He is a good man and has been with you for many years. Try to accept it. He is back in Cambridge, but when he heals up, you need to talk to him. We need him with us the rest of the way. He is quite a carpenter too. We still need to build houses before we get hit with more winter weather, and North Dakota has cold winters. We need him." Willie tapped Captain on the shoulder, and as he walked away, he said, "Good night, Captain. Think about it." He then said a bit louder, "Come on, girls. It's time to go."

The others left immediately and followed Willie and Della straight away. Laurie and I stayed a bit longer, so I announced that I will walk her back to her wagon and tent. I walked her back, and once it was dark and we were in between camps, we stopped and really kissed. We were making out when she stopped, looked at me, and said, "I do! I really do love you!"

And for the first time, I looked her in the eyes back; her blue eyes were sparkling off the moon, and I said it to her too, "I love you too!" We kissed a little more, and I held her hand all the way to her tent.

As we walked up, I heard Willie's voice, "It's time for bed, kids. Now." We smiled at each other and said goodbye.

I commented as I walked alone by Willie's tent, "Good night, sir." There was no response.

CHAPTER 17

A Grueling Pace

Everyone in the community was up before sunrise, every water barrel filled with clean fresh water, and all the horses and wagons lined up ready to head out. Mikey had breakfast done and loaded before the sun was a finger above sunup. Chris was gone and back already with a great scouting report. "The roads are clean and mostly dry. If we push and we do have a strong east wind, which is kind of rare in the spring, we can make it past Zanesville and almost to Columbus, sir." Chris was optimistic in his voice, and when Captain realized it was going to be a perfect travel day, the decision was made.

"Let's go for the record, one-hundred-mile days, back-to-back." Captain then looked at Mark and me. "You guys find spots to cross the rivers. It's better to travel five miles to a bridge than to try cross where there could be trouble." I think Captain just wanted us to ride and not be bored, as the road we were on is well groomed and sure to have good crossings. Chris had traveled one hundred miles ahead, and he already knew this road had bridges all the way past Indianapolis, Indiana. Mark gave me our fishing head nod look, so we then quickly grabbed our fishing rods, and away we went. All the snow was melted; it was a beautiful fifty-degree spring day, and we hadn't fished for months. Mother smiled as she saw me digging through the wagon looking for my water boots and fishing gear. "Your boots are in the back of the wagon, and your rods are on the side. Be careful, and bring a rifle in case of trouble." Mother was enjoying watching me scramble, as if I would get to the river two minutes later, one fish might get away.

Mark and I arrived at the first bridge only forty miles ahead of the wagon train. There was no ice or snow, and after a little searching, I found a perfect rock to perch up on and fish for a couple hours. We started casting, and after changing lures a few times, they finally started hitting on a white-painted lead jig with a white piece of plastic. After ninety minutes, we each had five on our stringers. "Let's fish more, until we can see the wagons," I suggested to Mark smiling from ear to ear. Just as I said that, I caught another dandy walleye. "Must be at least ten pounds I figure. It's almost thirty inches and fat as our spring heifer ready to pop out a calf!" I yelled to Mark. He laughed and gave me a big thumbs up as he too was reeling in a beautiful fish.

He yelled back, "Daily double!" We each caught a few more and decided to clean and wash the fillets so as Mikey went by, we could just give him the fish. Our plan was just right, and we had everything cleaned and washed. As the wagons approached the bridge, both Mark and I were mounted and ready to ride. We handed the fillets to Mikey, and he figured it was enough for the entire community; all he needed was some lard or vegetable oil. We were pretty close to Zanesville, so Mark and I, along with Willie and Laurie, rode into town. We asked Mother and Mikey if they needed anything else, and just like that, we had a big list, and a few more riders accompanied us into Zanesville.

It was only a thirty-minute ride if we cruised, and everyone who was riding along knew that Mark and I were going to ride like we were on fire, and Laurie was going to ride right with us. We arrived at a nice general store and were barely there when eight other riders joined us. To my surprise, Carol, Ole, Ox, Doc, and several others needed supplies too. Like the other general stores, the owner met us at the door and helped gather our list, and every list, quickly and with a smile. In his window, like the other stores, there was a poster "Horse Racing" in big letters, and right there on the poster was a picture of me and Flash. It read, "Final Spring Race. Two-Man Teams, Twenty Miles Start at 10:00 a.m., and the One-Hundred-Mile Race Starts at 5:00 p.m. All the Day Before the Kentucky Derby."

I looked at Mark and commented, "Looks like we are teaming up!"

The store owner looked at me and Mark and then said, "Ah, you are the Gross boys?" He looked at me, shook my hand, and asked, "And you are the fastest rider in the land?"

I didn't say much but pointed at Mark and said to the store owner, "He has won nearly every shooting event this spring, and if he could race and shoot, I may not have won every event."

He looked at Mark and said, "Well if you intend on being his partner in the final race, you probably won't be able to shoot. The one-hundred-mile race and the shooting event finals are at the same time."

He looked at me and said, "It's probably better anyway. He should be your bodyguard if he can shoot like that."

Everyone in the store looked at the owner and was immediately concerned and started asking all sorts of questions. "Why? What have you heard? Will there be security there? Who is threatening? Will it be safe? What have you heard?" A barrage of questions followed by everyone toward the store owner, except by me; I never said a word. He handed everyone a betting sheet or two and said, "There are bets and horses coming from all over the world. There are more bets on your races than the derby so far!" He continued, "Louisville will be packed with every walk of life, and even though it should be a fun-filled time, there will be several outlaws and thieves looking to make a quick buck or two. Lots of big gamblers. Biggest race in the western hemisphere!"

I asked, "Why did they change the format? Why two-man teams now?"

He shrugged his shoulders and said, "I do not know, but I heard they are trying to make it more competitive, and there are so many good entries they are trying to make it a bit more exciting. This will draw bigger crowds and bigger bets!" I'm not sure if he was trying to make me nervous, but he was.

I tried not to show any emotion, walked right up to the store owner, paid for our supplies, and said, "We will win. No way I lose," and walked out. Mark followed, and very efficiently, everyone paid for their supplies and headed out the door and back to the wagons.

We did not ride as fast because we were talking about the Kentucky race the entire way. Mark was trying to decide whether to shoot or to ride. Laurie wanted to ride partners with me, and I was wondering whom I should partner up with. Teams are a different race. *Should I go first or second? Will they allow a girl in the race, or should I ask Chris? He did win one of the first races.* All these things were going through my head. *Who is betting on me? I don't want everyone to bet on me to win and then I lose.* I was getting so nervous. After unloading our supplies, I just grabbed Flash and Strike and rode away by myself. I didn't think anyone followed, but I was kind of hoping Laurie would. I stopped in a small meadow with tall grass all bent over, got off Flash, and just let him walk away. I laid down in the grass, and as I was petting Strike, I asked him, "What should I do? Who should I race with?"

A deep familiar voice said, "Do what you think is best for you and your family." It was Captain, and he knew I was nervous and having anxiety about everything. I could not see him, but I heard him get off his horse, and as he walked up, he smiled at me and said, "It's not Laurie." I laughed. He knew how to ease the tension. He too had a lot of stress, and he also wanted to be at the race. He explained to me about the safety and how important safety was to our entire community. His duty was to keep the wagons and the families safe. Captain went on to explain to me that it was not my duty to worry who bets or how much. As far as whom to choose, he convinced me that Mark and his horse would be my best partner. "I am recommending Chris stay with me and the wagons. Willie already requested three days away, so I'm sending him, Mark, Brad, Russel, Anthony, and you of course. I will insist you all stay together and leave immediately after you gather your winnings." Captain and I laid in the grass until near dark that day. We knew the wagons would travel until complete darkness.

We talked about a lot of things: racing, winning or losing, returning to the wagons safely, and even a little bit about Laurie. We briefly talked about Diane and Janet and how not only will it make Captain a grandpa, but it will also make me an uncle, something I had never thought about. "*Wow*, I'm going to be an uncle!" I yelled. We talked about how much money I have, how much we all have, and how it's more than enough to buy our stock needed. "Every one of us that is over eighteen has bet on you to win, and you have won. We all have land. I'm encouraging everyone to minimize their bets. We have won enough. No need to blow everything if something happens." Those words stuck with me, and as we started walking, Captain noticed. "Our horses are nowhere in sight," he said.

I looked at Captain and asked, "Are you serious?" He looked at me and said, "Well, where are they?" I let out a whistle, and within five seconds, Flash and Strike were at my side. Ten seconds later, Captain's horse came walking up. Captain said, "That is really cool how your horse listens so good!" We mounted our horses, and as we rode back to the wagons, we both felt better.

The wagons did not ever make it one hundred miles in a day, but that week, we did travel eighty miles every day. There were some long days, but every river had a bridge or good crossing. No one was sick anymore, the weather has been perfect, and Captain was confident we could make it nearly through Indiana, past Indianapolis anyway, and nearly to the Illinois border before the ten of us went to the big race. When I asked him how the number got from seven to ten, Captain just nodded and said, "I guess there are a few others that want to watch the race." I knew there were others who had not bet on me, and they want their chance to make some big money too. Captain knew it too; he just didn't want me to worry.

Mark decided that he would be my race partner at least in the ten-mile-by-ten-mile two-person race around the city of Louisville. It would be an all-out sprint with only a few obstacles and turns. Mark decided to ride with me. We practiced every day and timed ourselves. He was just as fast as me; half the times, he was faster. They also made it a rule that every rider must carry at least 150 pounds in total weight on the horse. This eliminates the thoroughbreds with ninety-five-pound riders, and they think it might slow me down. "With my saddle and me, I'm nearly 150 anyways. I'll bring a rope and a couple extra boxes of rifle shells. That will put me at 152." I looked at Mark and said again, "It will be the exact same for you. You can even weigh less." Mark was reading the rules, and as he was reading, I was spouting off, "They are writing rules just to try to catch me. It won't matter. We will dominate this race. Is there any other new rules or rules I should know?"

He looked at me and said, "Yes, there is." He continued, "No women allowed in either race. All bets must be paid from the first race before any bets can be placed on the second race. All bets must be settled immediately after every race. *No exceptions*, no fighting, no guns allowed around the race track or stables. Only riders and horse trainers allowed in the stables. No camping on the fairgrounds. It goes on and on."

I looked at Mark and said, "Lets ride in the day of, race and leave. No camping, no drinking. Just win, collect the money, and get the heck out of there." He agreed. He wasn't sure everyone else would agree to that. He did think Captain might try to make it pretty clear. "Ten men away from the wagons will be dangerous enough, and then with threats that are dangerously real, we must have a plan and good guideline on how everything should go," Mark said with an almost exact sound of Captain. "I can hear him already, barking out orders. Willie, you ride with Glen and Mark. Anthony, you and Russ ride point. Stagger your speed, and always watch out for ambush and funnel points. Communicate at all times!" He did sound so much like Captain that if I didn't know better, I would have thought it was our father.

As the days began to have a little more sunlight every day and even after a few rain delays, we were making good time. We were several hundred miles ahead of schedule, and spring has sprung. Everything was starting to grow. The wildflowers were getting buds, the grass was turning green, and even walking all day, some of the stock were grazing themselves fat. Captain figured the one really fat cow might give birth any day soon. The wagons had been doing great. No lost stock, and we were still averaging nearly eighty miles a day. The community was ready for a break. The derby was coming up, and one of the cows was about ready to give birth. The birth would be earlier than originally planned, but between Mother and Captain, they could tell when it's time. Captain announced, "As soon as we find a nice camping spot, we will take a break. We will set up a good, safe camp before the guys head to Louisville. We need a safe place for the cows and horses to graze and rest, and maybe have our first calf." They were welcome words, especially to the pregnant women.

Janet was quick to point out, "We have traveled fifteen days without a break. We need a break." Diane agreed, and so did several others.

Chris then spoke up, "There is a beautiful grove of trees near a clean river only eighty miles ahead. One more good day's travel, and we can make camp there safely for a week." There were some groans of disappointment, but everyone knew it was best, so we forged on. The next day, we arrived, and the grove of trees was perfect even though it was a rough trail in and a rough trail going out. Trees and shrubs were fifty yards before it opened up to a beautiful pasture—tall grass and wild flowers throughout the huge meadow with lilac trees on the south edge just starting to turn purple. Just perfect for a weeklong break, so I thought.

CHAPTER 18

The Final Race

Mark and I had been training every day, and it's five days to the final race. We had a perfect track around the big grove of trees where we were camping at, and we added obstacles every time. We practiced who goes first, and we rotated each time. We had hand signals made up so if we need to communicate along the race, we would be able to. The hand signals were more for after the race in case we can't talk because of crowds and fireworks or we get separated or something. Captain would always say, "Be prepared for everything." Laurie had been there every day training with Mark and myself. She would time us, put out obstacles, and had learned all our hand signals. Mark and most of the guys still call her "Hay Hauler" instead of Laurie, but she earned her nickname, and to hang out with the guys, she needed a nickname.

Our current camp has not turned out to be as nice as the oak grove trees that we stayed in before we loaded onto the ship. All along the river and the north end of the trees, the entire ground was covered in poison oak and poison ivy. Several of the girls and a few of the guys who walked through the poison ivy on the way to the river now had a rash. Strike and two horses smelled horrible like a skunk, and Linda and Mother were horribly unhappy. Strike was in their tent right after getting sprayed, and now their tent and anything that was in the tent—like pillows and blankets—had to be washed and hung on a line at completely the other end of the trees.

Doc had run out of lotion to put on all the people who had rashes and can't find the ingredients he needs to make a home remedy lotion that would help with the itch. Some of the lovebirds have it in places Doc would never say out loud. Like Ox, his white complexion with a horrible red rash all over his back and butt looked painful. Russ asked Ox how he got it all over his ass and back. Ox just gave him the hand signal with one finger. Mark spoke up laughing, "Don't let Captain see that. He already knows Diane has some poison ivy, and he will put it together!"

Ox was quick to point out that Captain and a few others rode out this morning heading to town looking for more lotion and a few more supplies. Ox suggested, "Like a new tent and sleeping supplies." A quick chuckle turned into an outright laughing outbreak. Ox was a good sport and really took the jokes well; he was also quick-witted enough to give it right back. Hay Hauler and I were the butt of a few jokes too, but neither of us had any rashes. The two horses were walked in the river for about an hour, and I think they only walked through the grass where Strike had gotten sprayed. They didn't smell as bad, but all three animals were then tied up as far as away from the tents that they could be to still be safe.

Captain did not get back to camp until after dark, and Mother insisted that Mark and I sleep outside. She and the girls got the tent and our bedrolls. We did not complain as we knew Captain would not return empty-handed. Everyone was expecting him; even Mikey saved a supper plate for each of the men and Captain. The dry firewood was hard to come by, so only one nice fire per night. We were gathered around the fire when sure enough, Captain showed up just as the girls were talking about going to bed. The lotion was needed by many, but not everyone was willing to strip down and rub lotion on their privates right by the fire where everyone could see, especially Ox. Captain had several bottles, and everyone that needed some got some and even extra for Doc to hang onto if such a thing happened again.

Captain gave Mark and me the signal to come help set up the tents and distribute the supplies. He bought new bedding for all the girls and himself, and as it turns out, it was a lot nicer than anything they had prior. We distributed the supplies and returned to the fire. The girls and Mother quickly moved back to their own tent, and just like that, we were back in our tent that had a more-than-unpleasant damn skunk scent the girls had brought in. I looked at Mark and said, "I'm sleeping by the fire. It's not that cold. We will leave our tent up until we return from Louisville. Maybe it will smell better." Mark agreed, and we brought our saddles a bit closer as to prepare to stay close to the fire.

Laurie went to her tent and returned with a nice blanket. She said, "I will snuggle with you as long as your father will allow. I will keep you warm," she said. We all went on one last firewood search of the night, but Laurie was quick to point out, "Stay out of the poison oak and ivy."

Captain looked at me with a "be careful" look and then said, "Before you boys leave for Louisville, gather enough wood down by the old tent. When we get a good wind, I will have all the stinky crap burned." He gave a guilty look to Ox, gave him a good slap on the back, and said, "Good night, Ox." Anyone who was still around the fire laughed out loud hard, but Captain walked away without a smile. Ox felt it for sure, and without any emotion, he just said good night. Captain then crawled into the tent with Mother and the girls. As he was closing the door, he looked right at me and said to my surprise, "Keep your clothes on under that blanket tonight." Captain was on a roll tonight as everyone cracked up laughing again; he just shut the door and went to bed. The last thing we heard him say was asking Diane how her rash was; again, we giggled.

The day of the race was finally approaching. We were camped about fifty miles from Louisville, and we figured we would get an early start and just ride in slowly on the morning of the race. Mark and I were both confident that a leisurely walk before the race would only warm up our horses. We concealed our rifles and had our pistols and ammo stored in our saddlebags. Every one of us carried a rope and two saddlebags. As we rode into town around nine, Dave met us at the outskirts and showed everyone just where to go.

It seemed like every person we saw wanted to bet lots of money. Almost like we couldn't win the ten-by-ten relay race. I took Captain's advice and did not pay attention to who was betting what, but there was a lot of betting going on. I mostly talked to Dave, and he told us we were signed up, Mark was running first, and we were getting pretty good odds, if I wanted to place any bets. I told Dave I wanted to wager with every racer here, and I would give ten-to-one odds. He explained, "There are over one hundred racers. What do you want to bet?" I will bet each one of them any wager they want, up to $1,000 per team. Dave did a quick calculation and said, "If you don't finish, you could potentially owe one hundred thousand dollars. If you don't finish…" he said again.

I looked at him and said with confidence, "We are ready. We will win. Place the bet!" Dave disappeared, and we settled around the start line.

Around ten minutes before the race, Dave returned and said, "The bet is placed." He looked at Mark and said, "Yours is too."

I was explaining to Mark how the race starts fast. "Let's move our way to the front of the pack and listen for the countdown and the pistol."

Mark looked at me and said, "Thanks for the advice, little brother. We have already been through all this. Let's just win!" He reached over to give me high five, and just like that, "*Three, two, one,* and *bang!*" The race was started. Mark took off and had a great start, with only one horse in front of him; I knew we had a good chance. I waited around and noticed every guy waiting on me to set up for the exchange. I looked across to where Willie was, and in just a few minutes, he signaled me. Mark was still in second, but right on the tail of the leading horse. I worked my way clear, and the other top ten racer did too. It was clear that barring any problems, it's a two-team race. The last mile of the track was visible, and several wagons and hay bales were being put on the track for distraction and obstacles, something we had practiced and something Mark was really good at. *It is usually where he would gain time on me in practice*, I said to myself, and just like that, I could see the horses. As Mark maneuvered through the obstacles, he passed the other rider, and as he was racing toward me, he was an easy horse length in the lead. He did what he was supposed to do; now it was my turn. As he came racing past me, Flash and I took off.

Flash did not like to run behind anyone, especially Mark, and as we got up to speed, Mark purposely rode in front to get Flash at full speed. The plan worked. As I passed Mark, he gave out quite a yell, "Don't look back! Just ride! Stay right of the wagons and left of the hay bales!" I didn't know what he meant at first, but as I approached the obstacles, I figured out what he meant. I did exactly what he said, and Flash did *not* disappoint; he just knew when it was time to race. The last mile, I could see more obstruction than what was there when Mark went through, but by this time, I had a five-horse lead and was waiting for the change. Flash was moving around the obstructions before I even directed him; for me, it was just "stay low and hang on." We didn't miss a step and finished the biggest race in the country in first place! The German Gross boys were cheered on that day, and a banner was even hung in the town square already: "German Gross Boys Win in Kentucky."

As I passed the finish line, there she was! My lucky lady! Laurie was standing in her spot waiting to give me a hug and a kiss! Willie was there along with all ten from our community. Russ and Brad had bet everything they had. Mark had bet most of what he had, against Captain's recommendations, and along with a huge purse, what I won from Dave sponsoring me and along with my bet with the other riders, I was coming home with quite a pile of money, and there was still another race. My favorite moment and what I was looking forward to the most was a winning hug and kiss from my sweetheart. Everyone cheered a bit louder when she gave me a huge hug and kiss. Every bet was paid up within two hours. We were loaded with cash and were starting to get a lot of dirty looks. Willie recommended that we ride out of town until the other race got close. Dave agreed, so we headed for the stockyards.

It was a few miles from town but a good place to hold up, if no ambushes were waiting for us. No one knew where we were going except us, but as we rode away, several horses were following. At first, Brad and Russ were drinking and having a great time, but then they were pulling out their rifles and pistols; Brad even had his sword. Willie called out formation, with Laurie and me in the middle. We were the youngest, and although I did have my rifle and pistol with, I felt good about keeping Laurie close to me. Mark was right behind me, and Russ and Brad were in the rear. Willie and Anthony were on point, and the others were roaming carefully keeping a watchful eye. We were quite happy, of course, and with some quick math, we were riding with over one hundred thousand dollars, with another race to go.

We made it to the old stock yards, but it was obvious we were in for a battle. As I dismounted to open a gate, all hell broke loose. There was gunfire coming from everywhere, and Captain was not with us. This was a first for Mark and myself. Willie proved why he was a lieutenant; he was commanding as good as Captain. Laurie's horse spooked and took off full speed. Willie tried to go after her but was shot and fell off his horse. Brad took two shots, one to the shoulder and one to the chest, both rounds aimed directly at me. Russ took off after Laurie, and neither was nowhere to be seen. The rest of us were pinned down. Willie was wounded, Brad was badly wounded, and both Russ and Laurie missing. Brad's horse lay dead, and it looked like Willie's horse took a couple rounds too. He was still standing but bleeding badly. We had cover because we were in the stockyards and had a decent shed to stay safe in, kind of. Several fences and corrals surround us, but still, as long as we had rifles and shells, we could hold off quite a few attackers.

Brad was unable to travel and needed immediate medical help. It was obvious that we would not make the second race, and hopefully, someone would come look for us. None of us had even placed a bet on the second race yet, and I knew there were a lot of people who wanted a chance to get their money back. Hopefully, someone would look for us out this way. As we gathered to make a plan, we heard a voice, "Give us your money, and we will let you go."

Brad, with what seemed like his last breath, said, "Never. We will never give criminals anything. Try to come and get it." Although he was still breathing, he passed out; we all looked at each other and agreed, "They get nothing."

I thought of a plan, and Willie agreed. We needed help, and my plan was to go for help. I told Willie, "I can sneak out. They will never see me, and once I'm far enough away to escape, I will whistle for Flash. He will come running to me, and I will go for help. Mark will do the same, but go back to town and try to find the marshal. I will be back with reinforcements as soon as I can, and I will bring help and a doctor."

My plan worked perfectly. When I was out of range, I whistled for Flash, and he came running. The thieves who had us pinned down did not even know what happened. As Flash came running, I made a quick mount, and I was gone. I knew Flash and I could make it back to Captain for help and back again by morning if we rode fast. We were trapped there for three hours before I got away. Mark tried the same escape move, but his horse didn't run as fast to him as Flash did to me. I did hear some gunfire as he rode away, but I was riding hard and fast and could not tell if he made it. It was pretty dark, but we had a pretty good moon.

Flash seemed to know where we were going, and he was running wide open. I knew that time was very important if Brad had any chance to live, not to mention a pretty severe leg wound on Willie's lower leg. I let Flash run. I had escaped and headed for our wagons and Captain when I saw a very welcomed sight. Chris and his horse were heading right for me, and it looked like he was heavily armed and ready for battle. Laurie had made it back to the wagons several hours earlier and had the majority of the cavalry riding my way. Every soldier was coming but Mikey, and the women were guarding the wagons. Chris and I rode back quickly and found Captain and the men and turned them toward the stockyards. Once again, I stopped out of range from anyone. I had Chris hold Flash, and I snuck right back to the men. Mark had not returned with the law, but Russ had about twenty men and were spotted coming from the other side.

Now we had them surrounded; we just needed to communicate with Russ. Chris made a daring ride through the yards and made it to Russ. He also found Mark and got him to the other side. He was shot, and his horse was dead, but now we had someone who could communicate by hand signals with Russ and Chris. Willie and me and Laurie was riding with Marcella, who was following Captain into battle, like she always had. Doc was riding with Marcella as well. Laurie knew all our signals, and once the sun came up, we would attack from all sides. I would give the signal to Marcella and Doc, along with Laurie, when all was clear.

The hand signals worked perfect, and shortly after sunup, Captain attacked from the west. Russ, Chris, and several others rode in from the east. Included in Russ's posse was Sergeant Francis. He was not 100 percent, but Russ found him and several others, including a federal marshal! The shootout ended rather quickly with very few others even wounded. The guy that shot Brad had been killed, and three others lay dead as well. The other few guys gave up quickly and were being handcuffed by the marshals when I gave the all-clear signal. Doc, Marcella, and Laurie rode in quickly and immediately went to the wounded.

Mark and Willie were both shot in the leg, and both their horses were dead. Brad had not moved since his last sentence, and he barely has a pulse. Doc announced, "Brad will not make it, but let's try to get him into the Louisville hospital as soon as possible. He is still breathing." Captain quickly responded, and a makeshift bed was tied up between four horses; we were headed back to Louisville. Our posse now counted at around fifty men ready to fight, and our wounded were coming in fast. The streets seemed empty as the Kentucky Derby was only a couple hours away, and most everyone was at the track.

Chris had already gone to the hospital, back to the race track, and was heading back to the hospital with the hospital surgeon. By the time we arrived with the wounded, the surgeon and Chris were riding up. He immediately went over to Brad and pronounced him dead. He then went to Mark who was looking quite white and was not doing well. He lost a lot of blood and had been lying for several hours before he got help. Willie was experienced and had a nice field dressing. With no bones broken, Willie still needed fourteen stitches to his lower leg and some rest. Mark was immediately taken into the hospital and had to have surgery; he had a partial of a bullet lodged just above his knee that needed to be removed. The surgeon completed the surgery, and Doc assisted. It went fine, and Doc announced that Mark would make a full recovery.

Captain insisted Brad can travel now, Mark and Willie would stay a couple days until they could ride, but the rest of us needed to get back to the wagons. Willie insisted that he would ride. "I've been wounded worse than this and fought three more battles. I have two other not-so-tough daughters and a wife back at the wagons. Let's ride."

Mark was sore, but he would not stay behind either. "Let's get the heck out of here now before something else goes wrong!" Brad was put in a box, donated by Dave, and was taken back to our camp in a wagon. Willie and Mark rode in the wagon too, and we all headed back without even hearing who won the Kentucky Derby or the fifty-mile relay. We had a quite a posse of men and experienced soldiers; no one would dare attack us now. Captain still sent Chris and the scouts ahead to make sure there were no more ambushes or thieves to deal with.

Captain and I stayed right with the wagon, and Laurie and Marcella rode close by as well. We rode into the darkness, and as we rolled into camp, everything was safe. Mother and Carol had made a makeshift hospital, and Mother was so distraught to see more wounded that she could not leave the makeshift hospital. Della stayed with Willie, but Willie wanted to go to his tent with the rest of his family. After another check on his wound, Willie, Della, and Laurie returned to their tent. Mother stayed with her oldest son in the hospital, badly wounded and had a close friend dead. She could not believe that all this death happened because of a horse race, and we heard her crying all throughout the night. Mark stayed passed out through the night and into most of the next morning.

Russ and Anthony were up early and had an appropriate grave dug before sunup. Mikey stayed up all night again and once again had a nice steel cross to mark Brad's grave. A funeral was held, songs were sung, and I think every person in the community cried. A young woman named Kari stayed by the grave site even after every person was gone. Verne, her dad, finally came and told Captain that Kari was pregnant with Brad's baby. Brad was a single soldier and had no known family. He won $15,000 on the first race he had ever bet on. He had 160 acres waiting for him in North Dakota and enough money to start a farm and ranch. Now there was more land to discuss with the authorities.

Captain announced that he would try to keep the land in Brad's name, keep his money safe, and when his child was old enough, he would be given this land and money. Verne and Kari could farm his land if they so choose to, but it would all eventually go to Brad's child.

The community began to dismantle the camp, but Captain announced one more day here, and we would get a fresh start the next morning. Everyone agreed, and Mikey served a nice dinner in honor of Brad. Willie was walking pretty well already, and Mark was awake when the subject of money and how much our guys won and what we sacrificed for that money. Willie had bet everything they had and then some. He came home with $20,000. He smiled and said, "Shoot me in my other leg for another twenty thousand, but I will give it all away to have Brad alive." Mark had way over twenty thousand and said the same thing. All toll, the count was well over one hundred thousand dollars in cash, and all of us would gladly give it all back to have Brad alive. Stories of what he had done for the soldiers over the years were talked about all afternoon. His bravery was second to none. I could not stop crying, and most of the day and into the evening, I did not say much.

Finally, come evening, Mother asked me if was okay, I cried, "*No!* I'm not okay! Brad purposely moved in front of those bullets to save me. He died saving me! I'm not okay!" I got up, walked over to Brad's tent, climbed in, and went to sleep.

The entire community was up early packing up our camp. I packed up Brad's things carefully and completely. He did not have a lot, but what was there, I packed as if to preserve it forever. We commandeered the dead thieves' horses for Mark and Willie to ride. I rode next to Mark the entire next day. We talked about the race and how our practice paid off perfectly and how bad we would miss his horse. He did tell me that he had made over forty thousand and now had more money than any nineteen-year-old should have. Plenty to buy a thousand head and still have money left over. Mark rode next to me until he couldn't ride any longer. By six o'clock, he rode in the wagon bed that Mother had made for him. I stayed by him. But he pretty much slept until we stopped. Mark stayed in the wagon bed until morning when we started west. He did get onto his new horse and rode with me the entire next day. He asked me what I was going to do with all my money. I responded, "Raise fast horses, fat cows, and hopefully have a few kiddos with Laurie in a few years."

He just laughed and said, "She is quite a little woman. I would marry her too."

CHAPTER 19

CHICAGO

As the emotions of the final race, the horrible shootout, the wounded, and the funeral wear away into memories, I couldn't stop thinking of how Brad had saved my life by surrendering his. It was my fault that Brad was dead. Mark and Willie were wounded, and all because I wanted to race my horse. I didn't think I was that obvious, but I must be. Mother and Doc had been talking to me every day about weird stuff they normally wouldn't. Things like love and family and stuff a young German cowboy just didn't like talking about. Several days, day after day, they would ask how I'm doing. I answered every day, "I'm okay." But on the inside, I was still mad and still wanted revenge. I was spending more and more time with Laurie, and everyone is okay with it; no one is even teasing me about puppy love anymore. Laurie and I were now best friends, and she was open about our love, and even though we are young, we will get married someday soon.

Captain pushed hard every day, and the wagon train was back ahead of schedule. All the roads and trails we had been on had been pretty good, and we had not broken a wheel or lost a horse, except Willie's stud and Mark's horse. No losses to the trail. Our cow had a calf, and even though it slowed the wagon train down a day, the calf was keeping up. We were near Chicago, and many of the men and families were looking forward to taking a day and going into Chicago. Captain does not like the idea of anyone going in and spending some money. It would be too obvious, and our wagon train would be tagged as having some money. Almost everyone that knows anything knows between the entire train, there was a lot of money—something very rare on a wagon train of immigrants. Also, everyone should know, it was a wagon train of ex-soldiers. All that aside, several men have announced they are going to Chicago. Willie and Mark both needed medical attention, and more than Doc and Mother could give. Willie was not healing, and although his wound looked good, he was not feeling well. Mark's wound was becoming infected. Willie told Captain he will be riding in and taking Mark with him. They were going to see a specialist at Northwestern University hospital.

Chris had found a good, safe place to camp alongside the river between Peoria and Chicago. The wagon train set up camp by nightfall. Captain has agreed to spend the next day to rest and let the wounded go to the hospital. He was not in favor of too many going to town, but if anyone needs supplies or to see a doctor, he would allow it. Oxford privately asked Captain to take Diane and Janet to see a specialist as well; neither were having a normal pregnancy, and both needed to see a doctor. Mother agreed, and Captain now insisted they all ride together with Willie.

Oxford then reluctantly announced that Francis will be going along as well. "His wounds are fine, but he is the father to Janet's baby and wants to know what is going on," he explained. Captain glared at Francis but agreed.

"You five men and the women then, get a list from anyone else that needs anything," Captain said.

Verne then spoke up, "Kari and I are riding into Northwestern as well."

Captain then said, "Anyone else, any of the others that are pregnant, any others with medical issues?" Two others spoke up, and the group going to Chicago quickly became a large group, and once again, Captain spoke out, "The wagon train could be in danger of another attack. Do not waste time, and stay safe. The rest of us will prepare for the worst and pray for the best."

Our campsite was really a cool spot along the Illinois river tucked into an oxbow in the river. Protected on three sides by a large river and only a narrow gap to get there, a safe spot but also a great spot to go fishing. The pregnant woman, now showing their larger than average midsections, several men, and the wounded were up and on the trail early. Captain announced to Willie, "We will wait for you, but if there are *any* problems, please communicate everything to me, quickly. I do not want to burry any more people." I could see a tear in his and Mother's eyes as they rode off. Mark, Diane, and Janet were all in the caravan heading to the hospital along with his top lieutenant and the only other captain in the wagon train. The camp was well fortified, and yet somehow Captain was still very nervous about the entire excursion into Chicago. As I watched them ride away with Captain at my side, all I could think about was how to ask to go fishing.

Once they were gone, I rode several laps around the camp. I mostly scouted for a place to fish and of course any spots anyone could come across the river to attack. I announced to Captain, "There is only one spot where any attackers could cross the river and no one in camp would see them, or it go unnoticed."

He looked at me with a "I know what you want" grin and said, "Yes, you can guard the trail at the crossing, with your fishing rod." I never said a word about fishing or Laurie, but he then said, "Laurie can go with you, but bring your pistol, and be safe. Shoot three quick rounds if there is trouble." I'm not sure how he always knows what I'm thinking, but he does. I grabbed my fishing rod and Mark's rod, and Laurie and I were off to the river. It was only a couple hundred yards to the spot I wanted to fish, and we could look for bait along the way. We left the horses in camp and walked to the river.

Along the way, we did not find any bait. The grass was tall, and we could barely see camp. We were only halfway to the river, and once out of sight, Laurie stopped me. She kissed me and told me we will be together forever. We held hands the rest of the way to the river bank, and once I was there, I realized, we had no bait. I don't think Laurie really wanted to fish, but she was all for me catching fish. She just watched and enjoyed a beautiful late spring day on the riverbank with her best friend and boyfriend. I began looking for frogs when Laurie reached into her lunch bag and pulled out an exact replica of a frog. She had made me a fake frog to fish with. Laurie said, "I was going to wait for a special day to give you this gift, but today is as special as any." I took the frog, tied it on my line, and started casting away.

I must have made a hundred casts without a bite. I decided to look for some worms, so I took a break and started to dig around for some riverbank worms. I only had to turn over a few logs, and I had plenty of bait. I kept my new frog on my line but attached a large night crawler to Mark's line and announced, "This is your line, so keep an eye on it."

Laurie asked, "What is it going to do if a fish decides to eat that giant worm?"

I laughed and said, "The rod will bend a little and look like it's getting pulled into the water. Don't let it!" I laughed again, and as she smiled at me, I stopped to watch her find a spot and stay comfortable and still be close to the rod. She was beautiful, I thought, and then I said it, "You are beautiful."

She just smiled at me, sat down on a nearby log, set her basket down, and said back to me, "I love you."

Captain Oxford, Lieutenant Willie, and the rest of the pregnant ladies had a thirty-mile ride into Chicago and then another ten miles through Chicago to get to Northwestern University hospital. The men did not push the ladies, and the ride went slow and steady. It took a few hours, but Verne had chosen to ride quickly to the hospital and tried to line up a doctor to see all the pregnant women at once. His hopes were to get everyone to see the Doc before noon. Verne is a very persuasive man, and Ox and Willie knew it. Willie also knew that the doctor he needed to see, along with Mark and the other wounded men, was not the same doctor that needed to see the women. Verne knew it too, and when the caravan of Germans showed up, they were met with hospitality and courteous nurses all ready to help.

The morning was filled with tests and more tests. There was crying, hugging, laughter, and more crying. Most of the caravan had made it back to camp well before dark. Mark quickly found me still down by the river, and Mark told me the story of the tests and crying. Then he told me all the good news. He saved the bad news for last. Mark has always been a good storyteller, but this story was full of information that everyone needed to know, especially Captain. Mark said, "My wound is infected, but the Doc gave me a shot and some pills and said to keep it clean, and I will be ok." He went on to tell me about everything else he knew, and Laurie started to cry. We had caught several fish that day. Mark helped clean them, and we were on our way back to camp.

Captain, Mother, and almost the rest of the camp were sitting around a beautiful campfire talking about the day. Oxford was there with Diane. Janet, Francis, and Willie were not there. As we walked into camp with bags of fresh fish, Mikey gave Laurie a hug, grabbed the fish, and walked away. I knew then that Mark had not told us everything. Oxford asked Laurie and I to sit down and began to tell us where the others were, including her father and why.

He started by telling us that Janet had major complications with her baby and had to have an emergency surgery. Something had gone wrong, and her baby had died. They must remove it immediately, and Janet was in serious danger. She was in the hospital and would be there for several days. Francis was with her. He went on to explain that a wagon train is not a good thing for a pregnant woman. When I asked him about Diane, he just smiled and said, "We are having twins." Laurie did not wait and asked where Willie is.

Oxford looked at Captain and then back to Laurie and said, "His wound is not healing, and he is much sicker than he led us to believe. He had been admitted to the hospital, and he wouldn't be able to join us the rest of the trip." Laurie, Della, and her sisters all were crying when Oxford continued, "He had asked me to ask Captain for his favor. He wanted Captain to watch over Laurie and his girls like his own daughters. He had asked Della and the girls to stay with him in Chicago and to use his money to find a more permanent place to rent until he has passed."

The entire group was totally quiet when Della asked, "How much time does he have?"

Oxford quietly with tears in his eyes said, "It could be a week, it could be a month, but he has a disease in which there is no cure, and his entire body is shutting down." I don't think there was a dry eye in camp; the news of Diane having twins and the other pregnant women being okay was bittersweet. Captain gave Diane, Carol, Linda, and all four of the Mayer girls a hug and announced, "I would take first watch. Anthony, you have the morning watch. I will take the Mayer family into Chicago early tomorrow and find them a place to live. Anyone wanting to say goodbye to Willie, write me a note, and I will deliver it to him. Willie is a great man, and I can think of several times when he risked his life to save ours. He will be missed!" Captain was choking up worse than I have ever seen; he turned and looked at Della and said, "We leave at six tomorrow morning." He then went into his tent quietly, returned with his rifle, and walked to the river. Mikey had prepared a delicious fish dinner for everyone. We all ate good; everyone thanked me and Laurie for the fish, thanked Mikey for preparing it, and slowly retired to their tents. Laurie asked me to sit with her the rest of the night. I did.

Laurie and I were sleeping next to the fire, and she was in my arms as the sun came up. Mother had brought us a blanket sometime during the night and covered us up. It was going to be the last time I see Laurie, and her me, for a long time. We were not sure how long, but more than either of us wanted. Della had everything packed and was ready to go before anyone even woke us up. Mother and Captain knew this would be hard on me as I was taking a lot of it very personally. I kept thinking it was my fault, and I could not take it any longer.

I gave Laurie a kiss goodbye, hugged the others goodbye, and got on Flash and rode away into the orange sky of the sunrise. Willie was like a second father to me, and now he is dead, because of me. Captain caught up to me and tried to explain to me it was not my fault. I did not understand. Captain went on and said, "Life is hard. Love everyone every day like there is no tomorrow. Tomorrow is not promised, and part of life is losing friends and family. We had lost several loved ones on this trip, and the hardest part is still to come."

I looked at Captain and said, "Let's make sure we don't lose anyone else. Tell Willie I will miss him. Tell him I will take care of Laurie the rest of her life. Tell him after we are married, we will name our first born after him."

Captain said, "I will do that. Now come on, back to the wagons. We need you to help get our wagons moving, and everyone would need help crossing the river. Do not stress. It is not your fault." Captain rode away, and as my tears started to dry, the sun poked over the horizon. I watched the sun came up that morning, and I realized Captain was right. I slowly walked Flash back to camp. I watched as Laurie and her family rode away into the sunrise.

They disappeared, and Mark rode up next to me and said, "She will be back. Let's get this wagon train rolling."

We returned to camp, and nearly every wagon and every family was ready to move out. Chris had found a good, safe place to cross the river, and Mother had the team ready to go. Doc made sure that every pregnant woman knew he will be ready at a moment's notice if any of them had any problems. Mother took the team and led the wagon train once again, and we were off. We only had a week or so to the Mississippi River, and once we cross, we will be entering what most consider to be the Wild West. No more roads, no more hospitals, and several Indian renegades that have not agreed to stay on the reservations and are known to attack wagon trains. The US military has a strong presence, and yet every day there were people dying by the hands of the wild Sioux Indians. There were a few other tribes in Iowa. The Sioux and a few wild Cherokee still remained.

Carol had been worried about getting west of the Mississippi. As once we cross over, we will be in Iowa. Carol had all the girls scared and some of the men nervous. Everyone wanted Captain back before we cross into Iowa. Her history books were a few years old, and Doc was quick to point that out. It does not ease much of the anxieties the community is feeling. Her books had stories of how the Indians steal the women and make them into slaves. How they scalp the men while they are still alive. Finally, Mother put a stop to it as Linda is crying and wanted Captain there before we go any further. Mother did not stop but did not push the team like she normally does. We traveled forty miles that day.

Chris, Mark, and I had been riding point while looking for a safe camp spot for the night. We had found a good spot and circled the wagons. We set up a camp even Captain would be proud of. Mark and I had noticed all day the deer trails and have discussed hunting for some fresh venison. It was spring, and the doe should have fawns, so no shooting the family pairs. We also decided it might be difficult to determine which were bucks and which were does because most every buck is hornless. We tried anyway that night, but no luck; we only saw doe. The little spotted fawns were so cute. I wanted to catch one and keep it as a pet. I thought we could just wean it with a cow and calf. It should drink cow's milk, I figured. Mark and Chris did not like the idea, so we returned to camp empty-handed. I did not give up on the idea but figured I would wait until Captain returns so I can talk to him about it.

That night was very quiet, and no one even had a fire. We had a well-prepared supper and went to bed. Mikey kept some food out in case Captain returns late; he did not return. The community was up at daybreak, and we were heading west; it was only a couple days to the Mississippi. Mark and I rode all the way to the Mississippi and back that day. We found a great spot to camp along the river.

We knew no way all the wagons would make it in one day, but if we push hard, we could make it in two days. We convinced Mother to push hard and set up along the Mississippi until Captain returns. The wagons rode into the night and only stopped for a quick rest and were pushing west before daybreak.

Captain had been gone for a few days now, and Mother was starting to get nervous. We had a great camping spot along the river. Lots of trees and a good fishing spot nearby. We had safety in the trees and surrounded by river; it was a safe and good spot to stay. It had rained a few days lately, but looks like we were in for some rainy, stormy weather. Mother and a few others decided to stay here until the weather passed and Captain returned. The warm rainy days gave everyone a chance to wash everything, rest up, and most importantly relax. It gave me and Mark a few days of fishing. Everyone joined us fishing at one time or another, and in a couple days, we had caught so many fish, even Mikey said we had enough. To me, the best part of fishing the Mississippi was I was catching fish on Laurie's homemade lure. I must have caught ten fish with that frog-looking lure. It started to get chewed up pretty bad, so I put it away and caught real frogs, night crawlers, bugs; the fish were biting on everything.

The fifth morning, Mother was up early and asked Anthony, Doc, Mikey, and the others over breakfast if we should wait any longer. The decision to break camp was made, and this was to be our last day in camp. Chris and I were to find a safe place to cross this mammoth of a river—somewhere for everyone to cross safely. Chris already knew where we needed to go, and he told everyone, "We have an extra day drive in the wagons, but the safest place to cross the river was near Moline, Illinois. There was a good trail across Iowa straight through Iowa, and we will turn north near Omaha." Mother knew that was what Captain would do and that was what we are going to do.

The next morning, we started for Moline. Mother was showing that she was nervous and asked Chris to ride toward Chicago and check on Captain. I wanted to ride with Chris, but I also knew Mother wanted Mark and me to stay near the wagon train. She wanted us to take turns and ride point and report back to her often. Mark wanted to ride with Chris too, but we both knew we had to stay with Mother and the girls. The community needed us to keep them informed, and so we did just that. Mark and I took turns riding miles ahead and returning every time with good news. Chris took off toward Chicago, and about the time the wagon train was near Moline, Chris had returned. He rode right to Mother and reported, "Captain will be here with the Mayer family and their wagon in just a few hours. Janet and Fran are with him too. She is okay and feeling much better." He then lowered his head and reported, "Willie has died. The hospital wants to keep his body for research because he died of a rare disease that very few had seen before and Della agreed." He then continued, "I will let Captain and Della tell you the rest, but they are planning a funeral service in his honor."

Camp once again had mixed feelings. A man that had saved many lives and had been a dear friend to all of us had died. Janet on the other hand was okay and will be able to make the trip with the rest of us. Captain and the others rode into camp just after dark. Janet and Francis rode in first, then Captain, and then the Mayer ladies, all in the wagon except Laurie. She rode in on her horse alone. The fire was glowing, and there was still plenty of fish for the new arrivals to eat. The girls in camp worked quickly and diligently and had made a makeshift sign that read, "Welcome Back. We Missed You." Everyone in camp signed it, and it had a picture of Willie sewn to it; it was perfect. The glow of the fire reflected off Willie's picture. I could not take my eyes off Laurie. I was glad to have her back in camp.

CHAPTER 20

INDIANS

Moline, Illinois, and we crossed the river, and we were directly in the middle of Davenport, Iowa. Captain was very paranoid going through towns, and Anthony knew that. A few days earlier, while riding point and looking for a safe river crossing spot, he had found a family camp five miles north of Moline. The camp looked hidden and no trails in or out. He snuck in close enough to see it was a permanent camp almost like a small city or community similar to what we were. No wagons, but lots of horses, and several families with children. Anthony knew who these people were, and yet he also knew we had what they wanted, and they had what we needed. They had two large ferries big enough to carry our wagons, horses, and our stock across the river. It was the only safe place. After inches of rain and high river levels before that, a bridge or a ferry seemed the only way.

He showed Captain the spot and explained the situation. Captain told Anthony to remove any and all remnants of the cavalry that he has. Dress as close to a farmer as you can, and I will do the same. He then said, "Today we are not cavalry. Indians didn't really like the cavalry. You and I are riding down there and making a deal to get our entire community across the Mississippi safely, on those ferries." He let on to the rest of the men to prepared for war as quietly and without letting the women and children know. Captain and Anthony prepared their wardrobes and were off as quickly and quietly as possible. Captain knew Mother was on to him, but she also knew crossing this giant river was not safe and knew what Captain was preparing to do, if necessary.

Anthony and Captain were off to the river where four men were standing. They spoke poor English but good enough to understand what Captain was trying to do. The odd-looking men were happy to help, and two dollars per wagon, one dollar per horse was the cost. Every person must pay ten cents to ride. Captain was happy with the price; the long-haired men were happy and seemed eager to get started. The men soon identified themselves as Indian, and although they looked a bit different, they were very similar. Captain hit it off perfect with the Indians, and the deal was complete. The last of the Winnebago tribe, now friends with the white settlers in the area. They were small farmers and a tribe of horsemen. They were friendly with immigrants trying to cross into Iowa. They trade and buy supplies up and down the Mississippi and had not had trouble with the local immigrants for nearly one hundred years. They know their place, and yet they were friends with the Texas Cherokee that also travelled up and down the river, and they were not so friendly. They stayed quite hidden and usually only, if ever, migrate south for a few months during the cold winter months of the Midwest.

Captain had appointed me and Laurie and Francis and Janet to stay on the ferries as they carried our entire wagon across. Two ferries and a couple on each one, every trip. It was not a bad assignment. I would be spending the next few days with Laurie, and the families seemed friendly. Most speak English, and I had lots of questions. The young men working the ferry ropes when we started actually struggled to get five horses per ferry or one team and wagon per ferry. We had twenty-five wagons and sixty-five horses; it would take quite a few trips. So it began, the first trip across. I was actually a bit nervous. Five horses, five men including me and Laurie. When we got to the other side, the ferry men switched, and the women grabbed Laurie immediately. They were friendly, and she complied. By the time we unloaded the horses, food was prepared along with a jug of tea and were on the ferry for the return trip. It was much easier, and the new pullers were friendly and talking, asking us where we are from, where we are going, and how did our trip go so far. They gave us food and tea, and we enjoyed each other's company for the next three days.

These families were not hostile like in Carol's books; they were very similar to us. They had a community of nearly one hundred people. Everyone, including the women and children all have a purpose, as did the German families. They had a chief as we did, they had warriors, scouts, and a medicine man. They had small farms and horses. They did not have cows but were very good hunters and live off the land. They actually had assigned hunters during the fall season that were basically required to kill enough to eat throughout the winter. They had places to store meat similar to our cellars. When I asked about fishing, they said they had tried but not much time to fish and not much luck. We were floating back and forth for a few days, and I had an idea.

I was just riding mostly and wanted to show my new friends how to catch fish and work at the same time. I showed them my fishing rod and how it worked. I showed them how to catch night crawlers, and I gave them an entire spool of fishing line. I even gave them a couple hooks. After catching a few on my rod, I then whittled a few makeshift fishing poles. I attached them to the downstream side of the ferry, baited them, and as we were returning for about our fifth load of horses, we started catching fish. I insisted my new friends catch fish on their new poles. They had so much fun fishing, they forgot they were working. Captain and their chief watched what I had been doing, both with a bit of enjoyment and embarrassment. They watched the young Indians learn to fish while they worked. It did take longer to get across the river when the guys were fishing, not pulling, but no one ever complained of our slow times. The last day, the last of the horses and wagons were across but too late to leave. We had a large fish fry. Mikey had cooked for large groups before, and our new friends not only learned how to fish, but their cook also learned how to cook enough fish to feed the entire tribe. After supper, most of us sat around the campfire just enjoying each other's company. I did not understand why they don't have cows; they did not understand why we don't have any young children. We had so many beautiful women. Laurie tried to explain it and pointed out all the pregnant women, but we both left the fire that night with our questions unanswered.

The next morning, Captain had Mark and Chris bring their chief two horses. Captain already had paid the crossing fee, but this was a tip, and Captain knew it would be more appreciated than any amount of cash tip. The chief then had his men bring bags full of fresh vegetables, mostly fresh picked asparagus and other native vegetables that had already been harvested just in the last week. Chief then gave Captain a beautiful hand-carved bow with several arrows. One of the guys then gave me a bow and some arrows. The women redressed Laurie in a beautiful handmade Indian dress and explained to her that this was a wedding dress, and when we get married, she was to wear this dress. Women of all cultures want to get married to great men I guess, and as I mounted Flash that morning, a young Indian woman came up to me holding a baby. She said, "I have only seen fifteen winters. I am younger than Laurie. Marry her, give her children."

I smiled, nodded, looked at Laurie, and said, "I love her too. We will be married when the time is right." I'm not sure if the young mother knew what I said, but she touched my horse, smiled, and walked away.

As our wagon started to roll west, I had realized, we all did, that we made friends with native Americans. They were a great tribe that is well known even with the Dakota Sioux and the vicious Texan Cherokee. What Captain and the rest of us did in these three days of ferrying our tribe across the mighty Mississippi might serve us well the rest of our trip. We waved goodbye, and just like that we were in Iowa, heading west toward Omaha. The fear of Indians attacking us was lessened tenfold. Captain knew there was still a threat, but hopefully, word travels fast. The German's are Indian-friendly. They believe in God and would prefer trade than fight with every Indian tribe in the west; we are considered friendly.

Traveling had slowed way down. The roads had turned to trails, and it was starting to rain. Our next stop for supplies was Iowa City, only sixty miles away but will take three days to get there. We were not really hurting for supplies, but our beef supply to eat was gone, we had no pigs, and although we could eat fish, we needed food. Captain was already talking about buying cows and horses once we get to Omaha and Sioux Falls and then driving them to North Dakota. He doesn't think there was any one stop where we can buy ten thousand head of cattle and five thousand horses. He knew it was somewhat risky, but his plan was to put word out that the Germans were coming and want to buy every cow and horse for sale. Iowa City has a sales barn, and that was where Captain, Anthony, Mark, I, and several others were headed. We plan on buying some cattle, whatever Iowa City has, within reason, but want to make sure they get word to Omaha.

They would need to get word to their Oklahoma and Texas ranchers that we were buying cattle and would be hiring cowboys to help drive them all the way to North Dakota. There were ten men that rode into Iowa City that day, but we let Captain and Anthony do all the talking and dealing for us. When we left the sales barn, we had twenty cows, ten pigs, and ten more horses. Captain's plan went perfect, and before we left for the wagons, Captain insisted we all stop at the saloon and have a beverage. No one disagreed, and Captain, Mark, and I enjoyed our first beer together. Captain toasted to our plan, as if it had worked already. Before we left that saloon, the postmaster showed up. Captain slipped him a dollar and toasted one more time, postmaster included.

It continued to rain off and on for the next week. Our wagon train was slow going, and a few days we didn't go anywhere, Captain didn't even try. The mood of the wagon train was very good. It was not cold rain, several rivers to fish, and Captain, for the first time since Russia, was not in a hurry. He was sleeping in; we had lunch and dinner every day and night. We butchered a pig and a cow and had fresh beef or pork almost every day. We took time to train our new horses, and besides, the horse I picked out was getting trained. Captain was taking time, everyone was; we all loved horses but couldn't understand why we were traveling so slow.

Captain finally admitted that the sales barn manager told Captain that if we could hold off until June, Omaha and the others would have plenty of beef and horses to sell. We might have a tough time finding quality cowboys to help as most of the good cowboys just wrangler the cows to Omaha and head back to Texas to do it again. Somehow, Captain's plans always come together, and after he explained it, everyone understood. We had two weeks to get from Iowa City to Omaha. We took a week to get to Des Moines. We spent a relaxing day getting supplies and, again, sending messages by post. We were coming and wanting to buy cows and horses and were looking for cowboys to hire on. We took another week to get to Omaha, and it just so happens Omaha beef company was having a huge beef auction June 1. Our entire trip across Iowa went slow but well, and everyone was in pretty good spirits, even Della and the Mayer girls. Our first state west of the Mississippi went perfect. Our leader, even during the hardest times, had come through again.

CHAPTER 21

COWBOY UP

Monday, May 31, 1897. All of us were at the sales barn watching the cattle come in from all over the southwest, mostly Oklahoma and Texas. Our camp was two miles from the Omaha beef auction house, but there were cows and cowboys spread out throughout the entire area. I had never seen so many cows. When they move, it looked like the ground was moving. I was not sure how many there were, but it definitely looked like enough to get started. Captain figured over ten thousand heads of cattle and around one thousand horses would be auctioned off. It was an exciting time and yet a nervous time. Every man and woman in our camp can ride and ride well, but none of us, not even Captain, had driven ten thousand cows five hundred miles across rough terrain. There would be no more smooth roads, no more ferries to cross the rivers, and only two more cities after we leave Omaha before we were to our new home. As most of us were wide-eyed at the sheer amount of cattle, Captain was looking for cowboys to hire.

There was a group of wranglers that arrived the day before. Half were in the saloon; the other half were overlooking the herds. They had switched, and the foreman was with the herd today. Captain and Anthony were talking to the foreman, and it looked like they had hit it off. As they were riding back to camp, Mark and I rode up to Captain and started asking questions. How much do they get paid? Can they help us push the herd north? How many cowboys are there? Captain explained it briefly to us but also said he would give details once we were all back in camp. It was only five minutes to camp, and Mark and I were racing. His new horse was big and stout but does not have the speed Flash has, and so I arrived in camp quite a ways before Mark or the others. I did help out, and as the guys arrived, I grabbed their respective rides and put them on the stringer. With the extra cows and horses, our wagon train circle is not quite as tight. With the horses attached to a long rope on the north side, the cows stayed pretty close.

It wasn't long, and everyone buying cows or horses had gathered around. Captain was speaking for everyone to hear. First, he said, "I have hired fourteen hands and another cook to help us drive the cows. The foreman gets $50 a month, and each cowhand gets $40 per month. We have about five hundred miles from Omaha to North Dakota, and we could move the herd about ten to fifteen miles per day, twenty on a good day. The days are long, and we can move them only during daylight. It is about the same speed we crossed Iowa, so the pace will be slower than ever. On the other hand, horses run when they move, then rest, and can run almost all day. They average fifty miles a day or more. It sounds like we should get close to one thousand horses and as many cows as we want, but we need to find our budget, which includes the labor cost of about $1,500 total. I plan on taking five of our men and five of the new cowboys and run the horses all the way to North Dakota. Everyone else will be with the herd and the wagons. The wagons will follow the horse trail where possible, and the herd will follow the wagons, where possible.

"Once the ten men get to ND with the horses, they must immediately start building corrals. Build as big as possible on each man's homesteaded land. Look over where the house and barns will be built and build accordingly. Francis and Russ, you two must push the horses north and look over the land. I trust where you build the corrals will be where they should go. Glen and Laurie, you two, along with Janet will be pushing the horses. Glen, you and Laurie will need to be in the front. You have the fastest horses, you need to be on point and watch for any horse trying to pass while finding the best route. You will have five experienced cowboys riding with you, so if there are questions, ask them. They have just moved 500 horses and 2,500 cows from Texas to Omaha, so they have experience."

"Cowboy up," Captain said. "We are buying starting at 10:00 a.m. tomorrow morning and want to get our stock as far away from the stockyards as soon as possible. Once we buy a cow or horse and remove it from the stockyards, it is considered ours. Any strays that get back to the stockyards would be considered lost, so our first day or two is very important. We will have our cows tied to a wagon, and hopefully, it will be in front showing the stock where to go.

Horse sale starts at 10:00 a.m. As soon as all were sold, they start selling cows. The big question is, how many can we afford and how many do we want?"

Captain doesn't even know how much money Mark or I had, much less guys like Chris and the others. We don't want to blow everything either as we do have to build houses and barns before winter. Captain then started asking, "How much do we have?" Mark and I have nearly $100,000 each; Chris and a few others had just as much or more.

So I spoke up, "There is no shortage of money, Captain. Let's buy all the horses they have and five thousand heads of cattle. We will let Captain deal with the money, so everyone just gives him $25,000." Mother did not know about the giant amounts of money we made horse racing either. Captain knew it was a lot but did not know together his boys alone have a quarter million dollars.

He commented, "No wonder half of Kentucky were after you guys." The only person besides me that knows exactly how much money I had was Laurie; we counted it recently. I have $135,000 in cash, and I bought the stock at the Iowa City sales barn. Mark had around $120,000. But had been buying supplies, saddles, and lots of other tack for the horses. He had been gambling with a few of the guys at night, but they only play for dollars.

"Tomorrow is going to be fun. I can't wait!" I said. Mark agreed and so did almost everyone. "Yeehaw!" and "Giddyap" were our words; the excitement was everywhere.

About the time we were sitting down to eat, the foreman Dale shows up. He is about average height but really thin, gray hair, and every other word out of his mouth, he was cussing. Captain invited him to eat and said, "There are women and children everywhere. We say a prayer before we eat, so kindly watch the pirate talk." Dale did not have a problem with that and sat down to eat. For a man that is so skinny, he ate more than anyone. He did leave Texas over a month ago and had been on the trail for quite some time. After supper, Dale asked Captain to make a deal on his entire herd, horses and cows.

He explained, "He is charged to sell them. The auction house needs to make money too. But I will make you a deal on everything I have, and we can take off with our 500 horses, 2,500 cows and head straight for the Dakotas." Captain liked that idea, and the deal was made. The numbers stayed quiet in public, but the deal was we will pay Dale and his cowboys $100,000 to get his herd to North Dakota by July 1. A $50 bonus per man once we are in North Dakota and a $5 deduction for each dead cow or horse, and that included if any get away.

Captain then said, "That is half the cows we wanted to buy. If I buy another 2,500 cows, can we herd them altogether?"

Dale smiled and said, "My cowhands are as good as they get. The 2,500 more cows is not even an extra charge, but 500 more horses is one dollar per additional horse." And they shook on it. We all had given captain $25,000 each, and Captain went into his tent and came out with $50,000 in cash.

"Half up front, the remaining amount when we get there," Captain exclaimed.

Dale loved the idea but commented, "Don't tell my guys I got paid until we are miles away from Omaha. If you do, we would never get them out of the saloon." As Dale started to walk away, Captain shook his hand again.

Dale walked directly to me after that and said, "You are the horse racer with the fast horse?" I smiled and nodded. He asked, "How tall of a horse is your runner?"

I quietly said, "He is fourteen hands tall and built for speed."

Dale smiled and then commented, "Mine is sixteen hands tall. Let's race them for fun."

I smiled and nodded. "Anytime, for fun."

Captain nodded and said, "We have had plenty of trouble racing for money. Until we are in North Dakota, no more horse races, please."

I spoke up again and said, "I am going for a ride right now. Do you want to ride along? I want to find our trail out of here. I've never herded a thousand horses before, and I want a smooth run at least the first day." Dale looked at me and agreed to ride with me.

The next morning by nine, Dale had his fourteen hands and a cook ready to go. They were just west of our camp grazing. An amazing sight, and we were going to double it today. I wanted to go to the sale just to watch the horses, but we were buying every horse under ten years old, and I will be running them north for the next week or more. The excitement was in the air; everyone was up by sunup, wagons packed to the brim, and packed down good. Our twenty-five wagons were all packed and ready by 7:00 a.m. Mikey and a few of the girls rode out with breakfast and coffee for each cowhand. Mikey introduced himself to their cook, and they seemed to be instant friends. His name is Pedro and wears a big Mexican sombrero. He was always smiling, and his supply wagon looks overloaded for an ox, but they had come from Texas, so it should be fine. The cowhands could not believe how beautiful the girls were and commented how much better this trip is going to be. Mikey chuckled and said, "Yes, there are fifteen unmarried girls. None of them were here without a father, and most of them are pregnant." Every cowboy still liked their odds, if it's just to look at and watch. After two months of staring at cows, everything looks better.

The plan was to follow the Missouri River the entire way to North Dakota. I had the first fifty miles along the river planned, and several of our wagons were already heading north. It was beautiful country, with nice fields on both sides of the river. The horse auction started early, and our five hundred horses were out of the gate in fifteen minutes. By ten o'clock, five hundred horses came running by our few wagons. Mikey and Pedro's were still parked from breakfast. They ran clear past the cows and didn't even seem to spook them. It was an amazing sight for sure. We now had one thousand horses, and we immediately headed north. I had a really cool oxbow picked out for our first night on the trail, about forty miles away.

The cowboys running the horses would not use any tents, and someone always had to be watching the herd, day and night. Janet decided she did not want to do that, so she was staying with Mother, Linda, and the lead mules of the wagon train. She was on horseback, and so is Linda, Carol too, but she was busy checking out the nine cowboys watching the cows for the next month or so. Mark was still fighting infection, so he was required to stay with Mother, Doc, and the wagons. He was not liking it, but Captain and Mother would not give in, so until the infection was gone, Mark did nothing fun. Captain and Chris decided he may be needed with the horses, so he had joined up with us. I was glad. Chris was an awesome horseman and would do the work of two men. One thousand horses moving all at once was pretty rare and pretty cool. Our first five miles was actually perfect. A gentle trot, and not one horse strayed away. Laurie and I were riding point, and the herd just seemed to follow our horses wherever they went.

We stopped near a shallow stream, and the horses got a needed drink. Once done, Laurie and I took off again, and this time, we were pushed by the herd. We knew where we were going, but now we were passing Mother and the front wagons. The herd surrounded the wagons as they went past. Even Linda thought it was pretty amazing. We were running, so some of the horses pulling the wagons spooked. No damage, but the most excitement Mark had in a while. As we went by, we only then realized this would be the last time we see any of them for probably a month. It was a quick wave, and we were gone.

We made it to the oxbow where I planned to stop the first night. We were there early, so the cowboys took first watch, and I went fishing. Laurie and I managed to catch five big northern pike, and that was more than enough supper for all of us. We had our day packs with, so as I cleaned and deboned the fish, Laurie prepared potatoes and the fish fry. Supper was ready to eat before dark. The horses were resting nicely, and several even bedded down. We all ate together and got to know each other. Of course, we knew each other, but the five cowboys were interesting men. Three negros and two Mexican, none of which spoke great English but sure were fun to talk to. Russ told the cowboys the "Hay Hauler" story, and they all immediately agreed—she is "Hay Hauler." The older negro definitely was the leader, but it seemed like these five men were very good horsemen. It should be a fun week.

The next morning, we all were up by daybreak and were moving north along the river. Chris had already found our trail, and the herd seemed to follow him just as well. Francis rode back toward the cows, just to see if everything is okay. Captain appreciates the updates, but I think he wanted to give Janet one last chance to ride with him. He returned back in just a few hours and reported that the herd of cows was just over five thousand, and they were going to try to make it to the Oxford near the river where we were just the night before. They were making good time as well, and Captain was ecstatic about our herd. The wagons were traveling faster than the five thousand heads of cattle, just as planned. Our one thousand horse trail was pretty good to travel on, and it's easy to see where there was trouble.

It is calving season, and 2,500 of the cows were pregnant, and 200 hundred horses were, including Laurie's horse. At the pace we were traveling, we would be in North Dakota in a week. None of the horses should foal in the next week. Laurie's horse was expecting in three weeks or so; we were hoping the other were too. Most of the cows that were pregnant would have to have them on the trail. Captain and Dale were going to split the family pairs off from the main herd and bring them up the rear. The last bunch would be followed by wolves and coyotes, so all the cowboys are carrying rifles. Mark could not wait to start shooting varmints; he did ride out in the evenings with his rifle. The wild coyotes and wolves sure were vocal, but so far, no kills.

The weather had been absolutely perfect, and the third day, we traveled over two hundred miles. We had already entered into South Dakota, and besides a few drifters, the herd was doing well. We had our biggest task at hand. Crossing the mighty Missouri River with one thousand horses. The Missouri was by far the longest river in America, but it has quite a few good crossing spots, as it winds quite regularly. Our map shows crossing to the east side of the river in South Dakota would bring us right up to our land once we cross into North Dakota.

The herd was doing well, and I was elected to cross the river first. Flash and I had crossed many rivers, and he usually swims across with me in the saddle. We found a nice gravel and sand beach to cross at, and we can walk the herd right into the river. There was about a ten-foot channel that the horses would need to swim across; the rest, they will touch bottom. If they watch Laurie and me, we would be okay. "If there were any floaters, sound off. I would retrieve them immediately." After we cross, we had another 120-mile run for the next two days, and then we would be to our destination. We calmly walked the majority of the herd down onto the beach. They were drinking and just meandering on the beach.

Once all one thousand were on the beach, I started to head across. Laurie followed me, and just like that, almost in a line, but five by five or so crossed together; they all swam the channel without incident, and we were across. Laurie did admit that this was the first time her horse swam, and she remained in the saddle. The cowboys were all quite impressed with our riding. I'm not sure they know I was riding an American champion field racer, and Laurie was riding my horse's mother. Once across the river, we took our time the rest of the day.

We did travel seventy-five more miles, but even with this big herd, we had no problems. The cowboys keep the herd all in a group. It seemed like Laurie and I were up front; Chris is mostly up front but was constantly circling. The cowboys were always on the sides, and Francis and Russ were following. I think Chris was watching the horses, looking for the biggest, best, fastest. He was great at finding the good ones. I did ride beside him for a while yesterday, and we both had spotted a few really special-looking horses.

The next day was another gorgeous day, and we had the herd moving by 7:00 a.m. We were all excited to see our land. We each had a map of whose land is whose. We had twenty-five homesteads of 160 acres each, and Captain has another 35,000 acres signed up for purchase at ten cents an acre. All connected or close, all just east of the Missouri in southern North Dakota. Altogether we had nearly 50,000 acres connected and another 10,000 close by. No fences yet, no houses or barns, it was a virgin land. Besides the Lewis and Clark expedition floating by, no one had ever been on our land. We were all excited and should be on our land by 7:00 p.m. that evening.

Our maps indicated we had made it to our land. Willie's land, Captain's land, Mark's land, all were side by side, surrounded by the land we were purchasing. So far, I personally like Willie's 160-acre homestead, the Mayers had the most woods anyway. It was where we were camping. We would begin to build the corrals soon. *Welcome* to North Dakota. The cowboys were even excited for us. We were hooting and yeehawing and doing high fives the rest of the night.

CHAPTER 22

THE HERD TO NORTH DAKOTA

North Dakota was more beautiful than I even imagined, and the horses were enjoying their new home. The grass was tall, and the ponds were full of fresh water. The Missouri River was full to its banks, and the beaches were huge with soft sand and driftwood stacked as high as you can see. We finished a community corral that we can fit all the horses in with only two gates. We enclosed Mayer's entire homestead, all 160 acres. It included quite a few trees, a creek, and a pond. There was a slight incline to the top of the hill where there was a nice flat area for a house and a barn. All ten of us who moved the horse herd to ND had been working steady to build the corral. Wood seemed to be plentiful for now; the corral was built with wood and looked amazing. There were gates at either end, and Francis was talking about adding a few side corrals for mare and colt pairs and another area for training and working the horses.

We have had no communication with the wagon train, Captain, or any of the cowhands for seven days. It had been decided that a few of us would ride back, check on the wagon train and cows, and then ride back to ND and relay information about the horses and the wagon train and the cows. Laurie and I had volunteered to make the ride. Chris was riding with us. Three of the cowboys had decided to ride back to the cows, just in case they needed help. The other four were staying in ND and continued building corrals and putting up fence. Francis and Russ were excited to get started on their own homesteads and were staying to do just that. Their homesteads were about five miles to the east of where the horses were and where the corrals were built, so building corrals at their own homesteads meant leaving the entire herd with just two cowboys. It was not a problem so far as everyone ate breakfast and dinner together every night.

It was agreed that once the corrals at the other homesteads were built, we will split the horse herd among the corrals. The land between the homesteads will be fenced with barbwire, so once the cowherd gets there, they all will be fenced in, with solid wood corrals at either side. As we were about to ride away, heading back to find the wagon trains and cattle, I commented for all to hear, "Captain will be proud. We had a plan, we prepared for everything, and it worked. We have our horses on our land!" I was as excited as I had ever been, smiling from ear to ear. "It was a long, hard fight to get here, but we made it! Stay safe! And we will see you in a few days!"

The men all cheered, and Russ even spoke up with a chuckle, "He even sounds like Captain Matt!"

We rode early in the morning all the way until dark. Laurie and I enjoyed riding together and riding fast. We covered hundreds of miles a day; Chris usually was riding with us but once in a while would slow down and ride with the cowboys. They had never seen anyone want to ride so much, so fast, and love it. The cowboys asked Chris why we always want to run, and his response did not make sense to the trail-hardened cowboys. "They are teenagers in love," Chris said, but with a nod of their head, they just agreed, "They sure like to run."

We arrived at the wagon trains, and everything was going as planned. Mother had the team doing well and slowly moving along. Mark was riding right with Mother and the girls when we met up. Mark immediately said, "I'm glad you're back. I'm bored as a wagon." His wound was doing really good, and the infection was gone. Laurie went straight to Della as I stayed and tried to explain how beautiful North Dakota was—where the homesteads were and how we had corrals built and how awesome the river was. I was talking fast, and it was easy to hear the excitement in my tone. Others were gathering around and asking questions, but the answer everyone wanted was "How far away is it?" My answer didn't give the answer they were looking for.

I told the crowd, "We made it in just a few days."

They all know I like to ride fast, so they finally asked, "How many days will it take for the wagon train to get there?" I wasn't even sure what to tell them, but as I was trying to explain everything, Chris and the cowboys rode up and let me off the hook.

Chris responded, "If we can move a little quicker than the herd, we can have the wagon train to their homesteads in two weeks' time." Even though getting the wagons to North Dakota in two weeks would be a tough push with pregnant worn-out women and no men helping since they bought the cows, it seemed to bring a little happiness I hadn't seen in Mother in quite some time. She snapped the reins and gave a hardy, "Giddyap, let's go." And the mules picked up the pace.

The cattle herd was about a mile behind the wagons, and as I rode up to see Captain, his immediate response was, "Hello, you sure are riding fast. Even the wagons were moving faster since you got here."

I responded, "Yes, sir, North Dakota is waiting for you. It's too beautiful to get there any later than scheduled." I went on the explain the corrals and the fences and how we planned to drive the cows right into the fenced land between the homestead corrals. I explained as much as I could. I told Captain and Dale about crossing the Missouri River and that the herd should cross easily. The wagons may have a few issues. Captain and Dale looked at each other, both confident that crossing a river is not the biggest challenge.

No sooner than I could ask how the loaded wagons were going to cross a twenty-foot-deep crossing, a cowboy approached and said, "Another cow is giving birth. It is the fifth today. I will stay back with the pairs, but it's time to start the second group."

Dale immediately said, "Take a few men, and cut out the pairs and the cows that are due soon. We will keep driving the rest north."

Captain looked at me and Mark and said, "Grab your rifles and an extra box of shells each. Watch over the calve and cow pairs. Coyotes and wolves are already following too close for comfort." Mark was excited for the challenge, but I wanted to head back to North Dakota. Captain knew that too, and before I could say anything, he said, "You watch the cow-calf pairs for a few days, and then you can take Mark and show him his land in North Dakota." Mark was so excited, and for the first time, he realized he would have his own house. For the first time, officially, he would not live with Captain and Mother and the girls. He would be on his own, and he now was really excited and nervous.

Mark had planned out our coyote hunting for days, and I was actually looking forward to doing some shooting. We were assigned to watch the calves, but we also were pretty good at spotting funnel areas. The coyotes had to pass through if they want to grab a calve and get away. There was a bright moon our first night on guard of the calves, and I'm glad we had extra shells. The herd was stopped right at the basin of a tall hill and a creek to the east. A fairly safe spot to rest for the evening, and also, a perfect ambush spot for any hungry coyotes or wolves. Mark picked out a couple good perching spots to watch the herd and had a good eye on the funnel for the predators to try get one of our calves.

It was barely dark, and the wild dogs were howling. They seemed so close I could touch them. Their howling voices and the screaming of coyote pups sounded like there were hundreds of them. It wasn't long, and the first pair of coyotes came lopping along. Mark and I both saw them, and we signaled to each other that he take the one on the left and me the one on the right. Our kill spot was nearly the same. As the coyotes approached, we both made an easy shot and killed both animals simultaneously. The first one was the best of the night, and using the moon as our only means of light proved to be a bit more difficult than we expected. It's amazing how the coyotes knew how to move through the area and stay in the shade caused by the moon. We only killed one other coyote that first night but had several shots. I did manage to scare away several others.

By morning, we had ten more cow-calf pairs join our slow-moving family herd and now had twenty calves and nineteen cows, one set of twins. We were about one-half mile behind the main herd, but we were moving slower and stopping often. It was rather easy to keep the small herd together, but they really don't want to walk as steady as the main herd. Mark and I took turns sleeping that morning, and by evening, we were both on guard again. I was tired and wanted to ride north. Walking slowly along with cows and calves just wasn't what I considered exciting. Mark was busy planning our night ambush on the wild critters of South Dakota.

That evening, Mark did all the shooting, and he killed four more coyotes, and he spotted a wolf pack planning an attack on our calves. The wolves circled the herd five times that night. They never attempted to catch and eat any calves nor did they give Mark or myself any shots. They were now aware that there were now forty cow-calf pairs. The third night was my last night on guard, and the most exciting night of the three, if exciting was fighting off a pack of wolves and a pack of coyotes. The smell of fresh calves had the wild dog packs brave or hungry or dumb. Mark killed eight wolves, and I got two. Mark killed four coyotes, and I killed one. We both were out of shells by sunrise. Captain heard all the shooting and came to see how we were doing. The several dead carcasses were easy to see, and so Captain immediately asked, "How many calves did we lose?"

Mark proudly answered, "None, not one, but we were out of shells." Captain was really happy to hear we didn't lose a calf and gave us another one of his famous head nods.

"Great job, boys. Go ahead and take the next few days and ride up to North Dakota and let Francis and Russ know how we are doing." Mark was excited to see his new homestead, but he liked shooting coyotes and wolves so much he was thinking about staying back and guarding the calves. I convinced him to ride with me to North Dakota, and it didn't take too much convincing, and we were heading north. We stopped and grabbed some food, said hello and goodbye to Mother and Laurie, and off we went, riding hard the entire way. We hadn't been sleeping nights while guarding the herd, so we decided to ride through the night, and by the next evening, we were in North Dakota.

We were tired, our horses were tired, but we spent the next night on Mark's land, his homestead. We bedded down as the sun went down, and as we were lying next to a nice campfire, Mark said, "I hope there aren't too many coyotes around us tonight. I'm too tired to hunt tonight." I'm not sure if there were coyotes around us that first night in North Dakota as we slept without waking up until the sun was already in the sky.

Mark and I spent the next several days working on and around his ranch. He has picked out a spot to build a house and barn, and we had a nice corral built with two training areas for horses. We had fenced in a large area for cows where the creek makes a large oxbow. There was beautiful grass, plenty of water, and even a small grove of tall ash trees for shade. It was so nice; it was hard to leave to go check on the cows and wagons coming.

We left after seven days in North Dakota. We worked on Mark's ranch until heading south to check in with Mother and Captain. We only rode for one day, and we were there. The herd is a few miles behind the wagons, and the cow-calf herd was several miles behind the main herd. Mother was excited to see us, and Mark was excited to tell everyone about his ranch. The entire community was excited to finally get to North Dakota, and everyone wanted to know about their land, about all the land, and about how much farther.

The entire wagon train, cowherd, and calf herd crossed the Missouri, and besides a few of the calves floating off, no animals were lost. The calves that floated away were all found; one died later, and one was walking with a bad limp, but altogether, the crossing went well. The wagons and main herd were traveling good and should reach North Dakota in just a few more days. The calf herd would be another week, as we now have two hundred cow-calf pairs, and fifty more were ready to give birth any day. Captain had been with the calves since we left and vowed to stay with them until they all were in the North Dakota pastures.

Mother was the first wagon to arrive, and Mark and I had cleared a spot for Mother to start unpacking. We built a corral for our horses and mules, and for the first time, the horses were in their corral. The wagon train had made it, and for the first time in several months, everyone will be on their own farms and ranches in North Dakota. We were spread out, homesteads were 160 acres each, so by nightfall, we could not see most of the wagons. Several of the fourteen hands were already in Napoleon, checking out the local taverns.

Captain and the third herd finally arrived six days after the wagons and five days after the main herd. As Captain and Dale brought the final 250 cow and calf pairs into the hills of southern North Dakota, they saw the herd of cows grazing comfortably, they saw the horses, and as he came over the last hill, he stopped on the very top to look around and said, "We are here. Through sacrifice, hard work, and strong will, we are home."

CHAPTER 23

One More Time

It had been a few days, and every family had settled into their homesteads. Francis and Anthony had their houses framed, roofs on, walls built, and everything moving forward. Francis was quite a carpenter and knew exactly what needed to get done and how to do it. They even had piles of rocks piled where their chimneys were going. Francis wanted to hand carve the doors, windows, and that took time. The openings were obvious, but still open. Francis had an old buffalo blanket as the door for now. As soon as Captain announced he was ready to build his house, every other man joined him. Most had started construction on their own house, but they stopped what they were doing and helped Captain.

Captain's house was good sized with three bedrooms upstairs, three bedrooms on the main floor, and a walk-out basement as half the basement was dug into a hill side, and there were walk-out doors facing the corrals. The front door faced south with a large porch and deck, and an outdoor grill made with field rock. The house basement had a huge fireplace that was three stories high and openings for wood burning in the basement, the kitchen, and family area. There were vents for heat in the bedrooms upstairs. All the girls' bedrooms were upstairs. The master bedroom, boys' bedrooms, indoor plumbing, bathroom, and indoor sink with plumbing for Mother's kitchen were on the main floor.

As most of Captain and Mother's house had been completed now, just the carving of doors and windows left, Captain had invited everyone after church on Sunday for one last community celebration. He wanted to make one last announcement, and he hoped everyone joined him and Barbara on the Gross farm for a picnic. Mikey was roasting a pig and frying some fresh fish, making one last meal for everyone.

The entire group of cowhands Captain hired in Omaha were still around, and several of them had decided to try to homestead in North Dakota too. Sunday's picnic was a wonderful success with every single person attending. A few of the ladies looked like they will be having babies soon, but everyone was interested in what Captain had to say. Mikey and Mother prepared several large pans of apple crisp with fresh whipped cream for dessert. The plates were all cleaned, but before dessert was served, Captain spoke up, "Thank you everyone for attending. I only have a few things for you to think about, and you can let me know your decision after dessert. How many cows do you want? How many horses do you want? How much land do you want to buy?"

Captain was silent; there was a quiet hmm in the crowd, and finally, Anthony spoke up, "How much does the land cost?"

Captain answered quickly, "First come, first serve, ten cents an acre, and I believe there is plenty of land for everyone!" A loud cheer started, and the mood was very festive, and Captain yelled, "One more thing, enjoy your dessert. I want to leave for Bismarck tomorrow morning early."

Dessert was delicious, and there was a fire started for everyone to gather around. Captain sat at a table nearby with Mother and Linda nearby. Every man in the company, Mark, Oxford, and Della included, all came to visit Captain that night. They let him know how many cows, horses, and acres they each wanted. Everything was recorded. The men were informed that they should ride with him to Bismarck, the capital, to complete their land purchase and homestead paperwork. Almost every man did, including ten of the fourteen hired hands. It was quite a ride; nearly every man in the company rode with to Bismarck.

Monday morning, the cavalry rode in cavalry formation; they left the missing men's spot empty. Willie, usually directly behind Captain, was the most noticeable empty spot. Mark and I rode scout, as Chris wanted to ride with Anthony this last ride together. The fourteen hands didn't understand at first but figured it out quickly and just got in line behind the cavalry. They left early and traveled fast. The plan was to make it to Bismarck and back in one day. The cavalry men had traveled this fast many times, but the cowhands were used to taking their time. They did make it to the capital with Captain and the rest of the men, but none of them made it back before midnight.

Captain did not care, as long as they were back by Saturday. Captain made it known that we do not have enough cows to fill everyone's request. He did not bother to worry about it or say anything about it until the land was paid for and how much land we will have. Captain's plan seemed to be playing out as he had planned. Saturday, the fourteen hands and a few of us land owners rode to Sioux Falls and bought five thousand more cows. Omaha Stockyards had made a deal with Captain and will put five thousand more cows on rail and will have them there by Monday or Tuesday next week.

Captain told everyone, "We will make one last cattle drive and split up our stock once we are back home. Everyone that wants cows or horses will pay me for their stock. I will pay the fourteen hands and for the cows. Cost is $30 per head, and that includes the rail ride, the cow, and the cowboys to bring them to North Dakota."

Dale assured everyone that they do not need to make the drive. "I will make sure my men will get all the cows home safely. This I will do for all of you, and so will my men!"

The hired hands, Captain, myself, and Laurie all rode out together early Saturday morning. We were missing a few of the cowboys, but Dale assured us, they will be there once we start moving cattle. I thought it odd that Captain requested only Laurie and me to ride with him. Later that morning, the three of us rode off and talked for quite a while. Captain had something to tell Laurie, and it included me. Once out of voice range from the others, Captain began to speak. His first question directly to Laurie was really weird, "How would you feel about joining our family?" Out of the blue and with no warming up and then didn't explain, for it seemed like quite a while.

Laurie looked at me and shrugged. "I am part of your family. Captain, you are my father now. You always will be."

Captain nodded, and almost blushing, he said, "Della came to me and asked if Barbara and I will take you in until Glen gets his house built and you two get married." Captain went on and tried to explain, "She is giving you and Glen the land her and Willie planned on homesteading. It joins up perfect with my farm. Soon to be yours and Glen's, a farm on the south side. Mark's is north of my farm."

He noticed Laurie started to cry, so he went silent for a while again, this time for at least five minutes, and then Laurie spoke up, "Why doesn't she want me with her. Where will her and my sisters live?"

Captain then answered quietly and politely, "She knows you want to stay with Glen, but without Willie, she wants to move to a town, a big town, so the girls can get and education and jobs other than being a rancher's wife. She talked about Fargo and NDSU." Captain went silent, then looked at me and nodded. "What do you think, Glen?"

I didn't know what to say, but I tried to mutter out the words, "If Laurie is okay with living with my weirdo sisters until we are old enough to move into our own place, I'm all for it, hell yeah!"

Both Captain and Laurie got quite a laugh, and after they gathered themselves, Captain again looked at Laurie and said, "What do you think, Hay Hauler, you think you can handle the sisters?" We all laughed again as Captain has never referred to Laurie as Hay Hauler before.

Laurie then looked at Captain and said, "I will put up with the sisters until the time is right, but can I call you Matt or dad instead of Captain?"

Captain smiled. "You can call me Matt, Willie is dad." He looked back to Laurie and said, "You can call me Father or Dad or Captain, I guess, I don't care."

Laurie smiled and said, "Can I call you father? You will be my father-in-law one day. I would like to call you father." And she smiled. The tears dried up, and before Captain returned to the cowboys, Laurie smiled at Captain. "Thank you, Father, I would love to live with you until our house is completed." And she nodded to me.

"I will take the first bedroom on the top of the stairs, but as soon as my house is built, I want your permission to move out."

Captain, with a very surprised smile, said, "Deal!"

He looked at me and nodded, and before he could say anything, I said, "Deal!"

We all laughed again, and before Captain left us for the cowboys, he said, "We got a lot of work ahead of us, but I love both of you. We can do this." He smiled with a tear in his eye and again gave us his famous head nod and road away.

Laurie and I stayed quite a way behind the cowboys. Captain wanted to ride through the night, but as the cowboys were riding through Madison, their thirst and the girls standing outside on a beautiful June evening stopped the cowboys in their tracks. We did ride in and noticed the cowboys at the saloon; we stopped but decided to get a motel room. Captain didn't like it but once again was assured they will be ready to cowboy up when they are needed tomorrow. Captain didn't like Laurie and me staying in the same room, so he insisted separate beds, and he gets the adjoining room. We rode hard all day and knew we would be up early, so after a quick meal and putting Flash and our horses in the stables and a little too much of drunk cowboys, we went to bed.

I had decided to call Captain father as well. Laurie and I discussed it and decided even after we are married, we will still call him father. We came down for breakfast, and Father, Dale, and even a few of the cowboys were already at the table. The Vetter boys from Nebraska, three brothers that had all signed up for ND homesteads, were also buying some cows. We had a quick bite to eat, and we were off to the Sioux Falls, South Dakota, stockyards. Our ride was a nice gallop and took only about an hour, and we even stopped. Captain, Dale, and all three Vetter boys finally rode in around 7:30 a.m. The stockyard manager knew the routine well, and as we were looking over the stock, he joined our ride. He explained to Captain and Dale there were no pregnant cows, but fifty bulls, and those bulls will chase those cows all the way up to North Dakota. The entire herd had been on the train since last night, and they were nervous. "I hope you have more than three cowboys to wrangle all five thousand of this herd to North Dakota?" The Manager looked quite nervous.

Dale replied, "Before we get the paperwork done, they all will be here ready to go."

Captain looked at me and Laurie. "Go chase those bulls out of the pen and down to that creek just north of

Madison. We will be along with the cows. We will go from there."

The manager had a nervous look to him, and before we rode off, I heard, "Watch this, these two can ride, they have hand signals, and fast horses. They will have that heard of bulls up to that creek in a couple hours."

I smiled at Laurie, and as we road up to the pen of nervous bulls, I said, "We better not screw this up. Everyone is watching."

She said, "We got this," and reached over and kissed me and opened the gate.

The manager looked at Dale and said, "I thought they were brother and sister?"

He almost fell off his horse when he saw us kiss. Dale shook his head and said, "I believe that's his wife." A few more cowboys rode up about then, but we had the herd on a nice jog, so they just waved and rode into the stockyards.

Father and the cowboys had the herd moving, and by noon, they stopped at the creek for a drink. The bulls were very happy to see the cows, and the chase was on. We just kept the entire herd going the right direction, and the bulls did the rest. They were all over those cows, and rest assured, we have pregnant cows now.

It took five more full days of riding and keeping the cows and bulls heading northwest, but by the sixth afternoon, we were riding into our land. We had no casualties and a lot of mating going on. Several of the bulls were so tired, they could barely continue, but we were back, so they can rest. We herded all the herd into Father's land, which was completely fenced. A beautiful sight for sure. We are home.

CHAPTER 24

Building a House

Father's house looked amazing, and Francis had carved out a beautiful front door and had it hung and fitting perfect. He also built a beautiful huge front window and nearly had every room window ready to install. Anthony had completed the remainder of the fireplace, and as we rode up to the house, everyone was there to greet us. Mother and the sisters knew about Laurie moving in and were very excited to have her. On the other hand, Della and Laurie's two sisters were happy to see us, but they too knew that Laurie was moving in with the Gross family and were sad. Verne announced that he had decided to move to Fargo as well and is forfeiting his homestead. The two families will ride to Fargo together and start searching for houses to build or buy and look for jobs. Verne wanted to be a teacher at NDSU and wanted his daughter Kari to follow in his footsteps. They thought they would leave immediately, but Doc just announced that Kari wasn't going anywhere until she had her baby.

The excitement women got over a baby amazed me. Once Doc announced Kari was having her baby soon, the talk of moving to Fargo ended. The Mayer girls were excited but also sad to see Laurie stay on the farm. Della reached out to Father and asked if he would be okay with a few guys riding to Fargo with them for safety. Father complied, and a few of the cowboys were quick to volunteer for that job. Escort two Mayer girls and two Spitzer girls and help them find a place to live, even the Johnson brothers, who had been drunk basically since we got to Madison, said they will ride along. They had homesteads too but plan on waiting until at least next year to build or even own any cows. They make enough money, but they did not know us back in Flash's racing days and don't have the money we do. They are young and still want to cowboy some. They had plans to ride all the way to Mexico, get some cows, and drive them all the way to North Dakota next year. Father thought it was a good idea and a great adventure but was not going with.

The houses around the area went up amazingly fast. Francis, Anthony, and Father helped every person work on their house, barn, or fencing. Most of the houses were small or average in size, but not Chris's house, and the barn Chris was building was huge. He did win a lot of money betting on Flash; he purchased two thousand cows and one hundred horses. Besides Father, Mark, and me, he had the greatest number of cows. Mikey was amazing and had manufactured a brand for each ranch, and all with a small letter g attached somewhere clever to prove that these first cows and horses belong to the Germans. Father's brand was very uniquely manufactured with a big letters GR and with a small number 1 on the lower right part of the letter R. Mark's brand was very close, GR and a small 2 in the same spot, mine of course, GR with a 3 in the same spot. Gross Ranch 1, 2, and 3. He made a brand and a matching sign for every ranch out there, everyone special, but every brand had a small letter g on it.

We thought it best to live with Father and Mother, and although Laurie and I worked hard to prepare our homestead for a house one day, no construction had started. Mark had decided to build a log cabin for himself. Some day he would build a house up on the hill, but for now, he had decided to build a cabin in the hills and trees closer to Linton, North Dakota. There were a lot of hills and trees surrounding his cabin, and it was close to the Missouri River. The view was amazing, and the hunting and fishing was simply the best we had ever seen. Laurie and I helped Mark a lot, but I did manage to fish enough to keep almost everyone stocked up with fresh walleye and northern pike.

Kari had her baby on July the first; it took her three days to deliver, but it was our community's first "German from Russia" baby born in America. Father convinced Verne and Kari with the baby to stay until after the Fourth of July. Della and all the girls were staying with Mother and Father and were okay with staying until after the Fourth of July's celebration. It was North Dakota's first Independence Day celebration ever as a state and our first Fourth of July as American citizens. The nearest town, Napoleon, was planning a big celebration with horse races and fireworks, live music, and games for all ages.

Once I heard about the horse races, I was excited. I wanted to race so bad, and although it had allowed us to be the biggest ranches in all of southern North Dakota, the men who were killed protecting me and our money still haunted me in my dreams. Laurie's horse was pregnant and about to give birth to a true brother to Flash, sure to be another fast horse and a future race horse. Laurie said it was up to me, but she had to keep a close eye on her horse and will not be at the race. I did not want any trouble on the ranch, and Mother was begging me not to race. I had not seen any horse or horses that could rival Flash. I wanted to race.

Mark had completed his cabin and had announced he will not race. He would compete in a friendly gopher hunt. The team with the most gophers win a pretty cool .22 rifle. He knew of a pasture with so many groundhogs and flickertails, which both count as gophers, and we were sure to win.

Laurie and I picked out an engagement ring and were excited. She didn't know it, but I purchased the ring while she was in buying a new dress and getting her hair done for the big dance. I figured, we might as well be engaged. That way, no other cowboy or rancher would ask her to dance. *I think the dance will be a good time to ask her to marry me. I can't wait!* Laurie said she might be in the barn having a baby horse and might not even make the dance, but she smiled at me like she knew something was up.

I spent time with Father that morning too. We talked mostly about buying some equipment for next spring. Together at the MG ranch's, there were also several fields that needed work. We talked about the horse race coming up and if I should race, and we talked about Laurie. I was very nervous, and Father knew it. He doesn't know why, but he knew I was hiding something. The upcoming race, my wanting to race, even after Mother said she did not want me to, the diamond ring in my pocket, and the gopher hunt, and our first real American dance—I had reason to be nervous, and Father knew it.

The music had started, and the music was nice. The lead singer called for all the married couples and love birds to come out on the dance floor for a nice slow waltz, a slow song, with almost everyone from our community dancing. Even a few of the cowboys were dancing with the Mayer girls. Now was my chance, so I put my dancing moves on and slowly worked our way to the front. I looked at the singer and said in his ear, "I am going to ask her to marry me." The music did not stop, and I didn't even realize that it got a lot quieter. I whispered in Laurie's ear, "We will wait until our house is built, and I will build you a beautiful house. I have money. I will have as many children with you as you want, and I will love you forever."

She looked at me and asked, "What's going on?"

I got down on one knee, in front of everyone, and asked, "Will you marry me?"

We both had tears of joy running down our cheeks, and as the crowd cheered, Laurie shook her head yes and said, "Of course, I will marry you. I have loved you since the day we met!" The cheers went on for quite a while. Mother wept, and Father gave me a head nod...and a smile.

ABOUT THE AUTHOR

Born Glen Vetter in Wishek, North Dakota (closest hospital), but his parents lived in Napoleon at the time he was born. Glen is number five of six in his family, and they all were second generation *Germans from Russia*. He had lived throughout the Midwest but called North Dakota home, and he lives in Napoleon only a couple blocks from where his parents lived when he was born. Many considered him a redneck and not the "author" type. He enjoys the outdoors and sharing his skills with family and friends as much as he does participating. He is married, and they raised two boys, Zachary and Dylan Vetter. Four years ago on Father's Day, they were blessed with a grandson, Jaxon Vetter, another boy for him to educate and spoil.

Five years ago, he was diagnosed with an incurable disease that drastically changed his life. Glen went from a very active athletic outdoorsman to someone who was in a wheelchair and needed help to get dressed in the morning. He is no longer able to work, and his wild and free lifestyle had changed. Beer, whiskey, and primitive camping had been replaced with meds, needles, and infusion treatments. He is still able to hunt and fish; he just needs assistance. Glen enjoys visitors more these days, and telling stories of his many adventures keep the people around him smiling. He loves to make people smile; sometimes they laugh, and sometimes they cry, but most of all, they just want to hear one more story.

CPSIA information can be obtained
at www.ICGtesting.com
Printed in the USA
BVHW082304100222
628131BV00001B/4

9 781639 617371